THE GIRL I USED TO BE

J.A. BAKER

For Dawn. For always being there...

"Confront the dark parts of yourself, and work to
banish them with illumination and
forgiveness.
Your willingness to wrestle with your demons will
cause your angels to sing."
August Wilson

North Yorkshire Live

BREAKING NEWS 24th May 2019

A school in North Yorkshire is currently reported to be under lockdown due to a violent crime taking place within the school grounds.

Parents anxious about the safety and welfare of their children have gathered outside the gates of Westland Academy. One parent is reported to have said, 'We saw the police officers go in, but they haven't come out yet. It's all very worrying, especially since we've heard nothing about our kids and how they're doing.'

North Yorkshire Live has requested an update but the school and the police have declined to comment on an ongoing operation stating they will release any relevant information in due course.

This story will be updated as soon as more information becomes available.

PROLOGUE

She needs to get out. She cannot remain here all day, cooped up in this place, trapped and frightened while the sun begins its inevitable sluggish descent over the horizon, while the darkness sets in and shadows dance and stretch over her; eerie silhouettes reminding her of where she is and how long this has lasted. She has to get out.

A feeling of disquiet blooms under her skin, numbing her senses, dulling her reactions. She is groggy. Weak and unsteady. Soon she will pull herself round, try to reason with this person before they do something dreadful to her, something unthinkable. Something final.

She shivers and closes off those thoughts, shifting about to get comfortable, her clothing twisting and pulling. Catching underneath her. The ground is cold, hard; an unyielding surface under her soft flesh. She shuffles this way and that, tries to reposition herself, hoping to alleviate the ache that throbs and pulses in the lower half of her body, pinballing up and down her spine.

It's difficult to do anything, to move about or attempt to free herself. Her hands are tied behind her back, her feet held together with duct tape. It's a crude but effective method of containment. She hopes soon, to be able to wriggle free from it, but it is slowing her down, increasing her clumsiness. Hindering her dexterity. Straightening her back, she manages to find a more comfortable spot, letting out a low sigh as she stretches her legs. It gives her only a small amount of relief. The pain is still present, nagging at her. Reminding her of where she is.

And who put her here.

That is something she simply cannot comprehend, how it has all come to this. How she didn't see it before now.

She listens to the voices outside, to the frantic shouts, the cries of terror in the distance, the nearby whispers that are desperate. Urgent. Her ears are attuned to the authoritative tone of the negotiator, their pleas for the door to be opened, for the weapon to be surrendered, for her to be released unharmed.

Time has lost all meaning. How long has she been here? Minutes? Hours? At some point she blacked out, coming to as her feet were being bound together. She was too disorientated to do anything, too confused to escape or fight back. Fog had descended on her brain, muddying her thoughts, blotting out all logic. But now she is awake. Now she is beginning to think straight. She can remember what happened, what took place prior to her being trapped in here, and wishes she couldn't. The memory punches its way into her brain, lodging in her consciousness, forcing her to relive it. Everything is now horribly clear in her mind.

And with that clarity comes terror. Terror and fear that slither their way under her skin, clogging up her veins, turning her innards to liquid. Her heart begins to pound, a relentless thump against her ribcage. A vice tightens around her skull. She tries to slow her breathing, to take control of her senses.

A noise is close by. Too close. She can feel the heat from her captor. The air is thick with it. She can smell their rancid odour, hear the low rustle of their movements. She can detect their deteriorating mood; threatening, unpredictable, hellbent on some sort of warped revenge.

Thoughts of their capabilities, their need for vengeance knots her insides. She's fully awake now, roused from her brain fog. Aware of every sound, every movement. Her thoughts turn to escaping. To getting out of here unharmed.

She begins to hyperventilate, her breath escaping in tiny gasps. She is sure she is going to faint. Panic sets in. She has to slow everything down before she comes apart, before she unravels completely.

She blinks behind the blindfold, eyelids fluttering against the obstruction. The darkness behind it is complete. No gag. She is free to speak but can't. The words refuse to come. She is mute, too frightened to breathe properly. Too terrified to scream for help. Her windpipe has shrunk, her lungs like deflated balloons. She is useless, unable to do anything except focus on how frightened she is and how she ended up here. *Why* she ended up here.

She needs to find her voice, to reason with her kidnapper. She knows them well enough. Or thought she did. Today's event has stripped her of everything she thought she knew and held dear. About herself and those around her. Her knowledge and trust of others has been ground underfoot. Turned to dust. Humanity and hope have deserted her, making her question everything she takes for granted; friendship, happiness. Trust. They have all gone. Disappeared into the ether.

'Please,' she says quietly, her voice abruptly finding its way out, 'let me go and we can pretend none of this ever happened.' She means it. She is not about to make false promises or utter hollow phrases to gain her freedom. To be allowed to leave, she will turn a blind eye, forget everything. She would do her damnedest to put it behind her and continue with her life, to be the best that she can be. She has learned many tough lessons of late and that is one of them. Always be your best self. Her history cannot be undone but the future is something that can be moulded to recompense for past sins.

The breathing is closer now, harsh and rasping, gathering in strength and momentum. She can smell the reek of anger, the years of bitterness that have accumulated in her captor's pores. It wafts through the stuffy air, settling under her nose. She holds her breath, trying to stop the stench that is making her retch. She waits for a response, the sound of her thrashing heart, her own blood as it pumps around her veins, crunching and echoing in her ears.

'Please,' she says again, softly this time, her fear and desperation held bare. 'Please.'

Nothing. She waits, the atmosphere thick with anticipation, with expectation, with dread.

Then a deep grunt followed by the rustle of fabric as they move even closer. Her heart speeds up, expands and bounces in her chest until she is dizzy and hot, close to passing out.

'Just let me go and everything can go back to how it was. I won't let anybody hurt you or blame you for this, I promise.' Her voice is a whisper, laced with desperation.

She suppresses a shriek as the person lunges forward. She thinks of that cold sharp blade, wondering if it's still being held to her throat. She whispers again, her voice hoarse, 'Please, please, let's–'

'Shut up! Shut up or I swear to God, I will slit your throat and smile while I do it.'

1

1999

A small figure sits on the riverbank, slumped, defeated. Her heart thumps, her mouth is dry with fear, with an all-encompassing exhaustion. She's alone at last. They are far behind her. Thank God. She has managed to shake them off, to sneak deep into the undergrowth and salt herself away like a wanted person, a fugitive. Somebody who doesn't belong.

Despite her escape, every crackle in the woods, every snap of a twig, every whisper of wind that rustles through the treetops causes her spine to stiffen and her scalp to prickle. The rush of the water pounds in her ears, the strength of the current making her woozy as she studies it through a blur of tears.

This used to be her safe place, down here by the water; the special space she visited to get away from it all. They followed her into the tall shrubbery, shouting her name, dragging sticks through the long grass and the gnarled branches, doing their best to keep up with her, issuing threats, hunting her down like a wild animal, like a pack of salivating dogs going in for the kill, but she knows this area better than anyone and after a few twists and turns, they gave up. But they know now where she goes to which means her safe place is no longer safe. She has nowhere else to hide, nowhere to escape. Other areas are too far away or too exposed. Open fields, play parks and a village green provide no cover for her. She'll be a target for their threats and bullying. A sitting duck waiting to be shot at.

Her hands shake as she wipes at her face, clearing away the snot and tears with the tattered sleeve of her threadbare sweater. They despise her. She'd like to say she has no idea why they hate her so much but that would be a complete lie. She knows only too well why they loathe her and why they bully and goad her relentlessly. She's astute enough to realise it. A sharp thinker according to her teachers. She has a fast brain but an unattractive face. Her skin is grubby, her clothes old and unfashionable. She doesn't fit into their neat little world. And that is the problem. She's different. And people don't like different. They rail against those who don't conform to their ideals. They mock people who don't keep up with the latest fashion. They despise those who don't paint their nails or wear the flawless make-up that they sport with such breathtaking confidence, it makes her dizzy with envy.

It's how the human brain works. She read about it once in a psychology magazine. Different people pose a threat to the masses. They frighten everyone around them with their strange appearances and unconventional mannerisms. Somebody is always at the bottom of the pecking order. She is that person. No running with the pack, no fitting in with her peers. Just fear and isolation. And coming from a poverty-stricken family with a drunken, rage-filled father, she is powerless to change it.

She looks down at her hands, at her stubby fingernails caked with mud, at her filthy ill-fitting clothes. More tears well up. She can't remember the last time her mother loaded the washing machine. It's not allowed. The noise rouses her dad. Makes him edgy and unpredictable. So she remains dirty, her uniform grimy, her coat grey and worn.

She tries to stay clean, to be like the other girls at school. Last week she attempted to run a bath, tried to do something about her grubby appearance but her father pulled out the plug before the tub was even half full.

His face had loomed close to hers, his skin pasty, an atlas of red broken veins snaking across the whites of his bulging eyes. His voice was a roar. 'What do you think I am?' he had screamed at her, his tombstone teeth dripping with saliva, 'a fucking millionaire?' He had grabbed a fistful of her hair, rammed her head into the side of the sink and left her slumped on the bathroom floor, stars bursting behind her eyes and pain blinding her. Bathing is now forbidden. Bathing is something she will do when she carves out another life for herself far away from here.

She shuffles closer to the river, careful not to lean too far over the edge. She's not frightened of the water, not afraid of its power. She's in awe of it; mindful of its dark ferocity and the damage it could cause if she let it. It commands respect. She thinks about it often; about the harm it could do to her. Or the hurt it could stop. Perspective is important when it comes to considering the outcome. She's dreamed before now, of diving right in there and letting it sweep her away, letting the water drag her under until nothing else matters. No more fear, no more of anything. Just eternal darkness. An end to the misery. But then the moment passes, the sun appears, banishing the dark thoughts, pushing them away and she can once again see the light.

Recent rains have increased the speed of the current and caused a pulsing deep swell. She watches, mesmerised, held captive by the river's swirling eddies. She dips her fingers into the gushing river, letting them hang there in the icy water until her skin is numb, until pain shoots up her arms, whistling over her shoulders and into her neck.

She removes her hands, chalk white with cold, sits back on the ground, rubbing her palms against the long silken strands of grass until they're dry. Sometimes she enjoys punishing herself, seeing how far she can go before her nerve endings shriek at her to stop. It gives her a taste of how it could be, that alternative ending when her lungs fill with water and she gasps her last. It's what keeps her going; the thought of the cold and the pain and an eternity of nothingness.

Staring at her nails she is overcome by a wave of revulsion. They are the hands of a manual worker – dry, cracked, dirty. Her nails are ragged and bitten, chewed down to the quick. She dips her head, visualising the girls at school, their golden tresses and flawless skin, musing over how they conduct themselves, gliding across the playground with swanlike elegance. She isn't like that. She never will be. She is the antithesis of glamour and budding sophistication. That's why they hate her. That's why she hates herself.

One day she'll get out of this place, away from this village with its tight unforgiving mentality and she'll show them how she can really be. She will transform into something better, something prettier and more conventional. She isn't prepared to spend the rest of her life at the bottom. She has dreams and aspirations just like those pretty girls at school. Happiness should be available for all. But for now, she has to find a way of enduring it. She has to find a way of putting up with the beatings and surviving the hostile environment in which she has found herself, both at school and at home.

Standing up, she heads back. Back to her cramped dusty house with its reek of unwashed clothes. Back to the choking trail of cigarette smoke that lingers in the air turning the walls a sickly shade of yellow.

Once there, she will make herself scarce. She will hide out in her bedroom away from the noise and the chaos. Another survival technique she has mastered. Sometimes it works and sometimes it doesn't. It all depends on how much he has had to drink or whether or not the wind is blowing in a westerly direction and whether it's a Saturday or a Tuesday or a Monday. The rules are, there are no rules.

One day they will all realise. One day, all these people who have made her life a misery, will wake up and it will dawn on them what they have done. How they have treated her. All the damage. All the hurt she has endured. For now though, she has to grit her teeth, ignore it, bear the pressure of their cruelty. She will be the best she can be, given the circumstances. She will tolerate it all; the name calling, the sarcastic smirks, even the violence. But one day it will change. She knows it. She can feel it somewhere deep inside her gut.

She crosses the field, avoiding the park where the noise of youngsters playing in the distance causes her skin to prickle and grow hot with dread. It's not them, her aggressors, but even so. Her senses are raw, acutely attuned to every single sound. She's not about to take any chances. The park is exposed. She cannot risk being seen. Lying low, disappearing into the background is how she lives her life. This is who she is.

Across the expanse of green stands her house – a tiny terraced property, conspicuous by its neglect. Neighbouring homes with their gleaming white window frames and perfectly pleated curtains only accentuate how rundown and unloved her home is, how grimy and unkempt it looks, even from a distance.

She opens the door and steps into the hallway and her chest compresses as she hears her father bellowing in the kitchen. She stops and listens, preparing herself. He's complaining that his meal is late and is shouting her name over and over. Where is his daughter? Where the fuck has she taken herself off to this time? She should be here, giving a hand to prepare his food, helping out around the house, not sneaking off into the woods on her own.

'I'll bet she's down by that river again. What the fuck does she do with herself down there?' His voice is thunderous, filling the house, rattling off every wall.

She lets out a stuttering breath, a staccato rasping of warm stale air from her lungs, and braces herself, readying her small body for the inevitable blows. She can do this. She can withstand the punches, both physically and figuratively. She has an inner core of iron and is stronger than they could ever know. She has no choice. It's just how it is. But for how long? Even the sturdiest of steel girders perish eventually.

Closing the door behind her with a quiet click, she prepares herself for his fists, his acerbic, unforgiving tongue. She prepares herself for whatever is about to come her way.

2

I lie perfectly still, wishing the day would pass me by, wishing the weekend was upon us and I could stay here, spend the next few hours in my bed, revelling in the comfort and the warmth.

The rising sun spreads a blanket of ochre over me, a pool of warm yellow that covers my legs and feet. I stretch my toes and blink repeatedly, clearing the film that mists my vision. I gaze at the shadows that stretch across the sloping ceiling of the loft conversion that is our bedroom. They stoop and curve like elongated spectres staring down at me, their long spindly arms leaning out to snatch me up from my bed and swallow me into the darkness. I shut my eyes tight, then open them again. The shadows in the room shift and change shape, disappearing completely as the sun makes its slow but steady ascent in the sky. A greyness settles. The soft light is temporarily obscured by a ridge of thick clouds blowing in from the west. The mornings are getting lighter. That's one thing to be grateful for. I can rise, safe in the knowledge I will see some daylight before heading off to work. Blue skies make everything seem easier, even rising at 6am isn't so arduous, so bone achingly exhausting. Everything is manageable if I can see an azure sky above me, feel the warmth of the sun on my skin.

I turn over and stretch. Wade is still fast asleep, his lashes fluttering, his face twitching ever so slightly. I envy him, unable to relate to his mindset. No matter how busy or full a day he has ahead of him, no matter how difficult things are for him at work, he sleeps soundly every night and wakes up rested and refreshed, skin and eyes sparkling, his internal battery fully charged. But not me. I spend night after night thrashing around the bed, kicking off covers, worrying, making myself sick thinking about how I will make it through the following day with limited energy. But then of course, I do. Once I'm at work, I cope. Nothing bad ever happens. It's like many of the difficult things we undertake throughout our lives – the thought of doing them proves more intimidating than actually doing them. I'm a worrier, a planner, the sort of person who likes to be prepared. I wish I weren't, but I am. I cannot change how I think and act. If only.

I'm showered and dressed and onto my second cup of coffee by the time Wade joins me in the kitchen. He runs his fingers through his recently washed hair and asks, 'Anything for me?' He looks down at the small pile of post laid out on the table, a spread of envelopes, different shapes and colours, different sizes.

I flick through the stash and hand him a pale brown envelope. 'There you go. You can have the pleasure of opening the electricity bill,' I say, smiling.

He rolls his eyes and places the bill to one side before dropping two slices of bread in the toaster.

My eyes are drawn to a small white envelope that is addressed to me. Something about it is worryingly familiar. I scrutinise it closely, turning it over, looking for a forwarding address on the other side. As expected, it's blank.

Just like the other one.

I flip it back over and look at the front. A feeling of unrest nips at me as I stare at my name written in perfectly formed small block capitals as if to anonymise the handwriting. My face burns and a bubble of air becomes trapped in my throat. I surreptitiously open the envelope, my fingers fluttering wildly under the table. I stare at it, at the words on the small slip of paper lying idly on my lap.

Wade is turned away from me, his attention focused on making his breakfast. He can't see the tremble in my hand or the nervous tic in my jaw. He can't see the rising panic in my eyes as I stuff the letter deep into my pocket and sip at my tea, doing my utmost to act as if nothing has taken place, doing my utmost to quell the sickness that is rising in the pit of my stomach.

'Anything interesting that doesn't involve giving money away?' He opens the cutlery drawer, takes out a knife, inspects it and then delves it deep into the tub of butter.

'Nope. All boring nonsense,' I say, trying to sound confident and cheerful. My insides are shifting and swirling like quicksand. My head is buzzing, my voice disembodied, as if it's coming from somewhere else, from somebody else. 'Just the usual junk mail.'

I stand up abruptly, the chair scraping across the tiled floor. The noise is an assault on my ears. I stop, try to gather my thoughts, attempt to filter out the bad stuff.

Wade turns, faces me, the butter knife in his hand. 'Everything okay?'

'Of course,' I say a little too brightly. My face is tight with a forced smile. 'Why wouldn't it be?'

He shrugs, narrows his eyes, suspicion etched into his brow. 'You look a bit pale, that's all. Difficult day ahead?'

'Aren't they all?' I laugh, trying to keep the tremor out of my voice.

'Ah, you know you love it really, Miss Ingledew. You're a

natural.' Wade makes to hug me but I step back, pointing at the burnt crusts that are sticking out the top of the toaster. A small plume of smoke swirls about the kitchen. I almost laugh as he turns and wafts the grey tendrils about, waving his arms around manically, trying to disperse it.

'You need to lower the settings on that thing,' I say, giving him a stern glare, 'or you'll end up burning the house down.'

I leave him in the kitchen, swearing as he opens windows and tries to clear the smoke before the alarm goes off, and gather my things. A box of unmarked books sits by the front door. Fatigue and half a bottle of red got the better of me last night and despite my attempts to mark them all, I now return to school having made no dent in the backlog of work that continually nags at me and keeps me from sleeping at night. I stop myself from thinking about my friend Sarah, who isn't a teacher, the friend who continually tells me to leave, to find a job elsewhere. To quit moaning and have the courage of my convictions.

'Get a position in a bank or a call centre or even one of the big supermarket chains,' she said recently. We were in a coffee shop, consuming copious amounts of caffeine and chocolate cake while I moaned about my job. 'With your qualifications you'll rise up the ranks in no time and possibly even end up on more money. And you won't be expected to bring work home every night.' I had laughed. Sarah had rolled her eyes. She knew and I knew that I would ignore her suggestion.

She's probably right. And I do get sick and tired of hearing myself complain about how difficult the job is, how heavy the workload is. Both Wade and my friends must tire of it as well. I know I would, if I had to listen to me, day in, day out. Perhaps it's not as bad as I think it is. Perhaps teaching is an integral part of me.

I grab my bag off the newel post, head back into the kitchen where Wade is sitting eating his breakfast. The pungent smell of burnt toast still fills the air. I lean forward, plant a kiss on his forehead. He widens his eyes and smiles at me. Blackened crumbs cling to the corners of his mouth. I almost laugh but then I remember the letter. The letters. My stomach twists another notch, tightening until I can hardly breathe. I exhale softly, tell myself to blank it out, ignore it. I tell myself it's somebody playing a childish prank.

'See you tonight,' I murmur, hitching my bag up over my shoulder.

'Have a good one and don't let the bastards grind you down,' he replies cheerfully.

Every morning we say the same words, go through an almost identical routine. I like it. It helps keep me sane. Wade is my rock. I wish we could go back to bed, make mad passionate love until every breath has exited our bodies, until our skin is on fire. I want to wrap my limbs around his until we are so close it's as if we are one.

I think of the letter stuffed deep in my pocket, feel the weight of it despite it being featherlight. I'll have a closer look at it later, when I'm alone, safely isolated in class before the bell goes and thirty teenagers pile in. It's similar to the one from last week. The one that's hidden in my drawer at work.

I push it to the back of my mind. Too many other things to focus on at the minute. I can't allow a rogue letter from an idiot prankster get to me. A stirring of restlessness stabs at me. I think about the wording of both the notes, the fact that this person has my home address. I should tell Wade about it, maybe even inform the police. But what if they dismiss it? Or worse still, start probing into my private life, my past, the history I would rather remained hidden? Heat flares in my face as I unlock the door and head out to my car. The box of books can wait. No doubt I'll have more to add to the pile tonight which means my weekend will be spent marking. I shrug and sigh. I can't do anything about it. No point worrying over things I have no power to change. This is my job, my life. It's who I am.

A blackbird flutters off the garden wall as I open the car door. It flies above my head, circling and flapping before landing on the small hawthorn bush next to the driveway. It sits there, watching me intently, its yellow rimmed dark eyes following my every movement, scrutinising me as I slide into the driver's seat and shut the door with a gentle click. Oh, to be a bird, to be any sort of wild creature, to have the power and the ability to flit away and leave everything far behind.

I let out a shuddering breath and lower my head. *Push it all away*, I tell myself. *All the unmarked books and suspicious letters, push them to the back of your mind*, the small voice in my head whispers, *and concentrate on the moment. Be heedful but still forge ahead, press on with your day*. I wish I could, I really do but something tells me that more will follow. I can't settle. Not when I know those notes could be from him – that man, the one I've tried to forget. My big, dreadful mistake. One letter I can easily dismiss, two is another matter entirely. Two letters tell me he means business, that he won't give up without a fight.

Two letters mean trouble.

I turn the key in the ignition, listen as the engine kicks into life. What I wouldn't give to be able to just put my foot down, to drive away from here, far away from all this festering trouble and possible heartache and ruin. Far away from the undercurrent of fear and regret that is going to haunt me for the rest of my life. One night. That's all it was. One night that was one big fucking slip-up and now it looks like it's about to resurface and destroy everything.

Tears flow hot and fast as I reverse off the drive and head into work. My life is about come tumbling down like a house of cards.

And it's all my fault.

3

The car park at school is almost empty. I pull up into one of the favoured parking spaces that allows for an easy and, if I get lucky, early exit tonight. I'm always one of the first in which means I can have some time alone to contemplate how best to implement certain strands of the national curriculum in my lessons before more staff arrive and make demands on me, requesting my presence in unplanned meetings, before they corner me, standing chatting about nothing in particular when all I want to do is prepare for the day ahead.

I slip past the office undetected. Marion, the office manager is focused on the computer screen. I can pass by without being subjected to the usual tirades about her dysfunctional family, her selfish husband, her litany of ailments. This morning is not the morning to listen to her. This morning, my mind is elsewhere.

I stop suddenly, let out a small sigh and try to catch her eye, guilt pushing under my skin. I'm tired and anxious. It's not really Marion. It's me. And who am I to judge with all my moans and worries and constant angst. Who am I to decide what words and conversations are worthy of being aired? She's not so bad at all. Ready for retirement perhaps. Ready for an easier life, but not so ready I suspect, to relinquish control to a younger replacement who will substitute her carefully applied systems and methods with their own. Marion likes to be at the helm, to take ultimate control and the thought of being pushed into the background by somebody younger with more drive and ambition will slowly be tearing her apart. She was offered early retirement last year by the headteacher and chair of governors, and refused, spending the next six months indignant at being given such a proposal. Poor Marion.

She continues to type, concentrating on the screen, unaware of my presence. I slip away, my shoes making a soft squeaking sound on the floor as I head off for some sustenance to help me through the day.

The staffroom is empty. I make myself a strong coffee before heading up into class. I try to look busy in case anybody happens to spot me and wants to stop by for a chat. The school has a different feel to it when it's empty; slightly eerie and somewhat detached from reality. Dull floors once shiny, now scratched and ingrained with grit and dirt, echo as I head to class. Long dark corridors accentuate a crushing sense of isolation. I shiver and pick up my pace, keen to ensconce myself in the classroom and shut out the rest of the world.

My room is in darkness and has a chill to it, an icy edge that settles on me like a shroud. I switch on the light and turn up the thermostat, listening for the rush of hot air from the heater.

I am perched stiffly on my chair as I open my bag and remove a folder, placing it on my desk with a slap. I sip at my coffee, waiting for the place to heat up. My fingers are numb and refuse to work properly until the chill has dissipated. The weather has yet to realise that May recently arrived, that spring is here and people are ready for some heat, desperate for it even. Mornings still have an icy bite to them, the earth not yet warmed up after a particularly cold winter. I long for summer, for those long heady evenings when the air is filled with the scent of honeysuckle, when birds swoop and chirrup, their songs echoing across the landscape, when I can feel the warmth of the setting sun as it shimmers over the hills, a hazy orb of orange that turns the sky into a spread of comforting amber.

The letter hidden away in the back of my drawer cuts into my thoughts, nagging at me like the relentless throb of a rotten tooth. I pull out the one from this morning, open it up on my desk and read it, the message just as cutting and menacing to me on a second read.

I know what you did, you bitch.

Seven words that have the power to churn my guts and still my blood.

I slide open my desk drawer, reach into the back and drag out the letter that I found last week, stuffed at the back of my pigeonhole. I wish I'd kept the envelope. I threw it away before I read the note and by the time I got to it, Flora the cleaner had already emptied the bins. I wasn't prepared to chase after her asking if I could rummage through her rubbish for an envelope. And anyway, what would it tell me? Postmarks are vague and the handwriting is deliberately neat and unidentifiable.

I open last week's letter, straighten it out, place it next to today's poison missive, a disconcerting numb sensation beginning to settle in my stomach as I digest the words, feeling their threat like an icy stab to my heart.

I see you. I know you. I'm after you. Tick tock, tick tock.

I swallow, rub at my eyes, blink repeatedly. I'm worn out by these threats. I feel a hundred years old and the day has barely begun. I've got five lessons to get through – almost 150 pupils to teach, one of them a GCSE class involving lengthy Shakespearean texts that they despise with every fibre of their being. All I want to do is crawl back into bed and hide away from this person who wants to hurt me, to unearth my ghastly secrets.

A noise outside the classroom stops my thoughts. I snatch up both letters, shove them in the side pocket of my handbag. A shadow passes outside the classroom door accompanied by the thrum of distant chatter. More staff arriving. Soon the place will spark into life. My peace will be shattered. No more time for any further investigative work. No time to sit and ponder over who hates me so much, they took time out of their day to write these vitriolic notes. I have thoughts tucked deep in my brain of who it possibly is. I don't want to think about it. I don't want to think about *him*. Yet I have to. I have to tackle this thing; whatever *this thing* is. He is my main culprit and I wish to God he wasn't.

I take a slurp of coffee, shut my eyes tight, pray it isn't him. My brain aches at the thought of this whole thing rearing its ugly head. It's a physical pain that slices through me. I dread the thought of it crawling back into my life, that awful unpalatable episode, slinking its way forward and making itself known. Not now when everything is settled and back to how it was; how it should always have been. It was a blip when I was at a low ebb; a horrible mistake that shouldn't define me. Yet these letters are here now and I'm terrified that things are about to escalate, that I'll be powerless to stop it. My life, swept aside, me submerged, gasping for breath as I drown in a sea of deceit that is all of my own making.

I am suddenly torn between raw terror and white-hot fury. How dare he come back into my life and threaten me, holding me ransom like this? How fucking *dare* he? Heat blossoms under my skin. My flesh stings and burns with resentment and outrage. Because the more I think about it, the more certain I am that it's him. It has to be. The timing is right. I've done some stupid stuff in my life, made bad decisions, had good times, mediocre times, awful times, but at this juncture, my life is mundane; a regular existence. Except for that one indiscretion. That one time. That's all it was. Wade and I were going through a rough patch. My mum was causing me issues, trying to rake over a past I would sooner forget.

It was a tough time. I was at a low ebb. Wade was out of his depth trying to deal with my mood swings; he was worried, exasperated. And so, he moved out, just for a short while, to live with his brother in Southampton. I watched him leave; me huddled under a blanket on the sofa, fighting back tears. Him staring at me, his eyes piercing; filled with panic and confusion. I had made it nigh on impossible for him to help me, batting away his advances and suggestions and yet at the same time being desperate for them, frantic for his assistance. And so he took my advice and left.

And that's when it happened.

I met Glenn on a night out with Astrid and a few other friends. I was horribly drunk, my judgement more than a little skewed. We had been on jugs of cocktails for most of the evening. I hadn't eaten anything after a riotous day at school that culminated in a miscreant pupil throwing a chair across the classroom, and the alcohol went straight to my head.

After the chair throwing incident, I had spent the afternoon crying, my mind focused on my choice of career, Wade, my mother, my past. A man chatting to me, complimenting me on my hair, on my figure seemed like an appealing option. With hindsight I can see that he was anything but smooth-talking and more lounge lizard, and that his comments about my slim figure and shapely legs were totally inappropriate, but at the time I was taken in by his honeyed charm and easy manner, and wanted to get back at Wade for taking notice of my pleas to be left alone, for being unable to penetrate the self-made shield with which I had surrounded myself.

The man had been talking to Astrid before I muscled my way in. Apparently, she knew him from way back when she was a student and had eyed me suspiciously as I began chatting to him.

We talked for a short while although I was too drunk to recall any of it afterwards. I told the girls I wasn't feeling well, then left with him, a total stranger, while their backs were turned. We went back to mine and had the fastest sex ever. My head spun and my stomach roiled throughout. I threw up in the toilet afterwards while he dressed and let himself out.

That was over three months ago and now, it would appear, it is coming back to haunt me. In that three-month period, Wade and I have grown closer, so much closer than before. Him finding out about my ultimate betrayal would rip us apart. It can't happen. I won't permit it.

I close my eyes, unable to bear the thought; sickened by my own behaviour. That I allowed it to take place. We're settled now; a proper couple. We do everything together; eat, drink, watch TV, sleep, go shopping. He's even seen me having a pee for God's sake.

I had all but obliterated the thought of that night, that moment of impropriety, whitewashed it from my mind and now here it is, a reminder of my mistake, sitting crumpled up in my bag, ready to blow my world apart.

'Morning, Stella. Busy day ahead?' Jonathan Telford, the head of English is in the doorway, his smile broad as it lights up the shadowy room, his weather-beaten face beaming at me.

'Oh, the usual,' I reply, trying and undoubtedly failing to inject jocularity into my tone. 'I've got 10D this afternoon. Our friend Jack is back from his exclusion, so listen for his cries of protestation when I shove Act III, Scene i of *Macbeth* under his nose.'

Jonathan guffaws, shakes his head and sucks in his breath. 'If he gives you any trouble, you know where I am.'

'Oh, I love threatening them with Mr Telford. Worth it just to see their faces drop.' I laugh softly, leaning back in my chair.

'Seriously, Stella. If any of those little bastards cause you any problems, send them through to see me. My wife has got me on another diet so I'm full of hell and looking forward to a good fight with some jumped-up little shit who thinks he's well within his rights to hurl abuse at members of staff and chuck things around the classroom.'

Jonathan is a nice man, one of life's good guys. He and his wife Jeannie are a match made in heaven; a perfect foil for one another. She continually plagues him about his weight, how it's bad for his heart carrying all that fat around, how his midriff is too large, much like his appetite, and he offloads it onto us at work, moaning about how miserable life is now he can't eat whatever he wants, whenever he wants.

'Thanks, Jonathan. I'll definitely send for help if any of them play up.'

He waves, heads off down the corridor, his whistling disappearing into the distance until all I can hear is the creak of his classroom door and the deep thud of my own heartbeat as I lean down and lift the letter back out of my bag.

My hands shake as I scan the paper and then turn my attention to the envelope, scrutinising it for clues to its provenance. Nothing. Apart from the postmark which is barely legible, there is nothing to see. My vision blurs slightly. I swallow hard and blink back tears that are pricking at the back of my eyelids. I need to dismiss it, ignore it, get on with the rest of my day. So many tasks to get through and all the while, every second, every minute that passes, all I will be able to think about is that awful man and these stupid fucking letters.

I focus on steadying my breathing and stuff the letters at the back of my drawer, covering them with a pencil case I confiscated last week and omitted to return. A boy had been passing notes about, concealed inside the case, asking who fancied a beer at his house after school. His parents were away for the night and his older sister was working late. I took the case in a fit of pique and forgot about it. At least I now have a use for it.

I think about discarding both notes on my way home; stopping by a bin somewhere remote, tearing them into a hundred tiny pieces and stuffing them in as far as they will go. Then hope that I don't receive any more. It was good fortune that I was up before Wade to see it. What if he had got to the mail before me and opened it? What then? He would be curious, would start questioning me, possibly even want to take it to the police. That's just how he is; principled, tenacious. He would also be appalled that somebody was bullying me and scaring me senseless. He would want to protect his partner. He would want to end this whole awful debacle, even though I probably brought it upon myself with my reckless, selfish behaviour. How forgiving and compassionate would he be then, when the details of my hurtful infidelity came crawling out?

A wave of heat crawls over me, burning my skin, prickling my armpits and scalp. I rub at my eye sockets with the heel of my hands and shudder. I tell myself to put a halt to this behaviour, to stop being so fucking morose, to stop moping and second-guessing everything. Got to be positive, see beyond this, not make myself ill worrying and fretting. This could be the last letter. I could be sitting here, trawling over things that will never happen. I probably am. These letters are from a prankster, a desperate loner. They are best ignored.

I stand up, pull open the blinds, stare outside to the empty yard below. Soon it will be full of children and teenagers milling about, satchels slung over their shoulders, all prepared for the day ahead. I need to get myself sorted, be as prepared as they are. I can't let them see any chinks in my armour or I'm done for. They will have me on toast. Especially Jack Phelps. He watches and waits, like a ravenous predator, ready to pounce on visible weaknesses, ready to rip and shred his catch with his barbed comments, wicked smirks and a whole armoury of insults and unrefined linguistic weapons that he has at his disposal.

I rummage in my bag, pull out a comb and a lipstick. I stare in the mirror, apply some make-up then brush my hair and attempt to make myself look half decent. I smack my lips together, put everything back, take a deep breath and tell myself that everything will be fine. Which it will. It has to be. I have no other choice.

4

It didn't hurt. She's had worse inflicted upon her. He was too drunk to beat her with his usual gusto and strength. He ended up collapsing on the living room floor, his features contorted in an ugly inebriated grimace, a reek emanating from him that suggested he hadn't washed for weeks. Hygiene and taking care of his appearance were an anathema to him. Said it was for snobs and vain bastards and that anybody who thought themselves better than him could fuck right off.

Of course, she knows the truth is that he is too lazy and too drunk to ever pick up a bar of soap, comb his hair or change his rotten stinking clothes. Far easier to blame others and go through life like the filthy lousy piece of shit that he is.

She lies back on her bed, rubbing at her arm where his fist caught her. He missed more of her than he managed to hit. She was fortunate this time. Next time she might not be so lucky. It all depended how much alcohol he had consumed. Somebody in the pub has probably said something that riled him, or he may have just been feeling that way while out. No amount of begging or pleading ever stopped him. It's pointless even trying.

He is always deaf to her screams, blind to the horror of his actions. Unused to backing down.

She blanks out the shouts from the room below, closes her eyes and thinks about earlier events at the river, wondering why people do what they do, why they gain such pleasure from being cruel to others. If she were one of the pretty girls, one of the confident, well-turned-out girls who was in with the in-crowd, she would take somebody like her under her wing, help them along. Make them feel wanted. She wouldn't mock them, make them cower in her presence. She wouldn't chase after them like some feral creature hunting its prey. She would be better than that. Because she knows what it is like to be insulted, ignored, to be constantly pushed aside and trodden underfoot.

Overwhelming tiredness tugs at her, threatening to drag her off into the darkness where nobody can get to her, where nobody can hurt her with their words and fists. Not even her worst nightmares could ever be as bad as the reality she faces every single day, the stark cold harshness that is her life.

She drifts off, like a leaf floating downstream; weightless and free, off to a new land full of hope and promise. She suddenly feels peaceful, lying here in her tiny room, alone with her thoughts and musings, away from her father and his temper, away from the baying mob that gleans so much enjoyment from her misery.

The knocking drags her back to life, forcing her to leave a contented state of relaxation. She awakes, is immediately on edge again. It's the front door. Somebody is hammering on it, demanding to be let in. Rarely does anybody call. Her parents have few friends. She has none. Their family is small, fractured, lacking in the glue of happiness that binds other families together. There is an aunt she sees occasionally when her mum can be bothered to visit. Aunt Petra doesn't come to their house. They always go to hers. The girl has never asked why. There is no need. It's an unspoken truth that Petra hates her father. And who can blame her? A drunken brute of a man who regularly beats his family. A drunken brute of a man who loses more jobs than he keeps. Who would want to be associated with such a person?

As soon as she is old enough, she will leave him far behind. She will get a job, earn enough to find a place for herself and her mother and they'll be rid of him. It's been her dream for so many years now that she sometimes wakes up under the brief illusion it has already happened. Then the truth of her situation hits home and a heaviness descends, pressing down on her, crushing her soul and stripping away her dignity bit by painful bit. But it keeps her going, that dream, forces her up every day, makes her continue with her schoolwork, helps her through each and every day. It is a dream tinged with misery and hopelessness. But without it, she would have nothing. Her life would be unbearable. Worse than it is now if that is at all possible.

The knock comes again, louder this time, an insistent hammering that cools her blood. Scrambling to her feet, she pulls her sweater over her head and creeps downstairs. A quick peek into the living room tells her that her father is asleep, his body slumped on the sofa at a peculiar angle. Her mother must have dragged him up off the floor after his drunken rage dissipated. A lump is wedged in her throat. She swallows it down and steps back from the threshold before peering through the glass of the front door to see who is out there. It's not a face she recognises. The bevelled glass has distorted the features, but even allowing for the partial view, she can see that the face staring through is alien to her.

Swiftly, silently, she opens the door, pulling it ajar a fraction, and peers around it, keen to get rid of their visitor. If her father wakes, an unexpected caller will fuel his simmering anger. It will be like pouring hot oil onto a flickering furnace. And then they'll all know about it.

She nods at the woman standing there, juts out her chin to appear confident and authoritative. Displays of uncertainty and feebleness invite hatred and mockery and she's had a gutful of that, so she stands instead, hands on hips, jaw set, eyes narrowed in suspicion. 'Yes?'

She smiles, this woman, this stranger, her eyes creasing at the corners as she speaks. She has a kind expression, smooth clear skin. The sort of face that makes people open up, spill their secrets despite barely knowing her. The girl sucks in her breath, listens as the stranger speaks in a low voice. 'Hi there. Just thought I'd call and see if everything's all right?'

The girl doesn't move. A slithering sensation glides over her flesh, like a snake wrapping itself around her, sleek and cold, its unpredictable reptilian presence making her tremble.

'I live next door. I heard noises and I just thought–'

Her blood stills itself in her veins. What is she supposed to say? That everything is far from all right? That by speaking she is risking another beating when her dad gets wind of her blabbing mouth? That she wishes she didn't live here or belong to this family? Could she allow all their secrets to come pouring out to this kind-faced stranger who with just one look, clearly knows that something is amiss?

'Everything is fine but thank you for asking.' She blurts it out, her vision misting over at the thought of her father waking up and hearing this conversation, his eyes full of fire, his breath a noxious death stench as he stands behind her, fists balled up in anger.

The woman continues to smile, her gaze sweeping over the

girl's unkempt appearance, at the yellowed peeling wallpaper behind her.

She feels a flush creep up her neck and tugs at her collar to hide it. As much as she would like to confide in this lady, she knows it's impossible. Any intervention, no matter how well intentioned, would be catastrophic for her and her family. The only option is to smile, pretend everything is fine, that they are a normal family. Isn't that how many other families operate? Covering up for one another, papering over the cracks? Carrying on with their everyday lives as if shouting and beatings aren't a regular occurrence.

'I'm Valerie. We've just moved in. You know where I am if you need anything. Feel free to call around anytime...' The woman's eyes bore into her, a sparkle of recognition at the girl's plight evident in her features.

The girl swallows, tries to slink farther out of view behind the door jamb, acutely aware of her family's many failings, her own ragged clothes. Her bruises.

'Thank you but we're fine.' Her voice is a streak of desperation, thinly disguised. She is close to breaking, close to opening up to this perfect stranger. She can't. It's not possible. It's dangerous.

She nods and closes the door, leans back on it, relief flooding through her as she hears her father's deep rumbling snores in the living room. She has got away with it. This time. Batted away the help they so desperately need. Tears well in her eyes. She blinks them back, dreaming of being rescued, dreaming of an imaginary life next door with the smiling lady who probably has a wardrobe full of clean fashionable clothes and freshly picked flowers sitting in vases on every windowsill.

It's only as she creeps up the stairs that she realises how insular her world is. She doesn't know any of their neighbours. They are a family of social pariahs. Somebody new moved in next door to them and they didn't even notice. This is how small her world is, how limited her contact is with other people. She is truly alone.

Perching on the edge of her bed, she once again nibbles at her nails, already bitten to the quick. A miniscule arc of blood, ruby red, appears below the nailbed as she tears away a tiny white strip and spits it on the floor at her feet. Clamping her hands under her armpits, she begins to rock backwards and forwards, a line of pain, sharp and jagged, stabs at the end of the finger. So stupid. So childish. She has to learn to control the nail-biting, to stop her awful habits or she'll never break out of this self-perpetuating circle of destruction. Why is everything so damn hard? It's so bloody difficult growing up in this house surrounded by anger and hatred, held hostage by the violence meted out every single day.

Lying back, she stares at the ceiling, thinking about the kindness in the woman's eyes, the softness of her skin, how gentle her voice was. That's how she wants to be when she grows up. Not hardened to the ways of the world like her own mother, a woman who has had to endure many blows. She will meet somebody who lifts her up instead of constantly knocking her down. She will not marry a man like her father.

She closes her eyes, visualises a face smiling down at her; an attractive man, perhaps even beautiful, someone who will treat her with compassion, respect her, speak kindly to her. Someone who will sweep her off her feet. She doesn't care about feeling equal, about being a feminist or standing her ground. She just wants to escape this, to be needed. To be loved.

This is why she has to put a halt to her childish behaviour, her loathsome habits. Who would want to be associated with a dirty, grubby girl who bites at her nails, a girl who wanders around in filthy ill-fitting clothes? She has to find a way to drag herself out of this mess, a way to better herself and leave this lifestyle far behind.

She becomes caught up in the fantasy. She doesn't hear the creak on the stairs or notice the absence of the gurgling snores from the living room below her. She is deaf to the rattling breaths that grow closer with every passing second. Only when he is standing over her, the foul stench of his breath wafting towards her nostrils, does she snap back to the present, feel his presence in her room, and stiffen.

She remains rigid, doesn't bother opening her eyes or registering his existence. He sees things in her gaze that aren't necessarily there. Any excuse for an argument. Any excuse to ram his fist into her face. Instead, she lies still, preparing herself, bracing her body for the inevitable hit. She takes a deep breath, steels herself and waits.

5

2019

The registration period passes in a blur, as does the first lesson, time losing itself in the minutiae of teaching and learning. No mayhem, no backchat, no heavy drawn-out sighs when I presented them with a comprehension sheet about the literary life of Charles Dickens. A gaggle of girls seated at the back of the classroom gave a slight sneer as the paper was placed in front of them, and I could have sworn I heard a caustic remark about my hair as I turned away from them and made my way back to my desk, but that aside, it was an uneventful couple of hours.

The atmosphere changes abruptly as Year 10 bustle their way through the door. I should get up, ask them to go back out, to form an orderly line and then file back in one by one in silence, but I'm sapped of all energy, my bones like lead as a worrying ache sets in at the back of my head. I open a blister pack of painkillers that I keep in the back of my drawer, pop two out and swallow them down with a disgusting swill of cold coffee from the cup I made earlier this morning. I grimace at the taste and turn to look at the motley crew sitting opposite me. I'm met by a wall of noise and row upon row of dishevelled teenagers rummaging in bags, pushing each other off chairs and guffawing.

I stand up at the front of the class and fold my arms, hoping to convey an air of authority that I definitely don't feel. I'm too tired to exert masses of energy on people who don't seem to care what day of the week it is, let alone be bothered to study the subliminal messages hidden in the works of William Shakespeare, or to focus on the life of Dickens.

A surprising silence takes hold as I stand there, my face aching from the forced frown I always have to wear with this bunch of disaffected youngsters. I'm sure that deep down they possess some sort of empathy, some sort of concern and consideration for those around them. I'm also sure that in time, they will realise the importance of knowledge and how it can advance their lives but right now, those qualities are hidden, tucked so far down in their psyche, they aren't even aware that they are actually there at all. I remember that feeling all too well, the deep sense of being disconnected, isolated. The loneliness and utter despair I felt as a teenager. It's never left me. I wonder if it ever will.

I suppress a groan of exasperation as Sarah Peterson throws a textbook at another pupil, catching him on the back of the head with a loud sharp smack.

He rubs his head melodramatically, turns to her, his eyes brimming with rage. 'Fucking fat bitch! Your mum's shagged half of West Compton.' His remark brings a shriek of laughter from the rest of the class.

I heave a sigh of resignation at the incident unfolding in front of me. I can either shout louder than their collective shrieks or wait until it dies down, which it inevitably will. Their attention span is short. Not even the most puerile of jokes keeps them entertained for too long. Soon they'll get bored, notice that I am standing here waiting for their attention, and stop. I hope it doesn't take too long or Jonathan will think I'm not handling things as well as I should and make an unexpected appearance, his large bulk filling the doorway like the shadow of death. His help isn't unwanted, it's more a matter of pride. I don't want to be perceived as being unable to cope. In a department full of older teachers, I'm concerned about being viewed as inexperienced and weak. Weak teachers are a burden. They need continuous support. I don't want to be that person, the one who can't manage, the one who relies on others just to make it through the day with their sanity intact. I'm stronger than that, but sometimes the pupils in this place are enough to tip anybody over the edge, to make the most experienced of practitioners question their abilities. Today is not going to be that day. I'll make sure of it.

'Enough!' I'm surprised by the strength of my own voice, by the sheer ferocity of it. It has the desired effect. A deathly silence descends in the room. I stare out at an ocean of bewildered faces, wide surprised eyes that stare ahead, unblinking. That's the thing about not raising your voice too often, when shouting is a last resort, something that happens rarely, it has impact. The staff who shriek all day every day at the kids to get their attention simply lose respect and, eventually, their nerve. Children become desensitised to it, the raised voices sliding over them like the wash of the current over smooth pebbles, worn down and eroded after years of being bashed and knocked about.

'Right. Now we've all calmed down and decided to act our age, let's get on with the lesson,' I say, my voice a shard of ice. Being stern and austere is easy when you're anxious and exhausted. Despite an easy couple of hours, despite managing to calm the class down and take charge, I am still sickly and apprehensive. The matter of the letters won't leave me. Even as I assert my authority in front of a class of thirty fourteen-year-olds, the words written in the notes sit squarely in my mind, taunting me with what could lie ahead. Just a few short phrases that could blow my whole world apart. I try once more to shove it to the back of my mind. It's slicing through every single thought in my head, every emotion, every bloody thing that I am doing, and I have to stop it.

I pick up a black marker, write today's learning objectives on the board, drop the pen back on my desk with a sharp click. Determined to ignore the voice that is telling me something dreadful is about to occur, I carry on with the lesson. I have no reason to think this, no reason at all. Apart from those letters, my life is ticking along at a perfectly acceptable pace. Apart from those god-awful fucking letters, everything is as it should be.

Within five minutes I have handed out the relevant text, chosen people to read certain excerpts out loud, ignoring the odd frown and shrug of protest. I begin the lesson by explaining the importance of Shakespeare's use of alliteration and how the sibilance is crucial when reciting their parts, how readers should emphasise these language devices for the full effect.

A buzz of excitement pulses through me as I notice how uncharacteristically attentive the class has become. A new-found confidence settles inside me, firing up my senses, expelling the listlessness that has dragged me down all morning. I suddenly feel surprisingly strong. A surge of energy floods my veins, blossoming in the pit of my belly. I'm back on track and it feels good. That's the only way I can overcome this obstacle that life has thrown my way, by working hard and treating my secret letter writer with the contempt they deserve. Should I choose to shrivel up, to worry myself sick about a possible wrecked future, then they've already won. I refuse to let that happen, because if there's one facet of my personality I'm secretly proud of, it's that I don't like losing. I'm tenacious, robust and surprisingly tough.

I've had to be. I've overcome more than most to get this far. My life has been a hard one, full of serrated edges, twists and turns that led me down some dark murky paths and I'm damned if I'm going to let some shitty unhinged person ruin what I've worked hard to achieve.

My breath is hot and erratic as I address the class, a release of pent-up anger and terror leaving me, exiting my body, replaced with a steely determination to rise above my situation, to tower above those letters and the person who is sending them. They can go to hell.

The next forty-five minutes is spent examining the ever-growing madness of Lady Macbeth, studying the subtle shift of influence and control between Lady Macbeth and her husband, talking about the balance of power and how it moves fluidly throughout the play, painting Macbeth as a victim as opposed to the villain once his wife's true intentions spark into life. Even Sarah Peterson behaves herself and manages to get a few of her thoughts down on paper. I have no idea what those thoughts are, what it is she has actually written and whether or not they are relevant and make sense, but that she picked up her pen and opened her book is quite something and a definite improvement on the last lesson where she continually shouted out pointless, random insults across the classroom whilst banging on the window to startled passers-by outside.

The lesson ends in a flurry of activity with me running out of time and the bell cutting into my summing up speech which also included instructions on the homework I had planned to give out.

'Good lesson, miss.' Grace's voice is barely more than a whisper as she passes by, surrounded by her small huddle of friends. I glance her way, give her a look of gratitude. Pupils like Grace and Ravi and Damon make the job so much easier, so much brighter. They make it worthwhile. Ravi gives me a quick courteous nod and Damon gives me a broad smile and a small wave before they slide out of the door.

Breaktime is a welcome reprieve. I hurry to the staffroom, desperate for nourishment. My throat is dry, my stomach empty. I find myself hoping somebody has brought in cake or biscuits to keep me going until lunchtime.

Astrid is seated in her usual place, over in the far corner next to the window, mug in hand, eyes searching for any allies she can chat to. I make myself a coffee, give her a wave. She reciprocates and places her handbag on the seat next to hers to save me a place. I make my way over, sit down and am disappointed to find the main table in the centre of the room empty. No cakes, no sweets.

'Well, somebody didn't sleep too well last night.' Astrid eyes my face perceptively, gives me a disapproving glare.

'Oh God, don't.' A wave of heat rises up my neck into my cheeks, prickling my skin. I shake my head, determined to stay silent about it. Giving it airtime makes it real. All I want to do is get on with my day, power on through without opening up to anybody about my sordid little secret. And anyway, the whole thing is a nonsense. That's all it is. Complete and utter nonsense that is unworthy of discussion.

'Here,' she murmurs, leaning into her bag, producing a small pot of concealer. 'We all have bad nights. Shove on some of this and make yourself look half decent, woman. You're a disgrace to females everywhere.'

I laugh, take the make-up from her and attempt to dab some under my eyes, then rummage in my bag for a mirror. My reflection confirms the nerves that are still fluttering and swirling in the bottom of my belly. Despite my attempts at dismissal, despite trying to put on a show of bravado, I still feel quite sick and it is apparent in my worn-looking features. With heavy eyes, pale skin and deep grooves in my forehead, I look ghostlike, a shadow of who I usually am. My earlier attempts at applying make-up have done nothing to conceal the exhaustion and worry that is etched into my skin.

'Are you going to the staff night out next weekend?' Astrid's words are without judgement. I quietly heave a sigh of relief. She is a close friend who sees everything, knows everything. Says nothing until the time is right.

'Not sure yet. I'll need to check with Wade in case we have plans but I doubt I'll be going even if we don't. What about you?'

She shakes her head and screws up her face in disdain. 'Not if you're not going. I spend enough time with this lot during the day. Anyway, it's only a party to celebrate old bollock brain Smith's retirement. Hardly worth going to, is it?'

Casper Smith is old-school and should have retired many moons ago. He openly castigates the flood of young teachers that we have in school, believing his degree to be worthier than theirs. He is highly critical of their behaviour-management techniques, favouring his own method which involves bawling at kids for the tiniest of misdemeanours until they retreat to their seats mentally scarred by his six-feet four-inch frame, furious expression and exacting standards.

We drink our coffee in silence, my mind a maelstrom of thoughts; sharp, cutting emotions whirling around my head, knocking into each other, making me dizzy and disorientated. This could be my chance to speak to Astrid, to tell her about the letters. If I do it, I can take control, fool myself that it's no more than a blip, something best ignored. I spend the next couple of minutes mulling it over, marginally empowered by the thought of doing it. No more being a victim. Time to grow up and take charge. Even if it means taking a huge risk with everything that I hold dear. Not now, though. Not today.

I drain the last of my coffee and stand up. 'See you at lunchtime, Astrid.'

She gives me a weak smile and rolls her eyes. 'Only another three lessons to get through before I can get out of this place and go home.'

I give her shoulder a squeeze and shrug before heading back to class.

6

12TH APRIL 2019

Hello, diary.

I'm writing again even though I promised myself I wouldn't. It's a compulsion. I can't seem to help myself. It's mildly cathartic, this process of getting my thoughts down on paper. I threw my other diaries away. They were the manic overemotional scribblings of a failed serial killer. So I'm giving it another go. This time, I'll be calmer and everything will make more sense. I want to be able to look back at this time in my life as a turning point and when I read back through this diary, I want it to be legible. I want my intentions to be crystal fucking clear.

I watched her today from a distance. It's empowering, erotic even, being able to observe people when they don't know that anyone is watching. It's like being in the audience of a play, except I'm the only one there and she is the lead actor. I've shoved her in the limelight, given her top fucking billing but rather than shine like the star she thinks she is, she'll soon start to feel the strain. She'll realise what's going on and panic, wanting out of it. She'll try to escape, to get away from me. But she won't be able to. All the doors will be locked and I'll be the only one with a key. Just the two of us holed up together with no means of escape. She would like that analogy, I'm sure. She's big on metaphors and figurative language. She's big on things she can control. But not for much longer.

I've waited so long for this moment. It's going to be everything I've ever dreamed it would be. I can't wait to watch her unravel, to see her lose focus and crumple at my feet while she begs for mercy, for her life. It's no more than she deserves. She's had it coming for a long time now. Soon she'll know what it's like to be on the shit end of the stick. No more than the fucking bitch deserves...

7

In the end, I didn't speak to Astrid, my long-time friend, about what I have now to come think of as something best forgotten. I considered it, weighing up the pros and cons, but as my fear began to subside, I decided against doing something so drastic. I figured sleeping dogs are most definitely best left to lie. Why poke them with a big stick when they're slumbering comfortably?

The week passed without any more letters being delivered. Even walking through the school gates and into my classroom is not as overwhelming and gruelling. After the initial shock, the massive bout of anxiety I suffered, I find that I've slipped into an easier state of mind. The tight band around my head has loosened and for the first time in weeks and weeks, I've started sleeping properly. The world is a warmer, happier place to be.

I slip out of bed, limbs loose and supple after a full nine-hour sleep, pull on some clothes and pad downstairs to make a fried breakfast. I open the kitchen blinds, breathe in the stale air; the leftovers from last night's supper and the yeasty aroma from the dregs in a pint glass that is sitting on the kitchen top.

We spent Friday evening snuggled up on the sofa with a

couple of pints of beer and a bottle of Chardonnay, watched a handful of television programmes and crawled up to bed shortly after midnight, both too tired to even contemplate sex. We have all weekend to make love as often as we like. No hurrying to work, no coming home and flopping onto the sofa, too bleary-eyed to move let alone rip off one another's clothes and make mad passionate love. For two whole days we can do whatever we want.

In five minutes, I have cleaned up the kitchen and loaded the dishwasher. I open the window to clear the air. Above me, I hear the thud of Wade's feet hitting the floor as he climbs out of bed. He turns on the shower, the steady rush of water hissing through the kitchen.

The rattle from the hallway alerts me to the arrival of the morning post. I no longer feel that awful pull of dread as I stroll through and snatch up the wad of letters lying there on the mat.

I take the small bundle through to the kitchen and sort through them. A letter from my pension company, a reminder for Wade's car tax, a couple of polling cards for the local council election. And then I see it, the final one, tucked in at the back. The instantly recognisable white envelope, the same anonymised handwritten print on the front that forces me against the chair for support.

My heart crawls up my neck and there is a drumming sensation in my throat as I listen out for Wade coming down the stairs. Above me, the shower continues to pound against the tray. Time enough to open the letter, then hide it. Or throw it away. I didn't dispose of the other ones despite my promises to myself that I would because I know that it will be pointless. They are going to continue coming. Destroying the evidence won't expunge what I did.

I slide my finger into the corner of the envelope, slice it open with my nail, the ripping sound filling the still air around me, echoing in my head. The raw sharpness takes my breath away.

My chest contracts as I pull out the piece of folded paper and open it, swallowing repeatedly even though my mouth is as dry as toast. I read the words written there. They stampede through my head, a thousand feet kicking at my skull.

Fucking bitch. Watch your back. I'm following your every move.

I come close to tearing up the letter, stuffing it into the bottom of the bin, closing the lid with a resounding bang and pretending it never existed, but common sense stops me. Instead, I stuff it back into the envelope and slip it into the back pocket of my jeans. I'll put it into my handbag later but for now, I just want it out of my sight. The very thought of having such a nasty little note on my person makes me feel quite sick, but with Wade wandering about upstairs, about to make an appearance in the kitchen, I have no choice. Just when I thought it was all over, another letter arrives and once again my steady little existence is plunged into freefall.

I make breakfast, trying to ignore the rush of blood to my head, trying to ignore the screaming voice that is bouncing around my brain, telling me something is terribly wrong and this thing is not going to go away. This is the third note. They are stacking up. The others were revolting for sure, but this one has an air of menace to it. It's not just an observation, a stream of disjointed pitiful words designed to unnerve me. It's a threat.

I swallow, my throat thick with unshed tears. Why did I think this was going to come to an abrupt, unexplained end? Of course it isn't. These letters have a purpose. They are designed to scare me, to warn me. And they are going to keep on coming until I do something to stop them.

The familiar drag of slippered feet on the carpet makes me

go hot and cold at the same time. Wade is on his way downstairs. I straighten my posture, run my fingers through my hair, try to steady my shaking hands. I can't let this most recent letter ruin our weekend. If there's one thing my partner is good at, it's reading people. One tiny facial tic, the slightest of pauses in the conversation and he will see it, store it in his head and make a point of bringing it up when I least expect it. He is an astute man, clever and shrewd. It's his job to be perceptive. As an HR manager at a large bank, Wade deals with people's nuances and foibles for a living. The thought of having to keep up a pretence for the entire weekend fills me with dread. I could tell him about my one-night stand, get it out in the open, free myself of this heavy burden that is pushing me deep into the ground – and ruin both of our lives. Or I could lie through my teeth, enjoy our time together whilst feeling horribly remorseful, bone-tired and gritty eyed with all the play-acting and pretending that I will have to do.

'Morning, sexy. I thought you might have stayed in bed with me.' He comes up behind me, wraps his arms around my shoulders, plants a hot dry kiss on the back of my neck. I shiver, force myself to smile, then turn around to look at him, to stare deep into his eyes, my face tight with hidden emotions. Such a tension of opposites – absolute love alongside fear and betrayal. How far I have fallen in recent months.

'Thought I would leave you to sleep. It's been a busy week,' I say softly as I reach up to push a stray lock of hair out of his eyes.

'Certainly has.' He moves away, stretches, his navel becoming exposed as his arms are raised. The usual feelings that flood through me, the deep stirrings of desire at the sight of his toned torso and the spread of dark hair on his tanned skin are absent. Normally I would watch him, coax him back to bed. But not today. Today my mind is elsewhere, my emotions in a tight knot as I try to push the letter out of my thoughts once more. Every time I think I have this thing licked, the writer ups their game, leaving me in a state of panic and confusion.

'What do you fancy doing today, then?' His voice is so light, so innocent and unassuming it makes me want to weep. How could I possibly break his world apart by telling him what I did? The thought of sitting down opposite the love of my life and revealing the whole sleazy episode to him is unthinkable. I can't do it. It would break him, and Wade doesn't deserve to be broken. He's a good man, a solid reliable man with strong principles, unshakeable ethics, a man who trusts me implicitly. A man who doesn't really know me at all. Not the real me. I don't deserve him.

I shrug, try to look untroubled. 'We could go into town, amble around the shops and then have lunch at Cezano's?' My heart is flipping around my chest like a fish on dry land as my words come spewing out, rapid and unstoppable. I swallow, clear my throat then take a sip of coffee to disguise the tremor I feel sure is visible in my neck. A tiny gavel tapping away at my throat as I try to conceal my growing panic.

'Cezano's sounds good to me,' Wade says cheerily, seemingly unaware of my creeping distress. 'Now let's eat these eggs before they become totally inedible.' He bustles past me and takes over at the stove, humming innocently as he fries bacon and flips the already overcooked eggs. Hot fat spits and sizzles into the air. I step back, moving away from the heat and patting at my burning cheeks, my appetite waning by the second.

We eat at the kitchen table, Wade shovelling food away as if he hasn't eaten for weeks, while I nibble and poke at mine, hoping he is too engrossed in his own food to notice that I've barely touched mine. My stomach has shrunk and my throat is tight. Nausea nips at my gut. I sip at my juice and watch as he chases the last bit of bacon around his plate before mopping up the egg yolk with a slice of bread.

'Not hungry?' He raises an eyebrow. I suddenly see everything as an accusation, a finger of suspicion being pointed in my direction. I am becoming neurotic, paranoid. I am coming undone, tiny threads of my sanity fraying and falling around me.

I fight to get my words out. They stick in my throat, clunky and misshapen, like large boulders too big for my mouth. 'Guess I'm still full from supper last night,' I whisper, the sentence eerily distant and slightly distorted. I cough, take another swig of orange juice, my teeth knocking against the glass as I hold it to my lips.

'Well I'm starving so you won't mind if–?'

I shake my head and push my plate towards him, grateful he hasn't noticed my nervous disposition, the raw croakiness in my voice as I speak, the flush of crimson I feel sure is visible on my skin.

Wade manages to finish off my breakfast and sits back, replete, satisfaction evident in his expression.

'You won't eat your lunch,' I say with a slight smile.

He pats his lean stomach, winks at me. 'You reckon? You know me better than that, Stell. Always room for some more.'

I look away. A small amount of vomit begins to rise up my throat at the thought of eating anything at all.

I'm following your every move.

I shiver despite the warmth in the kitchen. Today, yet again, I got to the post first. I got lucky. It's only a matter of time before Wade gets there before me, finds the envelope and asks what's inside. Or worse still, opens it, releasing my Pandora's box of secrets and horrors into the open. Once released, they can never be put back. I visualise the arguments, the tears, the bitter recriminations that will inevitably follow just as surely as night follows day.

A dull thud beats at the base of my skull, a small pulse that continually taps away until I can stand it no more. I get up, the chair legs scraping across the floor tiles.

'What's up? You've not eaten anything. Hope you're not coming down with that stomach bug that's going around.' Wade's voice is brimming with concern. I swallow and fight back tears. 'We can give Cezano's a miss if you're feeling off colour.'

I shake my head and muster up a smile. I've got to stick to our initial plan. Any shift in routine will only exacerbate the problem, drive a wedge between us. Then the letter writer will have won; made me too anxious and frightened to live my life. I've got to carry on as normal and not give in to their threats.

My legs feel hollow as I head into the living room where I open the curtains and plump up cushions. I straighten the tie-backs and rearrange ornaments. Anything at all to take my mind off those stupid fucking notes.

'I'm just giving the place a quick tidy up and then we can get ready to leave,' I say to Wade, shouting over my shoulder as I continue my military-like tidy up of the lounge. My voice is a chirrup. It isn't me. It belongs to somebody else, somebody who is better at coping in a crisis than I am.

'Sounds good. As I said, if you're not up to it, we can give it a miss. I can get the food shopping if you would rather stay at home?'

Suddenly, the thought of being alone in this house, fills me with terror.

I'm following your every move.

What if he's outside, watching me? I let out a low gasp then tell myself to stop it, to calm down. I am my own worst enemy.

Strolling over to the window, I gaze at the empty street, the freshly laid, immaculately clean pavement, the recently tarmacked roads. This is a new area, loads of recently built properties. No trees and very few hedges apart from the recently planted tiny hawthorn bush next to our driveway. Nowhere for anybody to hide. As much as I miss the foliage and birdsong that an established neighbourhood offers, I'm relieved. Open spaces provide safety. Nowhere for possible attackers to crouch and hide.

Wade is behind me as I turn to leave the room. He stares at me and for one awful second, I feel sure that he knows. It's as if I've become transparent, my awful deed there for him to see, fully emblazoned across my features, etched into my skin, running through my veins. But then he smiles and the fog of fear that has been choking me, begins to lift. He knows nothing. Of course he doesn't. How could he know anything about what happened when he was hundreds of miles away? Hundreds of miles away while another man was here lying naked next to me in our bed. I shudder and attempt to smile back.

His voice is sharp and clear as he speaks, like cut glass. He runs his fingers through my hair, teasing out the long strands and rubbing at the base of my neck with his soft warm palm. 'Come on, Miss Ingledew. Let's get you into town and treat you for a change. I know exactly how to put the glow back into your face and the light back into your eyes.'

8

1999

Gingerly dabbing at her face, she plucks up enough courage to look in the mirror. A quick glance is enough to tell her that she needs to stop it. She winces at the red tear-streaked face that is staring back at her. A fist clutches at her stomach, twisting and tugging. She looks all the worse for crying. She has no idea why she does it; why she weeps and sobs afterwards. Yet as much as she tries to hold them in, the tears always seem to find a way out, reddening her swollen eyes, causing her cheeks to flush and burn. But only when she's alone. Not in front of him. Never in his presence.

She turns on the tap, swills her face with ice-cold water, shivers. She once read somewhere that having something cold against your skin can stop the swelling. Her jaw aches where he hit her with the palm of his hand. Not his fist this time, something to be thankful for, but painful nonetheless. She is diminutive, small for her age, he is a grown man, his bulk filling every room he enters.

Taking a towel, she dries herself, patting around the tender area next to her ear. She somehow managed to turn away as her father leaned over her, his anger a palpable force. The image of his drunken face pushes itself to the forefront of her mind, causing her to recoil with disgust. This time it was the side of her face that bore the brunt of his hit. This time. Not like last time when he caught her square in the nose. She had no idea there would be so much blood, that she could lose so much, bleed so profusely and not pass out; thick cerise fluid all over her face and hands, dripping between her fingers like warm syrup and landing in a gloopy mess on the floor.

She leans closer, scrutinises her reflection. There doesn't appear to be any lasting damage. No incriminating marks on her flesh. Nothing to indicate to any of her teachers that the person she lives with is a monster; that the person she lives with is capable of killing her. She is sure it will happen eventually. It's only a matter of time.

Tiptoeing back into her bedroom, she closes the door with a near-silent click, lifts up her bedroom chair, the stink arising from its unwashed cushions causing her to retch. How has she never noticed that before? She is aware that this house is a mess but does her best to keep her own room clean and tidy, to make sure that her tiny space is as good as it can be. It's like swimming against the tide, looking after and trying to care for items in a house that is falling apart. It matches the people who live in it. They are all, in their own awful way, coming apart at the seams, losing their grip, slowly dying, their bones corroding and turning to ash.

She jams the back of the chair under the door handle and steps back, wondering how angry it would make him if he tried to get in and couldn't. She smiles at the thought of it; his fat ugly face turning crimson with frustration and anger. Oh, how she would love to be able to climb down the drainpipe, escape from this place and leave it all behind her. And one day she will. As soon as she's old enough, she'll leave here, begin a new life where everything is shiny and new and nobody will ever hurt her. It keeps her going, that thought, stopping her from sinking into the abyss, a pit so deep she feels sure it could swallow her whole.

~

The rattle wakes her, starting off as a dull clank, swiftly growing into an intense banging that could rouse the entire neighbourhood.

She jumps out of bed, dizzy and disorientated, her head thumping at the rude awakening. And then she remembers. The back of the chair is still lodged under the door handle. Her stomach plummets down to her boots. How could she have forgotten to move it? Tiredness must have gotten the better of her and she dozed off, slept the full night without putting everything back to where it should be. And now she is in trouble. Big trouble. He will be behind it, ready and waiting, hands clenched, fingers itching to connect with her face, to finish off the job properly.

She races over to the door, the handle springing free as she drags the chair over to the other side of the room. Her heart bangs in her chest, solid and unstoppable as she waits for her father to come tearing in, furious at being denied entry. She stops, counts to five. Nothing. Complete silence. Then more knocking.

Reaching out, she pushes it ajar. Her mother is standing there, bedraggled and bleary-eyed, her face full of its usual angst and misery. The girl sucks in her breath. She needs to get ready for school. Being late is just another way of drawing attention to herself and that's the last thing she wants to do. Far easier to slip in unnoticed, head down and get on with her day. Anything out of the ordinary draws attention to her, puts her at the centre of the stage, and that's something she can do without.

'You need to come downstairs. Quickly.' Her mother's voice carries no emotion. The girl's innards contract. She visualises her father waiting for her, his face set like stone, his huge belly even more distended as he leans back on the kitchen counter waiting for her, a sneer on his face, a murderous expression in his eyes.

She heads out of the room, dread consuming her, making her weak and queasy. Her father is asleep on a morning when she leaves for school. He's out of work at the minute. Again. Another job lost. Another thing to drag him down. Another reason to drink. It's a vicious circle and they're all stuck in it, their lives on a downward spiral. All because of him. He forms the groove in their lives and they all have to follow slavishly.

It soon becomes apparent it's not one of her dad's outbursts this time. There's something else going on, something serious. Even more serious than a beating.

Sounds from the living room are sharp; metal grating, voices, clipped and efficient. Taking control of a situation, a serious situation taking place their home.

Leaden feet carry her down the stairs. Her mother is ahead of her, her footfall slow and clumsy borne out of years of anguish and alcohol, years of being bashed about resulting in a woman who looks and acts twice her age. She is punch-drunk; despondent and helpless. Unable to function in a crisis.

The girl stops at the door, her mother's body partly blocking the view. She doesn't need to see it all. Even without the advantage of a clear view, she can tell what's happening. The colour of the uniforms as the medics bustle about, their serious expressions as they kneel next to the person lying on the floor, she feels it keenly, somewhere deep in her gut. A stirring of emotions that she can't quite pinpoint.

'I couldn't wake him up.' Her mother's voice is hoarse and shaky. 'I tried and he wouldn't even open his eyes.'

The girl wonders if her mother is about to cry. It would be a new occurrence, something that she has never before been witness to. Her mother doesn't cry. Ever. They both know what tears bring. They've learned to keep their emotions and fears under wraps, to not answer back, to just keep their heads down and survive.

She peers around her mother's wasted body to the scene in their living room, tries to see her father's face, to work out whether or not he's conscious. No grunting voice or rattling of his tobacco-coated lungs as he struggles to breathe. Stretching on her toes, she manages a glimpse of his legs, his large cumbersome body, but is unable to see his face. Too many people in the way. Too much activity as they all gather around him, speaking quietly, using esoteric language that means nothing to her. She listens carefully, straining to pick up any morsel of information and hears the word 'cardiac'. She knows what that means for sure. They studied it in biology lessons at school. It's linked to heart attacks. The steady thump of her own heart, an erratic beat in her chest, rises up her neck, echoing in her thoughts as she considers what may lie ahead.

The crinkle of fabric and shuffling of feet fills the room. The medics are on the move. They lift the stretcher and manoeuvre his bulky unmoving body across the room, ready for exit. Her mother stays rooted to the spot, her face a sickly beige colour, eyes glassy with shock. Somebody should go with him in the ambulance, take charge, give the hospital his details. The girl knows this. Yet still her mother remains there, immobile. Neither of them able or willing to do anything. They stand and stare, bodies frozen, limbs locked in place. They are useless, can do nothing except watch as the medical team busy themselves in their scabby little living room and take charge of her father's lifeless body.

One of the medics comes over, speaks to her, his voice

authoritative, his eyes searching hers for a level of co-operation she cannot give. She can't hear his words. A buzzing fills her ears as she sees the body of her father disappear into the back of the ambulance. It's as if a great weight has been lifted. She is light as air, her body ready to float off into space.

He's gone. Been removed from their home, from their lives.

She doesn't know for how long, but already the lack of his presence has given the house a different feel. Everything is easier. Even the air feels thinner, easier to breathe, less toxic. The girl takes a deep breath and smiles. A heart attack. Her father has had a heart attack and is being rushed into hospital leaving the two of them alone in the house. She suppresses the smile that is clawing to be free. Just the two of them. No shouting, no swearing. No hitting or slapping. No punching. No more hatred and violence. For how long isn't clear, but at this moment she feels nothing but relief. At long last, they are free.

Leaning back against the wall, she lets out a lingering breath. No, not free. It's a reprieve. That's what it is. They've been granted a reprieve.

She perches on the edge of the sofa, tries to push away the one thought that is jostling for space in her brain. It isn't right, she knows it but can't stop it as it presents itself to her, teasing her with the thought of what could be.

A possible future without her father. Just the two of them here in this house and him lying in his grave, his body rotting, turning into fodder for the worms.

She finally allows the suppressed smile to escape then leans back, closes her eyes and dreams.

9

Lunch is perfect. A two-course meal of prawn curry followed by apple crumble and ice cream. I have a couple of glasses of wine to unwind after a stressful week. Wade insists on it. I finish my meal, even the pudding, eating it without my innards tightening every time my thoughts stray to those letters.

The sensation of my new ruby earrings, featherlight against my skin as I tip my head back to drain the remainder of my wine, gives me a warm glow. I had seen them a few weeks ago and admired them in the jewellers window before moving on elsewhere. I had no idea Wade had even noticed that I was staring at them longingly. And now they're mine because he has bought them for me. The guilt of owning them nips at me, softened slightly by the effects of the alcohol as everything mists over, like a camera lens blurred at the edges portraying the world in a more flattering light.

We finish our meal, settle the bill and spend the rest of the day ambling around town, picking out items of furniture to put on the wish list we have in our heads for when we eventually get an extension put on the house. That's another thing to compound my guilt and rob me of sleep. Wade is determined to cement our relationship, take everything a step further. Once we've got enough money set aside, he has spoken of marriage. It's not that I don't want any of it, it's just that the further we go with our plans, the deeper my guilt runs and the harder it becomes to reveal what I did. If indeed, I ever choose to speak of it at all.

I think about it on the way home. Wade drives, humming along to the music. I lean my head back and close my eyes, pretending to be tired after the wine and the food. I can't tell him about the other man. Not now. I can't risk losing what I have. No matter how much effort I put into mulling it over, raking over this whole thing again and again and again, I keep coming back to the same conclusion – that silence is better than speaking. Silence is better than shattering our neat little world into a thousand tiny pieces.

I keep my eyes shut, feeling the thrum of the engine, hearing the low drone of the wheels on the road as we wind through the country lanes. It's then that the idea comes to me, like an epiphany. It's so simple I don't know why I hadn't already thought of it before. My eyes snap open. The tight knot in my stomach begins to unravel. This idea is a workable plan, a way out of this mess, the efficacy of it so real, so within my grasp that I almost laugh out loud.

We pull up on the driveway and I am practically delirious with the idea that has been supplanted in my head. A great weight has been lifted. I glide into the house, light-headed and buoyant. Wade follows me, commenting on my giddy behaviour. He assumes it's the effects of the wine, or gratitude for my unexpected gift. How little he knows. And how guilty I still feel. Shame combined with relief. A heady mixture. A dangerous combination.

I spend the remainder of the weekend in a near-euphoric haze. We drink more wine on Saturday evening and spend

Sunday morning in bed making love before falling back into a deep dreamless sleep, the likes of which I haven't experienced since I was a child. In the middle of the morning Wade decides we need to replenish our spent levels of energy by eating a large continental breakfast which he brings up to bed. We eat, watch television, drink freshly squeezed orange juice and chat about our plans for the week ahead.

'Don't forget I'm away Wednesday and Thursday at the conference in London. I'll be back Friday afternoon,' Wade says casually as he dips his bread in his egg yolk. I honestly don't know where he puts it. 'I'll come straight home. I'm not going into the office just for a couple of hours, it hardly seems worth it, especially on a Friday, so I should be home by 3.30pm.'

Like a huge jigsaw puzzle, everything suddenly slots neatly into place. The urge to hug him is so strong that I have to restrain myself for fear of giving away my sordid little secret. I had forgotten about his visit to London. This makes everything so much easier, so much less fraught. With any luck, I will have this sorry mess sorted by the time he gets home. No more worrying that I'm being watched, no fear of being alone in the house. Wade's trip has afforded me a chance to bring an end to this episode. I cross my fingers, heart fluttering in my chest at the thought of what I plan on doing. It's a risk, but a necessary one. I can't go on like this, watching over my shoulder, wondering what's coming next. I have to put a stop to it, no matter how risky or unpalatable it may be.

'I've booked a taxi to take me to the station but if you could pick me up on Friday afternoon, that would be great,' he says innocently. 'Or if you can't get away from work on time, I can get a taxi back home again?'

'It's not a problem.' I am almost shouting; my smile stretched a little too wide, my voice a little too loud. I need to curb my eagerness, speak a little less enthusiastically, be a little more reserved. 'I'll leave work shortly after three o'clock so will be there in plenty of time. Everyone is only too keen to get away on Fridays. Even Holland. His car is usually already gone by the time I get to mine.'

Andrew Holland is the headteacher who seems to live at the school, such is his dedication to the place. He arrives at 7am and apart from his early exit every Friday, doesn't leave until well after 6pm. I once stayed behind to finish my lesson plans for the following week, leaving at five minutes to six. I passed his office. His eyes were focused on a wad of documents. I shouted cheerio. He didn't reply, didn't even notice I was leaving.

Wade squeezes my hand and smiles at me. 'Thanks. I don't tell you often enough how much I love you.'

A wave of shame washes over me, bubbling and lingering, turning me cold. I let out an involuntary shiver and nod lightly. 'Love you too, you big old softie.'

He laughs, pulls me closer to him, my head resting on his chest as I shut my eyes and fight back tears. Soon, these feelings will be gone and I will be able to live my life free of the tension that is always frighteningly close to consuming me. If I thought teaching put me on edge, it is nothing compared to how I feel since these letters have started arriving. What they have done, besides scare me, is stir up emotions I would rather stayed dormant. They have caused me to delve into my history, to try to work out who is writing them, and my personal history is something I would rather leave well alone. Mine isn't a pretty past.

I reach up and plant a kiss on Wade's cheek. He is oblivious to the negative thoughts and worries that continually collide in my head, bashing against my skull, bruising my brain. That's a good thing. Perhaps now I can tentatively replace them with positive ones. Focusing on what I plan on doing while Wade is away, I climb out of bed and step into the bathroom, the scent of sex coming off me in waves as I turn on the shower and step inside.

'I was thinking we could visit family this afternoon?' Wade's voice cuts through the sound of gushing water as I tip my head back and wash my hair. Despite the heat of the shower, I suddenly go cold. Every now and then he does this, springs a possible surprise visit on me unbidden in the hope I will soften my resolve. It won't happen. I admire his tenacity but he won't win. Not with matters relating to my family. My mind is made up and I'm not about to change it, especially after our last visit, after what it did to me. How it made me feel. I was wrung out. Humiliated and left despairing.

'Long way to go to visit your parents,' I reply, trying to inject humour into my tone. 'You sure we can make it to Southampton and back in a day?'

His silence says more than words ever could. I hear the shuffle of his footsteps, the slight click of the door as he turns and leaves the bathroom. He will be pondering over my remark, wondering what it will take for me to give in, to just blot out all that is bad about my mother and go and see her. As an intelligent man, he must realise that no matter how many devices, tricks and wily techniques he tries, I will never go. Ever. It is all a waste of time and energy. My past is exactly that; the past. It is a murky desperate place, somewhere I never ever want to revisit. Not even in my head.

I finish showering, get dressed and go downstairs to the kitchen where Wade is sitting staring at his iPad. 'Another storm on its way, apparently,' he says lightly. 'Sterling has risen against the dollar.' He raises his head, stares at me reproachfully. 'Oh, and an old lady may very well go to her grave having not seen her estranged daughter for years and years.' He is trying to make his words sound like the banter that we regularly pass back and forth between us, but we both know that this time it isn't that at all. It is far from that. His words are mean and sharp and cut deep; blades glinting in the sunlight, designed to wound.

I don't reply. What is there to say? My mother was an utterly useless parent. My poverty-stricken family and feral upbringing are something I would sooner forget. Things took place in that house, terrible unspeakable things that I have never uttered to anybody. Nobody knows my childhood secret. Not even Wade. Especially Wade. Our childhoods couldn't have been more different, and yet he still insists on bringing it up, time after time after time. Can he not remember how our last visit made me feel? Does that not bother or worry him?

I grit my teeth, fix my gaze on the fridge door, unable to look at him as I speak. 'Wade, why are you even suggesting this?'

He doesn't answer straightaway. I sneak a glance at him. He shrugs before eventually answering. 'I'm not sure really. I just thought that since you seemed more relaxed than usual, then maybe we could...'

I wait for him to finish, knowing he won't complete his sentence. He doesn't have to. I know by his tone what it is that he is implying, what it was he was going to say. He thought that he would suggest going while I was in a good mood, hoping it would make me more malleable, more forgiving of the past. But of course, Wade doesn't know the full story, does he? He thinks I'm just some poor kid from a rundown estate, some scruffy, snotty-nosed girl who worked hard at school and managed to shake off the shackles of poverty. And now he thinks I am a dreadful snob by refusing to go back there, to be associated with somebody who still lives like a pig, surrounded by furnishings of dubious origins. But that's not it. That's not it at all.

Wade's dad is an accountant, his mum a retired teacher. My dad was unemployed for most of his adult life. My mum was a cleaner, often coming home with pieces of jewellery and trinkets she had stolen from other people's houses. No amount of visiting my mother in my childhood home will ever change that and no amount of Wade asking me will ever make me go.

'Do you recall our last visit there?'

His silence speaks volumes.

Our last visit saw my mother so drunk that we had to put her to bed. Then we spent hours cleaning the house. At least a month's worth of dirty pots was stacked up in the sink; the house smelled like an old ashtray. My feet literally stuck to the carpet. My stomach had roiled, my sense of shame and despair had multiplied exponentially as I scrubbed and polished and disinfected every surface until they gleamed like new.

Shame burrowed deep in me alongside anger and exasperation. It sent me on a downward spiral, ghosts of my childhood filtering back into my brain, sitting there, refusing to move. I can't go through that again. I simply can't.

'She contacted you, didn't she? Asking me to go around there.'

A small nod, barely noticeable but a nod all the same.

'She wants money, Wade. She doesn't want to see me. All she wants is for us to hand over a wad of cash so she can spend it on booze and fags.' I am almost shouting now. If I am being honest, I would give her the money if she asked for it. I don't give a shit about the money. What I do give a shit about is what happened to me in that house. On our last visit, I promised myself that I would never go back there and I intend to stick to that promise. Going back into those rooms, remembering it all...

'Look, Stella, maybe if we can just go and–'

'No! Listen to what I'm saying, Wade. I'm not going back there. You think you know me but you're wrong! You know nothing about what went on in that house.' The words escape, a sudden shriek spilling out, a river of raging water gouging out a chasm between us.

He is stunned by the ferocity of my tone but his cautious

nature is telling him to back off. I hope he remembers how I was after our last visit, what happened to us. I don't care if she is my mother or not. She simply isn't worth it.

My head is pounding. Just when I thought I could begin to breathe easily again, my life takes another wrong turn, yet another twisting diversion that disorientates me, and I am redirected back to the start.

I sit down in the nearest chair, place my head in my hands and close my eyes, wondering where the next revolting surprise is going to come from.

10

'I just wish you would be more open to the idea of visiting her. And I also know that there's something else that you're not telling me. I'm not an idiot, Stella. I've got eyes you know.' Behind Wade's gentle tone there's an edge to his voice that tells me he isn't prepared to let this thing go.

I have news for him. Neither am I.

I've already managed to pull myself together. I have to, otherwise my life will be on a loop, my past forever dragging me back to that dark place. And that will mean that he has won. Instead, I will keep on with my life, try to forget how that man almost ruined me. For so many years I have tried to allow him no place in my life, and here Wade is, unknowingly, pulling him back in.

I'm up on my feet, my movements brusque and orderly. I think about Wade's words, the hidden meaning. I'm not sure whether he is referring to my childhood or saying that he knows about the recent letters. Or our brief time apart when I slept with another man. I shudder.

'I don't want to talk about it. I've said my bit, now can we just move on, please?' My voice is a hoarse rasp, my hands are trembling. I risk telling Wade everything if I stay in this frame of mind; everything about my childhood. That shadowy place that I never want to revisit. I've hung on to it for so long now that I honestly don't think I can let it go. I can't verbalise what happened all those years ago. Saying the words out loud, hearing them with my own ears would make it real. Better to keep it all tucked away out of sight; pretend none of it ever happened.

Wade's stance is neutral, his face impassive, but his brain is on fire. He is trying to figure out what I'm thinking, trying to work out why my hatred runs so deep. I won't hear the last of this. I just know it. And now a perfectly good weekend has been ruined.

'Okay, whatever you say,' he replies quietly. 'But remember this. When we got together, we promised there would be no secrets. I've kept my side of the bargain. How about you?'

The firm bang of the door as he leaves the room makes me go cold. I thought I had this all sorted, my past, my present. Our future. And now look at me. Look at us.

An unwanted thought slowly pushes its way into my consciousness, crouching and waiting. Biding its time. I don't want to think about it but it refuses to leave until I give it some consideration. Is this whole thing a ruse cooked up by Wade to trick me into coming clean? Does he know about the other guy and this is his way of getting me to admit to it? Was it him who sent those fucking letters in the first place and now he is suggesting this visit in the hope I'll unravel and confess? I dismiss such thoughts, let out a dry caustic laugh. Not his style. Wade is too sophisticated for such behaviour. But of course, how well do we really know those around us? Wade thinks he knows me and look at all the secrets I am hiding. Maybe there is more to him than I realise. Maybe I don't really know him at all. I shake my head, rid myself of such trashy thoughts. But then, if I don't give it some consideration, and Wade is onto me and all of this blows up in my face because I'm not prepared–

No. I refuse to go down that route. Wade is better than that. I'm not. He is not like me at all. I am the keeper of many secrets, the doer of many dark deeds.

Despite my efforts to push that reprobate thought away, it nips at me for the rest of the day. Wade is predictably quiet and distant, spending most of his time in the garden, weeding and tidying up our small patio area, sweeping it until it practically gleams. I can't change how he thinks so decide to leave him be. I too need some space, some time to clear my head.

I keep myself busy marking books, planning lessons, preparing for the week ahead. I briefly consider contacting Astrid about what I am planning on doing while Wade is away then decide against it. Too risky. If I text her, she will undoubtedly want more information then ring me. Wade will walk in and I'll have to clam up, deepening his distrust of me even further. That discussion can wait until tomorrow. It's not one that I'm relishing but as far as I can see, it remains my only option.

Astrid was there that night. She knows Glenn. I know nothing about him except his endeavours in bed, and even that is thankfully hazy. If she gives me the briefest of details, I might just be able to trace the source of those letters. It means telling her everything. The thought of doing it makes my guts flip. She is one of my closest friends. I know that I can rely on her to keep my secret. What I'm more worried about is her inner judgement of me. After expelling Glenn from the house, I hoped to forget about everything but now it looks like I have no choice but to reveal all to Astrid. Whether I like it or not, this problem will not disappear unless I do something about it. And that something has to come from Astrid.

I swallow hard, shut my eyes. The thought of the letters not being penned by him, that they could have come from somebody closer to home, sends me dizzy. I swat that notion away. Not Wade, my Wade. He wouldn't do such a thing. Even considering it as a possibility is wrong. I'm not thinking clearly. I need to slow down. I will go ahead with my plan, go and see this Glenn guy and then take things from there.

Wade wouldn't have even been on my radar had he not suggested visiting my mother this morning. I've interpreted his words as something suspicious and conniving. As usual, I'm putting two and two together and coming up with five.

The day drags by, the mood in the house cloying and oppressive, like a heavy weight has been placed over us, robbing us both of any light. I'm aware that I need to do something to alleviate the tension between us but can't bring myself to speak. Can I really tell him what happened in my childhood home? Will opening up that particular can of worms bring us closer or simply leave me feeling flattened?

We eat our evening meal in near silence and go to bed without speaking, both of us lying there, locked in our own personal thoughts, so near and yet so very far apart. It's only as I eventually drift off to sleep, that I make my decision. I have to tell him what took place in my mother's house. He deserves to know. I deserve some relief from carrying around such a heavy burden.

I drift off feeling easier, knowing that in the morning I will be able to see my past through fresher eyes. Unloading my worries onto Wade can only be a good thing, can't it?

11

'This is a joke, right?' Astrid's voice is a thin strand of scepticism and disbelief. Her face doesn't betray her disgust or incredulity at my revelation. 'You slept with Glenn Edwards?' She leans back in her chair, narrows her eyes. 'Jesus, Stella. What the actual fuck were you thinking?'

My whole body feels as if it's vibrating. An uncomfortable tingling sensation creeps up my neck, over my scalp, behind my eyes. I hoped for more than this. Perhaps some understanding, maybe even a tiny element of compassion but definitely not this.

We're sitting in the corner of a café close to the school. I figured it would be safer, easier to open up in here than in a crowded staffroom where walls have ears. I watch a couple sitting at the counter, giving Astrid a couple of seconds to digest my words. I focus on their movements, on how the woman dips her long slender fingers into her purse, how the man glances around, looking for a table. I focus on anything I can to avoid Astrid's unwavering and censorious gaze.

'Please don't judge me, Astrid. I was at a low point, and I *know* that's no excuse, but please don't shut me out or click your tongue at me.' The sentence tumbles out of my mouth, rapid and garbled, and the net result is a hideous coughing fit that leaves me shaking and bleary-eyed.

She lets out a loud sigh, leans forward, rests her small pale hand on my shoulder. 'I'm not judging you, Stell. I'm shocked. I'll admit that, but I'm not criticising you. I'm horrified at your choice, that's all.'

'Okay, so he was a bit of a slimeball, but we all make mistakes, don't we? I'd had a fair bit to drink and had an awful day and me and Wade were–'

'It's not that,' she says quietly, dipping her head before raising it again to look at me. Her eyes have taken on a different hue. They look darker, more serious. A worrying frown line has set in across her brow. I clear my throat and wait for her to continue, wanting and yet not wanting to hear what it is she has to say.

Astrid leans back and chews at her lip nervously. 'He's a real oddball, Stella. If I'd known you were going to hook up with him, I'd have done my utmost to stop you.'

'But you didn't know. This is all down to me.' I blink away hot tears brought on by shame and embarrassment. 'Now, what do you know about him? You have to tell me. This is important.'

A pulse throbs in her neck. Her tendons are stretched like catgut. I feel my blood pressure begin to build. *What in God's name is she going to come out with? What in God's name have I started?*

Astrid sighs quietly, turns away and blinks. 'One of my friends had to take out a restraining order against him while we were at university.'

The floor tips and sways under me. My airway shrinks and I have to grip the edge of the chair for balance. It's a few seconds before I can find the energy to speak.

'What did he do?' My voice is gravelly, my chest tight.

Astrid sighs, rests her hands on the table, her skin like

parchment as she struggles for the right words. 'He followed her around. Nothing too serious to start with. He even bought her some flowers and at first, she was quite flattered, but when she turned down his offer of a date, he started to get nasty, sending her threatening notes and messages. Then one day after she'd told him to sling his hook, he turned up at her flat drunk. She opened the door to him and he pushed her inside and slammed her up against a wall, placing his hands around her throat, threatening to kill her.'

All the air has been sucked out of the room. I hold on to my neck, my fingers splayed over my collarbone. Flames pulse behind my eyes. My heartbeat thuds around my chest, roaring in my head.

Astrid grabs hold of my hands, pulls me closer to her and catches my eye. 'He won't do anything like that to you, I promise.' She told the police and he admitted his guilt almost immediately. He was prosecuted and issued with a restraining order. He lost his job, left town and went to live back with his mum in Northallerton.'

'Whereabouts?' I'm shouting now. I can't help it. To think I suspected Wade, the faithful one, the other half of me. I'm consumed with remorse and shame. And anger. Why didn't Astrid tell me? She is meant to be my friend.

Astrid leans away from me, a flicker of apprehension settling on her features. 'Why? Why do you need to know his address? What's happened?'

I start to cry. Silent fat tears roll down my face. I wipe them away with the back of my hand, look into Astrid's wide eyes, to her stricken expression. And then I tell her. It all comes spilling out.

It's surprisingly easy, unloading my festering secret onto somebody else. Watching it float away is mildly therapeutic. Astrid is absorbing some of my problem, lessening my load.

'Are you sure the letters are from him?' she asks quietly.

I stare at her.

She blinks slowly and shakes her head. 'Yes, sorry. Of course they're from him. It follows the pattern of behaviour, doesn't it? Jesus, Stella, this really is totally shit, isn't it?'

She holds my hand over the table, her cool skin reassuring against my hot, clammy flesh. 'We'll sort this, I promise. This time in a couple of weeks, you'll have forgotten all about it.'

'Only if I go to his house and warn him,' I say quietly. I think of Astrid's friend and Glenn and how he tried to strangle her. A ripple of fear runs through me. Already I can feel his cold fingers against my throat, his strong grasp cutting off my air supply, the small bones in my neck snapping under his grip. I shake the thought away.

'Right, yeah. Maybe given his history we should go to the police instead.'

Blood thunders through my ears. *The police. Dear God, anything but the police.*

'Out of the question. I can't do that, Astrid. You know I can't. And you know why. Please don't make me. All I need is Glenn's address. If I go to the police, Wade will find out. I can't let that happen.'

Astrid looks away, peering through the window to the stream of passers-by outside. An exasperated woman with a screaming toddler hanging from her hand walks past followed by two men in suits, their eyes locked on to their phones. A gaggle of young mothers, a group of pensioners, they all pass by our window. The world, happily doing its thing while we sit here speaking about the unspeakable.

'His address, Astrid. I know you've got it.' I don't know anything of the sort but if I come across as nervous, she will try to manipulate me into doing as she asks and going to the police and that absolutely cannot happen. The police will probe into every little thing – my workplace, my homelife – their investigations will focus just as much on me as they will on this stupid fucking Glenn, who is doing his damnedest to ruin what I've worked hard to achieve. If I let some officer take a peek at the detritus of my life and ask me about the night I had sex with a perfect stranger while my partner was out of town, everything will unravel completely. My life will splinter, everything breaking apart with no way of putting it all back together.

Astrid lets out a ragged breath, reaches into her handbag, produces her phone and glares at me. 'I don't have his address but Maria does. She's the one he stalked. She made a point of keeping tabs on him after the court case, just in case he tried anything again.'

'And has he?'

The dismissive shake of her head doesn't convince me. She scrolls through her phone, her immaculately painted nails tapping against the screen as she searches for a contact. 'Not that I'm aware of. I'm pretty sure Maria would have told me if he had done anything untoward.' She keeps her eyes dipped, still searching, her teeth nibbling at her lower lip.

'Astrid, I'm not blaming you, but why didn't you tell me? Why didn't you stop me from leaving with him?'

Her head whips up, a strand of golden hair hanging over her right eye as she stares at me. 'Stop you? Stell, the last time I saw you, you were just chatting to him. I'd done my best to drag everyone away from him. If you remember, we kept moving around the place, changing tables?'

I think back to that night, a vague recollection of walking around the pub, Astrid's arm linked through mine as we moved across the room. I had no idea it was because of him. Everything was a blur, the floor like liquid as we moved and slalomed through a throng of people.

'I saw you chatting to him though,' I say. 'I presumed you

were friends with him.' My voice sounds weak and pathetic. I'm clutching at anything here to shift the blame away from me.

Astrid puffs out her cheeks and continues scrolling through her phone. 'Well, I wasn't about to upset him, was I? I thought that being nice to him and moving away would do the trick. I couldn't exactly shout at the top of my voice that he was a psycho, could I?'

I nod and fight back more tears. I'm lashing out here, blaming Astrid when the fault lies entirely with me. I should have gone home alone, not had sex with a perfect stranger just because I was lonely and upset.

'Sorry,' I mumble wearily. 'I'm just worried, that's all.'

'Believe me, if I'd known you were about to go home with him, I would have dived right in and stopped you.'

'But you didn't see me go, I know that. I deliberately left without you knowing. Sorry. Again.' My heart is hammering out a thick arrhythmic beat in my chest as Astrid taps a message into her phone and places it down on the table between us.

She looks at me, her face set like stone. 'We just need to wait for Maria's reply now.'

'What did you say to her?' I manage to croak. I pray to God she didn't mention me or anything that's happened. Humiliation drapes itself over me, a heavy cloak of disgrace and dishonour.

'Don't worry, I didn't say anything about you. I spun some tale about thinking I'd just seen him and asked where he was living now, making it sound like a casual enquiry. I told her I wanted his address so I could give him a wide berth.' She gives me a sideways glance; one I recognise well. 'Have a little faith in me, Stella. I'm not that stupid. I'm not about to drop you in it, am I?'

'I know. God, I'm coming across as so selfish and thoughtless. I can't thank you enough for this. For everything.'

She pats my hand, nods knowingly. 'We need to be back in

school in ten minutes. Keep your phone handy. I'll text you if she replies when we're back in class. Come on. Let's head back.'

Her phone buzzes as we're leaving the café. It's only been a matter of minutes. My stomach lurches. What sort of a guy is he that a casual enquiry prompts an immediate response?

'There's your address,' she says, handing me her phone. 'When are you planning on going? And who are you going to take with you because there's no way you're going on your own.'

I chew at my lip. 'I hadn't thought about it.' In truth, prior to knowing Glenn's history I had planned on going on my own but this piece of information about his past changes everything. Confronting a man with a prior conviction for violence isn't an appealing option.

'I'm going with you,' she says rapidly. I start to protest but Astrid holds up her hand, giving me one of her withering looks. I know better than to argue. 'You know I'm as hard as nails and you also know that you're as soft as shit compared to me. Don't try to stop me or I'll kick your arse, Stella Ingledew.'

She links her arm through mine, the earlier tension between us, dissolving. We've known one another too long for any disagreements to become permanent. I'm thankful for that fact. I'm thankful to have Astrid by my side.

Turning the corner into the staff car park, my stomach drops at the thought of spending the afternoon trapped in a classroom with thirty teenagers who don't want to be there any more than I do. The green metal fence stretched around the perimeter of the school is a formidable sight, stamping out any notion that this is a comfortable place to be and that people are welcome here. I've never been entirely certain of its purpose – whether it is to stop intruders from breaking in, or to stop the people inside from getting out.

I hear the remote chatter of teenagers as they wander about the yard, their voices dulled by distance. Astrid tugs at my arm, pulls me to one side, her fingers digging into my skin through the fabric of my sweater. 'We've got exactly four minutes left. Fancy a quick ciggie?'

Four precious minutes. I nod even though I haven't smoked since university, and follow her over to the corner of the car park where we huddle behind the school sign, lighting up like a pair of juvenile delinquents. I take a couple of drags, watch Astrid as she inhales rapidly over and over before throwing her cigarette on the floor and grinding it underfoot. I take one final drag and do the same, dropping the half-smoked cigarette at my feet. I stare at the floor; at a trail of pale grey smoke filtering up from the pavement where our cigarettes lie, crushed and broken, still smouldering. A metaphor for my life. 'Come on,' she says huskily. 'Lunch break's over. Let's head back through the gates of hell.'

12

1999

She hoped that once the news spread about her father, things would get easier at school, that everyone would back off, leave her be, if only for a short while. She couldn't have been more wrong. It provided them with more reasons to hate her, furnished them with the belief that she was too far removed from their flawless lifestyles to be considered normal. To be considered one of them with their perfectly manicured nails and coiffured hair.

'Morning, freak. How's your dad? Beaten up any nurses yet?'

She ignores the comment, slides behind her desk, busying herself with rearranging her stationery. A cheap biro, a chewed pencil and a broken rubber sit pitifully in front of her, the sight of them exacerbating her misery and sense of isolation even further.

'Come on,' one of the girls mutters, 'let's move away and sit at the back. Can't stand the smell around here. Makes me want to puke.'

The teacher is late. The racket in the classroom grows, reaching a crescendo; a wall of noise that halts as a ruler is thrown across the room, hitting her on the side of her cheek.

There is a crushing silence interspersed with an occasional giggle. Her face burns with mortification. A stinging sensation mushrooms over her flesh. She lifts a trembling hand to ease the pain, applying pressure, trying to play it down. She's had worse. Far worse.

'Hope you're not gonna cry, freak. We don't like cry-babies.'

Her eyes snap shut. She exhales. The same group of girls every time. They're relentless, following her, refusing to leave her alone. They have made it their mission to tear her down, strip her of what little dignity she has left, and make her life utterly miserable.

Relief ripples through her as the teacher enters, stands at the front, arms folded, wearing a thunderous expression. The shouting that ensues means nothing to her. She's impervious to the roars of Mr Waite as he tells the class exactly what he thinks of them. He explains his reasons for the delay, that he had to attend to a child who had fallen on the stairs. He had stopped to help her he says, because that was the decent thing to do, not that any of the immature young people before him would realise that. He continues with his tirade, yelling at them that it was about time the kids in this class started acting as responsible youngsters instead of carrying on like a group of toddlers when left unsupervised.

The lesson passes in silence, even the most challenging and volatile of pupils too afraid to speak out or misbehave or even breathe too loudly. Old Waitesy doesn't shout very often but when he does, everybody is wise enough to shut up and keep their heads down.

It's as she is leaving the building, slipping unnoticed through the throng of bodies at the school gate that a tug on her arm yanks her backwards, the vice-like grip filling her with dread.

'Off somewhere, are we? Why the hurry, freak?'

Her heart thuds in her chest, a deep thrum as she stares

down at the ground, at the mass of grey shadows gathered there, an ominous globe of darkness that surrounds her.

She pulls her arm free, yanking it away roughly and starts to walk away but is dragged back again. 'Not quite ready to let you go just yet, freak. Come on, we're going for nice little stroll.'

Doing her best to ignore the relentless barrage of insults thrown her way, she hones in on their methods, watches how they operate, feeding off each other using mob mentality to back one another up and fuel their collective hatred of her.

The taller girl is the leader, throwing insults at anybody who doesn't laugh at her jokes, pushing others aside as she strides past, her long blonde hair flowing behind her like strands of cotton. Beside her is a solemn girl with long dark hair who every so often, steals a glance the girl's way, a flicker of something remotely human in her eyes. Three others flock around the leader, vying for her attention with snippets of stories about their lives; dull witless tales that have no meaning or substance, designed to gain attention, to catapult them into her line of sight. They are like salivating dogs desperate for a morsel of meat. Desperate to be recognised and rewarded for their efforts.

'So, is your dad going to live then, freak? Bet you're hoping he dies, aren't you? My dad reckons he's better off dead. Said it's good enough for him.'

The ringleader stops walking once they reach the river's edge, keeping hold of the girl, her nails digging into the soft flesh on her upper arm.

'Tell you what!' one of the others shrieks excitedly. 'Let's dunk her like a witch. If she comes back up, her dad'll live. If she stays underwater, her old man'll croak.'

The girl's stomach contracts. Five against one. She stands no chance. She can only hope one of them sees sense and rails against the idea. Most bullies see sense eventually. They all have their cut-off point; an invisible boundary that should never be crossed.

A short silence descends, the air crackling with the anticipation of what could happen, what sickening event could take place in the next few minutes. The girl swallows down vomit. She can't let them see how frightened she is. Any chinks in her armour will empower them. That's how people like this function; they feed off the weak and vulnerable, like parasites, desperate to exist, to feel important. To feel alive.

She puts back her shoulders, tries to look unfazed by the comment. It's all bluff and bluster. It has to be. Even this lot aren't that stupid. She tries to take an unsteady step backwards but the hold on her arm is too strong; like a vice locking her in place on the riverbank. Running will be futile. The best she can hope for is that common sense and an ounce of decency prevail.

As casually, as surreptitiously as she can, she runs her eyes over all five of them. The leader is looking mildly amused while the others wait for her reply; vultures waiting, wanting. The one with the human expression is turned away from her, staring out at the fast-flowing water. A glimmer of hope stirs deep within the girl. That person is her only hope. She is the one who could possibly turn this scenario round, make them see that this could go so horribly wrong given the recent weather conditions, given the height of the water and the slippery riverbank. Two days of solid rain has turned the river into a torrent of gushing water, an unstoppable and treacherous force for even the strongest of swimmers.

'Right,' the ringleader says, her voice cool, detached, disconnected from the reality of what it is she is about to do, 'let's drag her down to the edge.'

The girl feels an army of hands pulling her across the wet grass, her feet grappling for purchase on the saturated ground. She lets out a roar of protestation. There must be somebody close by – a dog walker, a fisherman – anybody who can put an end to this horror and help her to escape.

A hot hand is clamped over her mouth. 'Shut up, freak. It's only a bit of water. What you scared of? You could do with a wash anyway, you filthy, skanky bitch.'

Her eyes swivel in her head. The leader is ahead of the gang, her long, slim legs striding towards the river's edge, towards the frothing, crashing water, dark and icy cold. The girl flinches, tries to dig her heels into the soil, resulting in a backward tumble. She falls, a soft body beneath her own breaking her fall.

'You stupid cow!' At least two of them yank her back up, her arms twisted high up her back until she feels sure they will break, popping out of their sockets in one rapid painful movement.

'Hurry up! Come on. Move it. Get back up before anybody sees us.'

'Do that again, freak,' a voice spits in her ear, 'and I swear to God I will rip every hair out of that stinking head of yours. Now move!'

She is powerless to stop them, feeling herself being dragged closer and closer to the water, her feet digging and slipping, twisting and writhing as she attempts to escape their clutches. Head spinning wildly, she tries to catch the eye of the quiet one, the only one who appears to have a conscience. Or a brain. She is close by, silent, her gaze vacant, hands dipped deep into her pockets. She keeps her face lowered as the rest of them pull the girl into the reeds that line the edge of the bank.

'Please!' she hisses at her. 'Help me?'

The quiet one doesn't respond, continuing to stand idly by as the girl is dragged into the numbingly cold water. 'I know you don't want to do this!' the girl screams. A hand is placed at the back of her neck. 'You're not like them,' she half cries. 'Please help me!'

Before she can check to see if the quiet one has responded to her plea, a sudden push forces her face underwater, heavy hands holding her in place under the freezing current that froths and roars around her, heavy hands that keep her dipped into the icy blackness, stopping her from breathing.

Her head is released after a few seconds. She feels like she has been under there for a lifetime. She surfaces, spluttering, sobbing, tears blurring her vision. She coughs and wheezes, barely having time to catch her breath before being forced down once more, her mouth scooping up muddy water as her face hits the river with a hard slap.

The cold is unbearable. She keeps her eyes closed tight, her chest ballooning with the effort of holding her breath. Her body bucks and twists as she fights to escape, to breathe and stay alive. Only when stars burst behind her eyes and she feels faint is she allowed back up for air.

Everything spins; the spread of trees overhead, the puffball clouds, they rotate manically as her brain struggles to cope. She falls back on the riverbank to the sound of laughter. A nearby foot nudges her ribs, pushing at her soft skin. 'Had enough yet, River Girl? See, the thing is, we still don't know whether or not your old man is gonna live or die so we might have to give you another dunking.'

She gasps for breath, blinking rapidly, trying to work out if the quiet one is nearby. She is her only hope. Or perhaps not. If she had wanted to intervene and help, she would have done it by now, wouldn't she? Maybe she was one of the ones holding her down, keeping her underwater, pushing her body to its limits as her lungs screamed for air and her brain went into meltdown thinking she was going to die.

Rolling onto her back, she is confronted with a sea of faces looming over her, eyes glinting with malevolence, expressions lined with hatred, their nostrils dark and wide, mouths gaping as they cackle and laugh at her, watching her closely as she gasps for breath. She tries to count them, to work out the ratio but her vision is blurred, her mind detached and disordered. Still, she tries. She has to. It's all she is able to do. Fighting back is pointless. So many of them. So much hatred.

Five. She thinks there are five of them but then blinks and sees only three. Or is it four? Too exhausted to think straight. Everything is unclear, too difficult to fathom. Her ribs ache. She wants to sleep, to disappear and wake up to see nothing but the glow of a russet sunset or a clear caerulean sky above her, unbroken by clouds.

She is hoisted up, dragged upright by rough pawing hands. She steels herself, certain that this is the end. That this is the part where they will hold her under until she stops kicking, the part where death will take her.

'Leave her.' An echo. An unrecognisable sound coming from close by. 'Come on, I'm bored now.'

The voice sounds distorted. An intangible noise. A warped string of words that could just save her. She has no idea who it is, who the voice belongs to, but has to stop herself from sobbing hysterically, hollering her gratitude as feet reluctantly shuffle away, voices muttering, complaining, leaving her like a wet rag, spreadeagled on the riverbank. Was it her – the quiet one? Did she finally speak and put a stop to their wicked, twisted game?

Only when they are all safely out of sight does she break down, her body heaving and convulsing as the tears spill out, dripping onto her already saturated clothes.

13

Wade sits opposite me. I tried; I really did. I wanted so much to tell him about my past but the words refused to come. The feel of them in my mouth made me gag; the thought of saying them out loud was so unutterably awful I thought I might pass out.

I had suggested a meal at the local pub, hoping a neutral environment and a glass of Chardonnay would calm me down, help me to open up but it hasn't worked. So here we sit, me rigid and uptight, making small talk about work, about the weather, about anything at all while a flurry of thoughts whirl around my head, distracting me, knocking me off balance.

The ill-feeling from earlier in the week seems to have gone and I had hoped the easy atmosphere between us would help me to speak more freely, but no matter how much I focus, tell myself to open up, to bare my soul to the person I am closest to in the whole world, I simply cannot do it. Every word and phrase sticks in my throat, choking me every time I try to make a sound.

Wade is away tomorrow at a conference and won't be back until Friday. Glenn's address is safely tucked away at the bottom of my knicker drawer. Not that I need to keep a hard copy of it.

I've Googled it time and time again, poring over the computer, staring at his house, wondering if there is some telltale sign, a clue as what sort of person resides there. The number of his house is embedded deep in my brain. Once I've made the visit, I will dispose of the paper, clear my search history even though I know Wade would never look. Deception is making me paranoid, turning me into somebody I'm not, somebody I never ever wanted to be.

We finish our meal and sit in companionable silence, sipping at our drinks, watching the sun as it dips over the trees in the distance, turning the sky into a swathe of burnt amber.

Wade grabs my hand as we walk the short distance home. 'Remember to lock all the doors and windows when I'm away. And don't let next door's cat shit on the lawn.'

'You're so romantic,' I laugh, squeezing his hand and fumbling in the side pocket of my bag for the house key.

'Yes well,' he says with a wry smile, 'somebody has to keep you on track, Miss Ingledew. Now let's get up to that bedroom.' He winks at me and despite my nervous disposition, I melt. A night of unbridled passion may be just what I need right now.

I wake up with mixed feelings about what lies ahead; relief at Wade being hundreds of miles away while I sort out the mess of the letters, and trepidation at the thought of actually doing it.

Breakfast is a cup of sour coffee that I have to force down. Wade is in the hallway, busily checking his briefcase, ensuring he's packed everything he needs for the next two days.

'Okay, my taxi is here.' He walks back through to the kitchen, tucking his phone into his breast pocket, tapping it lightly. 'Don't forget to lock everything at night. I'll see you Friday at the station. I'll text you to let you know if there are any delays.'

We hug, his body warm and sweet smelling as he leans into me. 'I'll call you tonight once the conference is finished. Love you.'

'Love you more,' I say softly, an unexpected lump rising in my throat. I swallow it down, plant a kiss on his cheek, enjoying his rugged skin against my lips. I want to hold on to this moment, to remember it, treasure it. Our last kiss before I carry out my deceitful mission.

I stand at the doorstep, watching as he clambers into the silver taxi. I think better of blowing a kiss, giving instead a hearty wave before slamming the door shut then slumping against it, my heart hammering wildly beneath my blue cheesecloth shirt. Why am I so nervous and out of sorts? I have a full day at work ahead of me before Astrid and I put my plan into action. I need to calm down and get a grip of my emotions.

Relief at not receiving any more letters seeps into my bones as I sift through the post before leaving the house. It has been a constant source of worry every day. I have had to ensure I was first up every morning and somehow manage to be the one who always collected the mail, quickly rifling through the stack of letters. And now, hopefully, today will be the day that it all comes to an end. I quash the small voice in my head that is whispering to me that Glenn is a loose cannon, and this may just be the beginning of something much bigger. Something that will rip my world apart. I can't allow myself to view it that way. I've got to be positive. I need to get my life back to how it was before that first letter arrived.

The day is a hectic one. Two meetings, one about possible staff redundancies due to budget cuts, a complaint from a parent about their child receiving too much homework, five full lessons, and news from the school's family support officer that I'll be getting two new pupils in my tutor class next week, both of whom come with social services involvement due to family issues with alcohol, domestic violence and drugs. By the time Astrid appears at my door, I am so tired I could curl up into a ball and sleep on the floor.

'Okay, partner,' she says with a smile. 'Ready to go?'

A pulse flutters up my neck at her words. Suddenly, it's real. We're going to face him, the man who is sending the letters. I won't leave until he admits his guilt and makes a promise to stop. I'll threaten him with the police and then see how he reacts, not that I would go through with it, but he can't know that. I just want him removed from my life.

I clear my desk, close the blinds, turn off the lights and shut the door.

'I've booked us a table at The Red Lion. No point turning up at his house too early. He'll probably be at work.' Astrid sounds a little too animated, excited even. Apprehension and a sense of mild dread swirls around inside me. Excitement is something I definitely don't feel.

'He has a job?' I fight to keep the shock out of my voice. Not what I expected. I imagined a sad old soul, sitting at home day after day watching porn movies, too unstable to hold down any sort of position.

'Last I heard, he was working as a sales engineer. Not sure whether they kept him on after the court case. Businesses usually find a reason to "let people go" rather than be associated with a proven stalker, a violent one at that.' Astrid stares at her hands, lifts a finger and nibbles at a nail feverishly. 'Better to assume he's working and turn up later, than turn up earlier and there not be anybody home, eh?'

She's right. She has thought this through. And she sounds so self-assured, so confident. I wish I had a quarter of her gumption. I haul my bag over my shoulder, head out into the daylight, our heels clicking on the tarmac as we make our way over to my car. I picked Astrid up this morning, brought her into work. No point in two cars making the trek to Northallerton this evening. At least I managed to do something right.

I can't seem to think straight as I slip the car into gear, stalling it before we even leave the school site. My hands are shaking and sweating. I grip the steering wheel, my fingers white, the skin stretched tightly over my knuckles, and restart the car.

'Come on, Stell. If you're in a state before you even get to his house, then he's already won.' Astrid's voice is cool and reassuring as she leans forward to catch my eye. 'You've already got the upper hand. He has no idea you're coming to see him. I actually can't wait to see the look on his face when he opens the door to us. He will quite literally shit himself.'

I take a deep breath. She's right. I do know that. I'm in control of this situation. I can't let this man get to me otherwise I've lost before I've even begun. I turn out of the car park, concentrating on my breathing as we crunch across loose gravel and stones, and out onto the main road. It's a forty-five-minute journey, involving a busy dual carriageway and various winding country lanes. I need to focus, to be on my mettle. I have to forget my nerves and just drive.

'Right,' I say with more confidence than I feel. 'Let's eat, and then visit his house, make this bastard face up to what he's done.'

'That's more like it,' Astrid laughs. 'That's my Stella. Now let's fill our bellies ready for the big fight.'

I let out a barking laugh that sounds more like a cry, take a right turn, head for the dual carriageway and put my foot down.

14

As hard as I try, I cannot summon up the strength to eat anything. Astrid on the other hand, polishes off a huge plate of fish and chips followed by an ice cream sundae smothered with chocolate sprinkles.

'Where in God's name do you put it?' I eye her slim figure, genuinely wondering how large her stomach is and how all that food can possibly fit inside such a svelte frame.

'It'll all catch up with me one day,' she says as she licks at the spoon like a small child, making sure every last drop of ice cream is consumed. 'My mum and her sisters all used to be slim and now they're as fat as butter. My Aunt Lucy can barely get out of bed because she's so big and when my Aunt Rachel died, they had to take her body out through the patio doors because she was too large to get through the front door. She truly was one humongous lady.'

I smile, shake my head and look away. I have no idea if any of it is true. Astrid is one for elaborating if it gets her a laugh or two. I guess it doesn't really matter either way; she's helping to take my mind off our next task and that is all that counts.

'Right, I'll get the bill.' Astrid makes a face and shakes her head while reaching for her purse. I wag my finger at her and shake my head in return. 'My treat, for coming along and helping. Don't try to stop me.'

She sighs, mouthing a 'thank you' at me as I fumble for my card and head to the bar.

By the time I have settled up, she is at my side, tugging at my sleeve. 'Right, come on. Let's strike while the iron's hot. I've got a full stomach and I'm in fighting mode after a day of teaching geography to little shits who don't seem to care a jot about the world around them. I mean Christ almighty, Warren Adams didn't even know the capital of France when I asked him. He asked if it was Madrid. I actually felt like walking out of the class.'

We both know this isn't strictly true. We also know that the bulk of the pupils at Westland Academy are decent kids. But all it takes is a handful of disaffected youngsters to play up and it feels as if the entire class is against you.

We step outside and it becomes even more apparent that I am not functioning as I should be. I've put on a brave face, but things feel horribly out of kilter, skewed and disconnected, like I'm trapped in a parallel universe, unable to properly connect with anybody and anything. I feel as if my life and everything I have ever done is about to explode in my face.

I take a deep breath and walk. The ground is spongy under my feet as we weave our way through the car park. I can barely manage to open the car door, to get in and fasten my seat belt. My hands are cold, my usual dexterity absent as I fiddle with the strap, trying numerous times before it finally clicks into place. I can feel Astrid assessing me, trying to get inside my head. Wondering if I'll come apart this evening. I am hugely relieved she has accompanied me here. I wouldn't have been able to do this on my own. Astrid is the perfect person for this – strong, challenging, even confrontational. Everything I am not.

'Take it easy, Stell. You'll be fine. Just remember, you're one step ahead of him. He doesn't know you're coming.' Her voice is like a cool breeze over my skin, her reassurances helping to put everything into perspective and calm me down. Astrid is exactly what I need at this point in my life.

'Thank you,' I reply as I start up the engine. 'I couldn't have come here alone.'

She pats my hand, nodding over her shoulder and eyeing up the oncoming traffic. 'Once this car's gone, you're good to go. Take the next right and keep on going for a mile or so before taking the next left. I'll just sit back and enjoy the scenery.'

I don't tell her that I know the route off by heart. Instead, I drive, letting the music wash over me, savouring the relaxing tunes of the early evening radio. The playlist is designed to soothe and calm, to still the nerves of drivers caught up in heavy traffic.

Ten minutes pass in silence, the music lulling me into a near hypnotic state, Astrid saying nothing. I suspect she has closed her eyes, is possibly even asleep. I don't glance her way, happy to leave her be. Instead I focus on the road, on the songs, listening intently as the presenter speaks softly into the microphone, addressing me as if I'm the only person in the world, the only one paying attention to their neutral beige words.

'Follow the road to the end then take the third exit on the roundabout.' Astrid's voice causes me to jump.

'You sound like the satnav woman. And you scared the life out of me. I thought you were asleep.' There's a distinct tremble in my voice. It doesn't take much to bring me crashing back down to earth, for the harshness of reality to hit me.

'Just resting my eyes. And I got you here, didn't I? Keep going for a mile or so once you take that third exit.'

We're getting close now. I remember this from my Google search. We chose a restaurant in the village next to where he lives. We can't be too far away now. I swallow and grip the steering wheel even tighter.

'Only a couple of minutes and we'll be there,' I say under my breath, more to steady my nerves and prepare myself than anything else.

I can see Astrid in my peripheral vision, watching me, gauging my state of mind, trying to work out whether I'm about to go into a meltdown, whether or not I will suddenly refuse to go through with the whole thing. That won't happen. I'm nervous. That's to be expected, but I've come too far to back down now. I've walked a long, dark path to get to this point but I can see a chink of light at the end of it.

We turn into a narrow crescent-shaped road. I take my foot off the accelerator, slowing down to take the bends.

I see it before Astrid does, having thought about not much else all day: a small bungalow with a low white fence. 'That's the one,' she whispers. The lawn is perfectly manicured and trimmed. A red Suzuki sits under a carport. My innards churn. Somebody is home.

My confession doesn't take Astrid by surprise when I make it. 'I looked this place up earlier on Google maps. It's not quite what I expected,' I say quietly as I chew the inside of my mouth pensively.

'What did you expect?'

I sigh loudly. 'I'm not sure really. But not this. It looks like a retirement home, like somebody twice his age should live here.'

We sit for a couple of seconds saying nothing until the silence becomes too much to bear. 'Come on,' I say as I wrestle with the car door handle. 'Let's get this thing over with.'

Every sound is amplified, an array of noises rattling around my head as we walk up the path towards the bungalow: the thud of our feet on the concrete driveway, the wild squawks of the birds circling overhead, even the sound of my own breathing is accentuated, a deafening oceanic roar that overloads my senses as I raise my fist and knock on the door.

A distorted shadow on the other side of the glass tells us somebody is approaching. I grip Astrid's arm, a sudden bout of dizziness threatening to take my legs from under me. The ground feels as if it is about to fall away under my feet.

The door is pulled open and there he is, right in front of me; the man I slept with. The man who has been prosecuted for stalking Astrid's friend. The same man who is now stalking and threatening me. My skin prickles and I'm suddenly hot and cold at the same time, my blood like fire and ice, meeting and merging, exploding in my veins. I let out a whimper, clear my throat to disguise it.

'Can I help you?' His voice is soft and welcoming. But not for long. Not when I tell him why we're here. He knows who we are; he has to. Somewhere deep in the darkest recesses of his brain, something is stirring, I am sure of it, and yet there isn't a flicker of recognition in his expression. He is standing there, his eyes vacant, his expression blank. Just standing there, watching us, calmly, nonchalantly. Like he hasn't got a care in the world.

Suddenly I am riddled with doubt, crippled with anxiety. I need to say something, not just stand here, mute, useless. Before I find the courage to open my mouth, Astrid steps forward, her hand resting against the door frame, her face inches from his, her voice a confident drawl. 'I think you probably can, Glenn. Remember me?' She turns then and points at me, her eyes ablaze. 'And more importantly, do you remember this lady? Please don't insult us by saying you don't know who we are because we all know that's an outright lie.'

My heart batters against my sternum, my skin shrinks against my bones, shrivelling like cling film as the colour drains from his face. He takes a step backwards with Astrid in close pursuit. 'I'm sorry?' His voice is a low joyless croak, echoing around the hallway, accentuating how fucking awkward and unreal this situation actually is.

I step forward so I can scrutinise his expression, watch as he tries to move away from Astrid's probing gaze.

'Don't act all innocent.' She is pointing now, her finger close to his chest. 'We know exactly what you've been up to. Now you can either let us in the house where we discuss this matter like adults, or we can do it here on the street where all your neighbours can hear. It's up to you. We're easy either way.'

My heart continues bouncing around my chest as he steps aside, ushering us into the living room, closing the door behind us with a muffled click. We find ourselves in the middle of a small room that is reminiscent of something from the 1980s. The window is adorned by heavily patterned brocade curtains. An array of twee ornaments sit on the flaking sill; porcelain cats, Toby jugs, a ghastly collection of bright teapots. The walls are devoid of any pictures or photographs and look freshly painted. The floorboards have been stripped back to bare wood and a tin of white paint sits in the corner of the room.

He holds out his hand, indicating for us to take a seat. 'Look,' he says as he sits down opposite, 'I did recognise you but have absolutely no idea what this is about. I honestly don't know why you're here.'

'Then let me enlighten you,' Astrid replies, her tone sharp as flint as she leans towards him, staring deep into his eyes. 'We're here to tell you to stop sending Stella threatening letters.'

He jumps up as if burnt, staggers backwards, his face creased, his veined, bloodshot eyes bulging. 'Excuse me? What the hell are you talking about? Is this some sort of sick joke?' His voice is a crescendo as he begins to pace around the room. 'I think you've got the wrong man here. You have no right forcing yourselves into my home. I'm asking you to leave. Right now!'

'We'll leave when we're ready,' Astrid barks, her voice thin and feisty like the snap of a rubber band.

It's my turn to step in, to stand up and speak hoping to defuse the escalating tension in the room. This is my problem; this situation is my doing and it's down to me to sort it out. Time to start talking, to dismiss my worries and fears, to open up to this man. Despite feeling anxious, I explain our visit, reminding Glenn of his previous conviction and the similarities between that episode and my situation.

'And you think I've sent those letters?' His voice rumbles through the room, resonating around us, his timbre powerful, authoritative, every syllable enunciated crisply and clearly.

'You've been to my house. You know where I live and you've done this sort of thing before. You have form. It has to be you.' I feel light-headed as I speak. Astrid is watching me, assessing my words and reactions, waiting to jump in if necessary. I ball my hands into fists and vow to keep going until I know the truth.

'Look,' he says as he suddenly slumps back down into the chair, 'I know what I did was wrong but I can assure you, this time it isn't me. I lost everything after that conviction – my job, my house. My whole life went down the bloody toilet. Do you really think I'm going to do anything like that again?'

I hold his gaze, wait for him to continue. I want to hear him speak, to listen to what he has to say. I need to know it all. Every little detail no matter how ghastly it is.

'I've never told anybody this,' he mutters, his face now a sickly shade of grey, 'but I had a breakdown at that time. I'm not using it as an excuse for what I did but it was a torrid time in my life and one I'd sooner forget. After losing my job and house, I had to move back in here with my mum. She died a few months back and left me this place. Without this, I'd have nothing. I'm self-employed now and slowly building up a portfolio of clients. I'm not about to ruin all that by sending out some stupid bloody letters to somebody I hardly know, am I?' He lowers his eyes and clasps his hands together in front of him as if in prayer.

A tight band of pain wraps itself around my head. He sounds so convincing; I no longer know what or who to believe. What if I'm wrong? What if we've come here making wild accusations and it isn't him? I know what Astrid will be thinking and can't bring myself to look in her direction. She's too fiery, too unwavering in her beliefs to back down, even when faced with overwhelming evidence to the contrary.

Glenn stands up, paces around the room, his feet thudding on the wooden floor. 'When did you receive these letters? If you give me dates, I might be able to prove that I didn't send them.'

'Thou doth protest too much.' Astrid's voice is a murmur but he hears it and spins around, finger outstretched as he thunders over to where she's sitting, his eyes ablaze with unconcealed rage. His body appears to have multiplied in size as he towers over Astrid's tiny slim frame.

'What?' he roars at her. 'What the *fuck* did you just say? Say it again! Go on. I dare you. Fucking say that again!'

A thousand horses gallop through my head, pounding at my skull. We don't know this man. He has a conviction for preying on another woman and now we've enraged him, pushed him to the edge and caused him to snap with our assertive manner, our wild unsubstantiated accusations. What the hell have we got ourselves into? I visualise him running into the kitchen, coming back with a large knife clasped in his fist and bringing it down into Astrid's chest or for him to lunge forwards and clasp Astrid's tiny neck between his large hands, pressing down on her windpipe until every last pocket of air has left her body.

Gasping and struggling to breathe, I bring a trembling hand to my mouth to suppress a shriek before slumping down onto the sofa, my body folding in on itself.

15

'Please,' I manage to say. 'Let's talk about this sensibly.' My throat aches just from the effort of breathing. Speaking is a monumental struggle.

Astrid sits perfectly straight, her posture rigid, her features unmoving. Glenn is still hovering over her, his eyes narrowed in anger. Only as he hears my voice does he turn to me and I think I see his expression soften a fraction. Or at least I hope so. I have no idea what the next few seconds hold for us. He will either become horribly violent and throw us out of his house or be the reasonable man I hope he can be.

'Wait here.' His voice is a bark. He turns and leaves the room. I hear him banging about somewhere behind me. I'm tempted to get up, to sit with Astrid but am afraid that the slightest movement or disturbance will infuriate him further. Out of the corner of my eye, I can see her watching me. I turn to her and shrug. She gives me a wide smile, looking every inch the self-assured woman who came here to confront this man; however, I know her well enough and can see beyond the façade. The tic in her jaw and the way she has her hands locked tightly together in her lap tells me that she, too, is frightened and wasn't expecting such a vocal reaction from him. We have no idea what this man is capable of. My instinct tells me he is a decent person but I have no proof of that. All I have is a glimmer of hope burning deep in my chest.

I let out a juddering breath as the banging stops only to be replaced by the sound of his footfall as he strides across the bare floorboards. His shadow looms over me, an ominous grey mass that covers my body. I shiver and look up.

'When did you get the letters?'

I close my eyes and try to think. 'They started a month or so ago. I got the first one in the middle of April and then the most recent one came last weekend.'

He thrusts out his hand and shoves an iPad under my nose. 'Here, take a look at this.'

I can barely move. My skin crawls as he continues to wave the iPad around so close to my face I can feel the heat emanating from the skin on his hand.

'I said look at it! Just look at the dates on the fucking pictures, will you?'

Snapping to attention and dragging myself out of the thick fog that seems to have descended on my brain, I take it from him, my eyes heavy and aching as I stare at a collection of photographs.

'Look at the dates,' he says dully. 'Just look at them, will you. I was in Thailand in April.'

'That proves nothing,' Astrid says from the other side of the room. 'Do they not have a postal system in Thailand then?'

To his credit, he ignores her comment and leans down to speak to me, his closely shaven beard near to my face. 'Was there a foreign postmark on the envelopes?' His voice is softer, pleading. More rational, less angry.

I shake my head. 'They were posted locally.' I stare at the

pictures of Glenn next to a group of people, posing in front of various temples and sitting on exotic beaches.

'Now look at the dates.'

I scroll through and stare at the corner of the photographs, at the dates on each one. He was in Thailand for most of April. He's telling the truth.

'And what about last weekend and the few days prior?' Astrid says, her voice dripping with sarcasm. 'Where were you then, eh?'

Glenn shrugs. 'Sorry if this is going to upset and offend you, but I was in Amsterdam meeting a new client. I've got proof if you want to ring the hotel or see the receipt for the plane tickets on my Visa statement?'

My scalp prickles with humiliation as I stand up to face him. I have no words. Instead, I give him a meek smile and look over to Astrid to indicate that we need to leave. He has said enough to convince me. The pictures – plus my gut instinct – tell me we've got the wrong person. Glenn is innocent.

'I'm sure you're a very nice lady, but I've never ever sent you any letters and nor do I plan to. I've got a partner, a good life going for me now. It's taken some time, but I've managed it. I'm not going to ruin it, not for you or for anybody for that matter. Now if you don't mind?' He holds out his hand towards the door and nods at Astrid who remains seated.

Time seems to stand still as we wait for her to get up. I find myself counting the seconds, willing her to do as he asks. Eventually the rustle of fabric booms in my ears as she rises from the chair and walks over to the door. Relief washes over me. I thought she would never get up. She glares at him, her eyes wide, accusatory, intense.

'If we find out that you're lying, we'll go straight to the police and then I'll be back here with my six-foot-three, seventeen-stone boyfriend who will personally remove your bollocks which I will then feed to my dog.' Astrid's voice is like ice, her expression cold and calculating as she continues to stare at him, her jet-black pupils never shifting from his face.

'Like I've already told you, it wasn't me. So if you don't mind...' Glenn points to the door, his eyebrows raised. His skin turns from grey to a pale pink as the shock of our appearance at his house leaves him. It's replaced by a growing sense of calm as he takes control of this situation and ushers us out of the door, his hand resting on the frame, his bulk blocking our way back in.

A flush takes hold on his neck, spreading up to his face; an intricate web of fury peppered over his flesh before he slams the door shut with a resounding bang.

I suck in a lungful of fresh air as I step outside. The cloistered atmosphere of the small bungalow has oozed in through my pores and is weighing me down. I don't look behind to see if Astrid is following me. All I want to do is get in the car and drive away as quickly as I can. I feel dirty and stupid and I just want to go home and shower and scrub at my body until my skin is raw.

'What a creep.' Her voice is gravelly with an edge to it. She also knows it isn't him. Not that she will readily admit it but deep down, we both know Glenn did not send those letters. We were wrong. I was wrong. And now I have no idea what to do.

I refuse to consider other suspects as I shove the keys in the ignition and put the car into gear. I can't go down that route. Too painful. Too raw. I press my foot down on the accelerator, the engine roaring in protest as I pull away at speed.

'Thanks for coming along, Astrid,' I mumble, my voice croaky with a multitude of emotions as I head out onto the winding country lanes that will lead us back home.

'What now?' Her voice is weak. No more the confident accusatory woman from a few minutes ago. She sounds as if all the life has been sucked out of her. I suspect her brazen act has left her mentally flattened and physically exhausted.

'Well, this is my problem so it's down to me. Thanks for all your help but I guess I need to sort it out on my own. At least we can rule Glenn out now.'

'Can we though? Photographs can easily be doctored.' Astrid turns to me as I take a bend too sharply.

'I think so. He didn't have time to alter those images. I've been barking up the wrong tree and now need to rethink,' I reply quietly as I manoeuvre the car along the tiny twisting lanes, hedges and shrubbery poking out at unpredictable angles that are proving difficult to avoid. Foliage juts into the road, broken tree limbs, gnarled branches, spiky hedgerows that reach out like deathly fingers, they all seem determined to stop me from leaving this place, blocking my exit and limiting my line of vision. I clutch the steering wheel even tighter, my palms slick with sweat.

We're almost at the junction that leads us onto the dual carriageway when it happens. I have no idea whether it was a lack of concentration, whether I was going too fast, or whether he was taking up too much of the road.

A blink of an eye, a singular beat of my heart, a momentary lapse of concentration, that is all it takes and before I can do anything at all, the steering wheel slips out of my grasp and I clip the side of the huge green tractor that is coming towards us on the opposite side of the lane. A breath is suspended in my torso, trapped beneath my ribcage, our bodies shaking with the impact, the car bouncing and spinning off across the lane, screeching and swerving until we eventually come to a halt, my poor vehicle sloping off to one side, the engine jumping and wheezing under the strain. We're lodged in a ditch, our bodies leaning awkwardly, my head angled painfully as I lean forward and yank the keys out of the ignition.

Seconds pass, minutes perhaps. Time loses all meaning. I swallow, rub at my eyes with tight knuckles, shake myself out of my fugue state and look around us. A wall of branches and shrubbery press down on the glass as I struggle to open the door. Panic sets in, my skin prickling, my head thumping. I try to control my breathing, to keep calm and think clearly. Wiping my palms on my clothes, I give the door another push. There is a dull but definite clunk as it gives slightly, a strip of air leaking into the space around us. I almost cry with relief, then think about Astrid, about her silence, her lack of anything resembling shock and fear at what has just happened.

'Astrid? You okay?' She doesn't answer. A physical sickness takes hold in my gut until I see a movement in my peripheral vision.

'I'm fine,' she says with a sigh. 'Fuck's sake, Stella. What happened? One minute you were on one side of the road and everything was normal and the next we're bouncing around all over the fucking place and now we're stuck in a bloody great ditch.'

'Sorry,' is all I manage to say. 'Really sorry. I don't know what happened.'

Silence. No reply. I feel as if I'm going to pass out as I wait for her to say something and then, 'It's okay,' she says wearily. 'Neither of us is injured. That's the main thing.'

Fighting back tears of relief, I manage to wrestle my way out of the car, the door jamming against the side of the ditch as I push it open further and slither out of the narrow space. The passenger door is stuck and Astrid has to clamber over the centre console, over the gear stick and onto the driver's side to make her escape.

Our bodies collide, both of us attempting to scramble out of the ditch. At one point we manage to laugh, a hysterical shriek at the predicament in which we find ourselves, at the state of our hair and clothes. At the fact we are having to haul ourselves up on our hands and knees, our dignity in tatters, still at the bottom of the ditch.

'You okay, love?' The driver of the tractor looms overhead. He leans down and holds out his hand to pull us up.

We scramble our way out, brushing soil and grass off our clothes. 'Thank you,' I murmur, my breathing laboured as I catch his eye. 'We're fine. No injuries, thank goodness.'

'This is a narrow road, pet. And I don't want to start apportioning blame, but you were going at a lick. There's plenty of blind bends round this way. You can't speed in these parts.'

My face burns. Loath though I am to admit it, he's probably right. I wasn't concentrating. My mind was focused on what just took place in Glenn's house, on the letters, on anything but the actual road.

'We need to exchange details, I suppose,' I say quietly, already thinking about how I'm going to explain this away to Wade. Right now, he thinks I'm at home, on my own, sitting in front of the TV eating sausage, egg and chips.

I pull out a notepad from my bag and scramble at the bottom for something to write with, my hand sweeping around and coming up with old receipts and broken lipstick holders. Astrid stands beside me, uncharacteristically reserved and quiet. She stares over at the horizon where an orange glow filters into the clear sky before reaching into her pocket and handing me a battered pen. I scribble down my name, address and phone number and pass the pen and paper to the tractor driver who does the same.

'Do you want me try to get it out of the ditch for you? Got some rope back at the farm. I can attach it to the back of your car and pull you out if you like? Worth a try.' He steps away from us and walks to the rear of the vehicle, surveying it closely. 'Doesn't look like there's too much damage. A dent on the driver's side and you've got some scratches off that hedgerow on the passenger side as well, so you'll need to get them seen to.'

'It would be wonderful if you could pull it out,' I say, breathless with relief. I had envisioned ringing for a tow truck and having to wait for hours in the thick darkness of a strange country lane.

He flashes us a smile, telling us he'll be back in less than fifteen minutes. 'It's just over there,' he says, pointing to a speck of a building in the distance.

We watch as he walks back to his tractor, rocking from side to side on legs bowed with age. He clambers up to his vehicle with all the agility of an athlete and not somebody well past retirement age who can barely walk, then gives us a brief wave before starting up the engine and disappearing around the corner.

'How do we know he's coming back?' Astrid says with a pout. 'He might go home, forget about us, pour himself a large whiskey and fall asleep in front of the TV.'

I can't help but laugh. Despite the rotten situation, I find myself giggling at her comment. 'We'll give him twenty minutes. He said less than fifteen so we'll allow for twenty. If he's not back by then, I'll ring my insurance company and get us towed home.'

His tractor rumbling around the corner exactly fourteen minutes later is the most comforting thing I've seen all week.

16

The car starts up first time. I half expected it to splutter into life and then fizzle out again after a few seconds, but the engine is running sweetly and shows no signs of stalling. It certainly shows no signs of having a collision with a much larger vehicle, nor of it ending up by the side of the road, covered with brambles and then having to be hauled out of a ditch. I only wish the same could be said for the bodywork. A large gouge runs the length of the wing on the passenger side and the driver's door has a deep dent in it as well as also being badly scratched.

'Thank you,' I say to Arthur, who waves at me as he hauls himself up onto the seat of his tractor.

'I'll wait here to make sure you get back onto the main road. I guess our insurance companies will sort the rest,' he shouts over the roar of the engine. I nod and give him a thumbs up, then fasten my seat belt and head off for home.

'He would be an Arthur, wouldn't he?' Astrid says sourly. 'He suits the name. And I'm pretty sure he's going to blame you when he contacts his insurance company so be prepared for a hefty excess and a hike in your premium.'

'Well to be fair,' I reply with a smile, 'it probably was my fault. I was chewed up and driving too quickly.'

'If you say so.' Astrid puffs out her cheeks and runs her fingers through her hair, tugging at the tangles and freeing up strands with her long nails. 'Anyway, accident aside, what do you make of our little venture? You completely satisfied that Gormless Glenn isn't the mysterious letter writer?'

I nod and sigh heavily. 'I'm totally convinced. Which still leaves me with a big problem...'

'Exactly *who* is the letter sender and what do they want?' Astrid interjects.

I nod and rub at my face with my free hand. It's been a long day. I ache everywhere and my eyes are dry and gritty. It feels as if a sheet of sandpaper is lodged behind my eyelids.

'What will Wade say about the car?' Astrid asks. 'Are you going to tell him why we were here?'

'I honestly have no idea,' I whisper as I bite at my lip. 'I'll have a think about it while he's away. Now we know that Glenn didn't send those letters, I don't have to say anything, do I?'

She doesn't answer. I can't say I blame her. I will actually have to find a way to explain this crash, to tell him why we were here. He is going to see the insurance documents, the statements. There's no easy way out of this. Either I come clean and tell Wade everything; or I make up some pathetic lie and continue to deceive him. Another lie. One after another. I visualise them, stacking up like a game of Jenga, ready to topple at any given moment.

We drive home in near silence, both of us wrapped up in our thoughts. Astrid is right. I should do the decent thing and tell Wade, but then what will be achieved by dredging it all up? Sometimes ignorance really is bliss. I honestly don't think my head is in the right place to spill my dirty secret.

'Give it some thought,' Astrid says as we pull up outside her house. 'It was you who asked Wade to leave and go stay with his brother for a while. He didn't choose to leave.'

I whip around to stare at her, a buzzing starting up in my head. 'Whose side are you on?' My voice is loud and my temper is beginning to build. 'I only told you because I needed your help and now, you're turning against me.' My fingers are hot. I keep them clasped around the steering wheel. A pulse starts up in my neck.

'Stella,' she says as she leans forward and gives me a hug, her skin warm and welcoming and smelling of lilacs. I can't help but soften as she pushes me back a couple of inches and stares into my face, her hands still resting on my shoulders. 'I only want what's best for you but I'm also Wade's friend. I have to see this from both sides.'

I lean back into the headrest, letting out a low moan. I'm so tired. Being devious and duplicitous is exhausting. Every inch of me is weary. I feel a hundred years old.

'The split was temporary and happened after seeing my mother,' I say quietly. 'Wade said I was being unreasonable towards her and I just snapped. I'd had enough of him taking her side and told him to leave, to let me have some space. I was in a mess after he left. I was utterly miserable and had taken some time off work. I'd only been back in school for a couple of days. And that's when it happened. I had had too much to drink and Glenn was there. And it just happened...'

'What is it with you and your mother?' Astrid is watching me intently, her gaze never shifting. 'This argument has been going on for as long as I've known you. Maybe it's time to call a truce?' She's waiting for me to crack, for me to tell her everything.

I shake my head and look away so she can't see the tears that are fighting to be free. I cannot forgive that woman. I just can't.

'Okay. Well look, give me a ring if ever you want to chat about it. We all know you had a rough time as a kid but don't let it rule your life. You deserve better than to be held to ransom by a shitty childhood. You have a life to live.'

I shrug and let out a juddering breath, then give Astrid one last hug before she gets out of the car and makes her way up the driveway of their impressive home. Astrid's partner is a solicitor and has his own practice. They do well for money. Not that I'm complaining. Wade and I are okay financially, but every time I see this house, a little flicker of envy burns deep inside me. Astrid, like Wade, had a normal upbringing with model parents who worked and afforded them a nice life and generally gave a shit.

Biting back hot tears, I stop myself from thinking this way. I can't keep doing this. Wallowing in self-pity is a grotesque and deeply unattractive characteristic. Astrid is right. The time has come to move on, to forget about it. I'm not about to forgive but surely I have it within me to forget. As long as people don't force me to become best friends with my mother, then I'm prepared to leave it all behind me. She knew what took place in that house and did nothing to stop it. She enabled it, sitting right back and doing fuck all to help me. I can never forgive her for that. Ever.

By the time I get home, I'm so tired I could crawl into bed as I am. Instead I shower then check my phone. Three missed calls from Wade. My skin prickles. I should have rung him earlier, checked my phone at the pub and returned his calls. Now he'll be worrying where I am which in turn makes me edgy, anticipating his probing questions. Why are the simplest of tasks so bloody difficult?

I sit on the edge of the bed, press the call button, then wait. He picks it up after just two rings, his voice thick with concern. 'I was starting to get really worried. Thought maybe you'd gone out on the lash.' He laughs softly and my throat contracts. 'You know, while the cat's away and all that.'

I cough lightly and try to sound jovial when my insides are

coiling themselves into a small knot. 'You're half right,' I say a little too shakily. 'Astrid and I went for a meal after work. Thought it would make a nice change. I've just dropped her off and then come home for a shower.'

'Ah, okay. Well I hope it was better than the meal we had here. Our food was over an hour late. Cold fish and lumpy potatoes doesn't quite cut it.'

I chew at my lip nervously and grasp the nettle. 'I had a bump in the car on the way back. It's driveable but it's got a dent in the driver's side wing and the paintwork needs sorting.'

There's a slight pause before he speaks. I imagine his face as he thinks about what to say next. Wade is a cautious person, always choosing his words with the greatest care. 'And you're okay? No injuries? Nobody hurt?'

I smile at the sound of his voice. 'No injuries,' I reply quietly. 'We're both absolutely fine.'

'That's good,' he says softly. 'As long as you're okay, that's the main thing.'

A wave of guilt threatens to pull me under as I listen to him speak. 'So, what happened then?'

I tell him about the tractor and the ditch and the large scrape on the passenger side door, about the crumpled wing on the driver's side where I hit the tractor, aware that I'm speaking too quickly and repeating myself. Aware that my nerves are taking over, stripping me of any control.

'Whereabouts did it happen? I've been saying for ages that the back road through Morton needs widening, especially with that bloody huge drop on either side. And if–'

'It didn't happen there, Wade,' I cut in before I lose my nerve. 'It was on the way back from Northallerton on a lane leading to the main road.'

I wait for his reply, every second feeling like an age. When he speaks there is a shift in his tone, so slight I begin to doubt that I heard it at all. 'Northallerton? What were you doing in Northallerton?'

'Astrid thought it would be nice to go somewhere different for a change. We ate at The Red Lion and then went for a drive afterwards.'

Liar. More lies. You just don't know when to stop, do you?

Wade sounds happy with my explanation, heightening my sadness and disgust at being so dishonest with him. It seems that no matter what I do, I'll always end up riddled with guilt. I'm damned if I do and damned if I don't.

We spend the next few minutes chatting about insurance policies and his conference, and work in general before he tells me that he has to shower before the evening session which is a less formal affair but something he needs to attend regardless.

'Don't worry about the car, Stell,' he murmurs. 'Accidents happen. Nobody was hurt. That's the main thing.'

I want to scream at him to stop being so reasonable and caring. I want to tell him that I'm a scheming, cheating shit of a woman and that he would be better off without me. I also want to tell him that I grew up in a house with a man who regularly beat me and abused me in the most intimate and violent way possible and that I'm a truly damaged being. But I don't. I can't. I don't know how to say it. I have no words.

So instead, I tell him that I love him and miss him. At least I'm capable of some sort of truth.

'Love you too, Stella. I'll see you Friday.'

I end the call, throw the phone onto the floor and weep.

17

1999

The funeral is a small affair; a handful of distant family members dotted around the chapel, their murmuring filling the awkward silence that descends once the coffin is carried in and placed on a plinth at the foot of the steps that lead to the altar.

The life support machine that had been keeping her father alive had been turned off by the doctors after consulting with her mother and Aunt Petra. The girl suspected that Aunt Petra was secretly delighted and if given the opportunity would have turned it off herself. They had all filed in, one by one, standing by his bedside to say their goodbyes. The girl had leaned over him, looked into his face and felt nothing but relief. All she had thought about was a life without him. A better life.

The service is thankfully brief. A short eulogy is read out by the pastor and a nondescript song is played as everybody shuffles out, congregating in a small huddle in the foyer. She doesn't recognise anybody and none of them makes any attempt to speak to her. She is thankful for that small mercy. Masking her hatred for her father would have proved too difficult for her. A step too far.

She watches as her mother mingles with a handful of

mourners, each wearing excessively sombre clothes and grief-stricken expressions. She wonders why they are all so solemn, so respectful, talking in whispers about a man who cared about nobody but himself. Where were they when her father was alive, when he was drinking the bar dry and taking his temper out on his family?

She wanders outside, shielding her eyes against the glare of the sunlight. The recent thunderous downpour has left flowers and undergrowth coated with myriad droplets of water that shimmer like crystals under the midday sun, releasing a strong earthy smell of petrichor. She stands for a few seconds, breathing in the aroma, enjoying the blend of wet soil and the heady fragrance of flowers.

It's peaceful here. She wishes they could stay a little longer but knows that soon she and her mother will have to leave. They will go back to their little house and carry on with their little lives, just the two of them. No more violence. No more hatred. Just a quiet still existence; day after day of peaceable happiness. Deep inside her is a glimmer of hope that things will get easier now he's gone. A great weight has been lifted and a flicker of something resembling contentment glows bright in her gut, augmenting and multiplying at the thought of how easy life will be without her brute of a father around. No more fear, no more hiding out in her room. No more of anything except an air of calm where his anger used to be.

They walk the short distance home, neither of them speaking. What is there to say? The silence is occasionally broken by children laughing and shrieking in the park on the other side of the field. She stares over at the huddle of small bodies, envious of their freedom, their happiness. The happiness she has missed out on. The same happiness she hopes will be present in their house now he is no longer around. She has plans. Plans for her and her mother. They are going to go places together – shopping, visits to the park. She visualises it and is mildly giddy as a frisson of excitement pulses through her.

She considers linking arms with her mother but something stops her, an invisible barrier she cannot seem to clear. They need more time together before their fractured relationship can heal, but that's okay. Time is something they have plenty of.

The midday heat begins to build as they pass by the main road and take a right turn onto the path that runs parallel with the river. She shivers as she turns then catches a glimpse of the water through the foliage. It sparkles and glints, pushing its way through the landscape, bouncing and sliding over small rocks before snaking off in the distance. She is no longer compelled to go down there to the riverbank, once her favourite place, not after what happened. Her memories of it have been spoiled, crumbled into dust.

A nagging ache sets in the back of her skull at the thought of that day, at the thought of what could have happened had they not got bored and left.

After the gang of girls had gone, she had lain for a few minutes, trying to get her breath back, trying to work out whether or not they would have actually had the courage to hold her under until every last bit of oxygen had been pushed out of her body, replaced by dank foaming water. Are they really that stupid and arrogant? Or did they know exactly how long it would have taken for her to drown and let go of her just in time? Are they really that clever and devious? Or just lucky.

Letting out a soft uncertain sigh, she blocks it out of her mind. All in the past. She's a different person now. She has grown, changed. They'll realise that when she goes back to school. She'll be viewed in a different light, perhaps given some lenience. Even bullies have their limits. She's in mourning. Her father is dead. No matter how much she hated him, no matter how much they all hate her, surely she will be allowed some peace at a time like this.

The girl and her mother leave the rush of the river behind them and head for their tiny neglected house. It is still unwelcoming and incongruous amongst the tightly packed cluster of neighbouring houses with their freshly cleaned windows and whiter-than-white front doors.

Stepping over the threshold, the girl is tempted to lean into her mother, to embrace her and whisper into her ear that everything is going to be fine, that they will make it together and be a stronger family unit once this is all over, but something stops her. She wonders later whether she should have taken the dead-eyed look her mother gave her as they closed the door behind them as an indication of what was to come. She wonders later whether as a family they had simply endured too much, been put under too much pressure for things to ever be put right again.

18

Well here I am again. Writing. About her. I can't seem to stop myself. I'm becoming obsessed with her. I wish I could write darker, more damaged disconnected prose that when read at a later date, after it's all happened, would give everyone an insight into what was going through my head. They would say it was unavoidable what took place, given my unhinged state of mind. They would look at my mad ramblings and shake their heads despondently, asking themselves what they could have done to stop it. 'Nothing' is the answer to that. Nobody can put a halt to what I have planned for that bitch.

Still, this is something I enjoy, the build-up, the gradual release of tension as the time grows nearer. It's a wild feeling, an uninhibited sensation as I think about the power I'll be able to wield. I often dream about the look on her face, the complete look of terror in her eyes. It's so fantastic. The best feeling in the world. And she has no idea. Not a fucking clue. That's part of the appeal. It's like a game, watching how she interacts with me, being all coy and smiling at me, while I'm picturing her dead with a great frigging knife sticking out of her ribs.

Soon she'll realise. Soon enough she'll know who it is that's been messing with her head. I just have to be patient and wait. Soon the time will be right. Not long to go.

19

2019

The postman is earlier than usual. I hear the metallic squeak of the letterbox and a gentle whoosh as the mail drops onto the mat below. I lie in bed, my eyes too heavy to open, my head tight with anxiety. I have a meeting before lessons begin and if I don't hurry, I won't make it in time. Unease ripples through my veins. I hate meetings, I hate being late but most of all, I hate checking through our letters, looking for that small white envelope that can wreak so much havoc, tearing my life into tiny unrecognisable shreds.

Dragging my weary body out of bed, I step into the shower, get dressed and head downstairs where a stack of letters await me, fanned out like a peacock's tail on the hall floor.

I lay them out on the table. No time for food. No appetite for it. Instead, I make a coffee and sit at the kitchen table with my mug, scanning the letters laid out there, their pale envelopes in stark contrast to the dark wood of the tabletop.

Pale envelopes.

I take a deep gulp of coffee, wincing as it burns the roof of my mouth, then run my hand over the pile of post, knowing it's there. I don't even have to see it. I take a deep breath before spreading the letters out on the table. It's there. I knew it would be. The same generic handwritten address, the same small white envelope.

Snatching it up, I rip it open, a surge of annoyance flowing through me. How dare they? How dare somebody try to make me worried and frightened in my own fucking home? Now that I know it's not Glenn who is behind this sick act, my fear and uneasiness has been replaced by fury and a sense of incredulity that somebody somewhere is taking time out of their day to do this to me. And not just that. The fact that they are too cowardly to reveal their identity really irks me. What in God's name are they hoping to gain from this puerile exercise? It's not as if they can even see my reaction to their notes.

I open out the folded piece of paper, lay it out on the table, scanning the words.

Not long now. You are a total bitch. The time is nearly here.

A week or two ago I would have been terrified at seeing those words, now all I feel is pure anger. White-hot rage. Soon replaced by another wave of apprehension as another dark memory resurfaces.

No. I will not go down that route.

Scrunching it up, I hold the note tight in my hand, the paper cool against my hot palm. I decide against throwing it in the bin. Something makes me keep it, an instinct, a sixth sense. I have no idea why, but I smooth it out, take it upstairs, open my jewellery box and place it in the bottom drawer. My secret drawer. I'm becoming quite the master at hiding things. Quite the master at lying. Even to myself.

I run a brush through my hair, apply a slick of lipstick and head downstairs, forcing myself to not think about those words. I'm going to ignore them and get on with my day. I will go to work and then tonight I will come home, eat, perhaps even have a glass of wine. I will watch TV and then go to bed and then the following day I will do the same and then afterwards, I will drive to the station and pick up Wade. I will do all the normal things that people do. I refuse to cower to an invisible threat. Whoever is sending them can go to hell. I've dealt with far worse than this in my life. A few measly notes are nothing compared to what I have lived through. The dark memory tries again, muscling its way into my head, a face from long ago, swirling, disappearing then reappearing again. A nasty little thought, a nasty little person. I won't think about it and I won't think about them because it simply isn't feasible that they could be involved.

Or is it?

Grabbing my keys, I head outside, slide into the driver's seat and fire up the engine.

The morning meeting is thankfully brief. I get to class in time to prepare for the first lesson. I place worksheets on desks as a starter activity, pile textbooks on my desk and then wait.

I'm sitting at my desk as Damon and Ravi file in. They smile broadly and place themselves in the middle of the room.

'Punctual as always, lads,' I say as I pass them the textbooks. 'May as well hand out these while we wait for the others to turn up.'

'Pfftt,' Damon replies softly. 'Child labour's illegal you know, miss.' He gives me a slight wink.

I turn away, my face hot as Ravi laughs, saying, 'We'll do it 'cos it's you, Miss Ingledew. We usually charge the going rate. Don't tell any of the other teachers we did it for free for you though or they'll all end up taking a lend of us. You know what they're like.'

I'm laughing out loud now. It's a mixture of relief coupled with euphoria. I wish all pupils were as thoughtful, as laid-back and companionable as these two. Teaching would be a walk in the park if every pupil was as easy to get on with and as keen to learn as Ravi and Damon. Thoughts of my own childhood flit into my mind, stabbing at me, reminding me of who I was. I run my fingers through my hair and banish those thoughts. Not today. I won't allow them to drag me down.

A sudden bang kills the moment as a throng of youngsters barge in. The noise of the door hitting the wall is so loud that I get up to check the glass panel, making sure it's still intact. I heave a deep sigh and turn to face the class, hands on my hips; a stance I hope is enough to quell the mayhem. It continues, an impenetrable wall of noise, loud enough to shatter glass, until I slam a hardback book down onto the table with as much force as possible. They look my way, their expressions bemused.

'Sit down!' My voice cracks with the effort of shouting and I end up having a coughing fit. I wipe my eyes and take a drink from the tumbler on my desk. The water is room temperature and has been there for at least two days. It tastes of a forest floor but has the desired effect and the dryness in my throat is quickly alleviated. I grab a tissue from my bag to blow my nose, then stare at the sea of faces watching me as I take a final splutter before throwing the tissue into the bin.

A snigger spreads around the room. This time I use a large metre ruler and bring it down hard on the desk with a crack. Jack Phelps jumps and I suppress a smile. It's not often I get the upper hand with that one. I enjoy the moment, glaring at him for added effect before sitting down and nodding at him to do the same. He sneers at me then lowers his gaze, his face reddening, highlighting the patches of acne spread over his badly inflamed skin.

Once I've regained control, the lesson passes without too

many hitches, until that is, the final five minutes when Jack rears his head once more. I am recapping on the lesson, explaining why Lady Macbeth is a conflicted character and although desperate for power, still has a conscience that she struggles with, when Noah, one of Jack's long-time friends, lets out a loud and attention-grabbing guffaw.

I stop speaking, glare at him and raise an eyebrow to indicate my objection at his unwelcome interruption.

He widens his eyes in protest. 'What? What you looking at me for? I never did nothing!'

'Didn't do anything,' I say loudly. 'I didn't do anything. If you're going to disturb my lesson by shouting out, at least be grammatically correct.'

Bollocks to sarcasm having no place in the classroom. On this occasion it is warranted, if only to let kids know that they're being exceptionally rude. But mostly to let them know how pissed off I am at being interrupted time and time again. This sort of behaviour happens every lesson with the same pupils and it's wearing. Everyone has their breaking point.

'It was him anyway,' Noah says sullenly, pouting after being publicly humiliated. He leans forward, points at Jack and gives him a shove before slumping back into his chair and crossing his arms over his chest defensively. 'He said Lady Macbeth was just like you – he said you're both a pair of complete bitches.'

A wave of dizziness forces me to lean towards the desk for support. I slump, placing my hands on the smooth wood, glad of the cool surface against my burning skin. I'm hoping to mask my shock with an authoritative stance. I tell myself that everyone uses the word *bitch*. Especially teenagers. It's just a word. Nothing more. It has no link to those notes, those repulsive toxic missives that have taken over my life. Just a word, that's all it is. Nothing more, nothing less.

The silence in the class is deafening. It drains me, robbing me of energy. There is a collective inhalation of breath as everyone waits for me to do something, to say something to him. I do nothing. I can't. After receiving that note this morning and then hearing that phrase being fired at me, I can hardly breathe. I tell myself it's just a coincidence. It has to be. There is no way Jack Phelps has the brains to cook up such an idea. He is of average ability and although he does his utmost to disrupt every lesson, he is just a child; a disaffected youngster who refuses to engage in learning. He is an irritant, no more, no less. He is not a stalker. He is not a dangerous, unhinged individual who has the balls to send threatening letters to his teacher's house.

Or is he?

I am literally saved by the bell. It rings loud and clear around us. I wave my hand to let the class know they're dismissed, keeping my head down, my eyes lowered to the floor. Half of them head for the door in a riotous fashion while the other half file out in a more genteel, orderly manner. I glance up, feeling somebody watching me. Ravi and Damon are close by. They give me a courteous nod and a pitying smile as they leave, followed closely by Grace. I feel sorrier for them than I do for myself. They have to put up with Jack's boorish behaviour in many of their other lessons. I only see him a few times a week. I get off lightly all things considered.

My head buzzes as I stumble to the staffroom. Hopefully I'll see Astrid there. I can corner her, speak to her about this incident. Something else to feel guilty about. Every time I see her, all I do is push my problems her way. Poor Astrid. She must feel glued to the ground, weighted down with my troubles.

Astrid isn't in the staffroom, her usual seat occupied instead by no other than Casper Smith, our resident ageing portly maths teacher, a man with all the charm and sensitivity of your average garden slug. Rather than brave a conversation with him, I sit next to Eve Chambers, a bright-eyed and recently qualified art teacher. Life has yet to drag her through the mud, make her question anything and everything about her choices and trajectory. Our brief attempts at dialogue rarely strays from the banal. Eve is an acquaintance, not a friend. Our talks are always casual and distant. She lives with her parents, two dogs and a cat. She likes to read and is a member of a book club which she attends once a month. She doesn't drink, abhors foul language and thinks that sex before marriage is a sin. Actually, I made the last part up but Eve is so strait-laced she would find life far easier if she lived in the nineteenth century. I have no idea how she will survive here at Westland Academy.

I can barely conceal my relief when Astrid finally makes an appearance. She slides down next to me, gives Eve a broad smile and then turns to me, her voice hoarse as she speaks. 'Jesus. Who the fuck thought up this smoking ban? I'd kill for a fag right now.'

Eve idly fiddles with the sleeve of her sweater, her gaze darting about, her mouth turned downwards in mild disapproval. Astrid mouths an apology to her then moves closer to me, out of Eve's line of sight where she pulls a face and rolls her eyes. I keep my expression neutral, trying not to smile. Eve makes her excuses and leaves, scurrying off to the far side of the room to sit with some of the student teachers who are doing their teaching placement at Westland Academy. She beams at them, shuffling closer to their tight little huddle and they all soon become immersed in conversation.

'Astrid, don't be mean,' I say with a slight smile. 'She's new and a bit wet behind the ears, that's all.'

'Well, she'd better hurry up and grow a second frigging skin working in this place, or she won't see the year out. Not with her sanity intact.' She leans over to me, her gaze flickering slightly as she speaks. 'So anyway, how did Wade take the news about the car?'

I blink, summoning up the strength to speak about it, thinking back to last night. To all those lies. 'He was fine.' I briefly close my eyes and shake my head. 'Actually, that's unfair. He was more than fine. He was brilliant. He's always brilliant. Said it doesn't matter about the car as long as nobody was hurt.'

Astrid puffs out her cheeks and nudges me. 'Jesus Christ, woman! I hope you know how lucky you are. Nathan would have a complete bloody hissy fit if I crashed my car. He's more concerned about a piece of metal than he is me.'

We both know this isn't entirely true. Nathan is a nice man and cares about Astrid, but she is definitely right about one thing – money means a lot to him. He enjoys the status it brings; the kudos of being considered wealthy serves him well when he attends legal functions or drives to the local country club for tennis lessons in his top-of-the-range Audi. It doesn't make him a bad person but it does often cloud his judgement of people and make him lacking in compassion in certain areas of his life.

'I told him we fancied a change from the usual so ate at The Red Lion and then went for a drive afterwards.' I turn and stare at her, making sure she's looking back at me. 'Just in case he asks.' She continues watching me. 'I'm going to forget the rest ever happened.' I don't have to tell Astrid to do the same. She knows me well enough now. I don't have to spell it out.

She nods and links her arm through mine and at that moment, last night's visit to Glenn, the lies I've been telling Wade and the letters I've been receiving and salting away, seem a dim and distant threat.

'Not saying I agree with what you're doing,' she whispers softly, 'but as the saying goes, I'll defend your right to do it.'

20

1999

'Morning, freak.' The voice comes from the back of the room. She doesn't look up, meet their eyes or sit near them. She has no idea how many of them there are seated there, in their regular protective throng. Always at the back. Better vantage point. And always together.

'How's your dad? Still dead?' A giggle erupts from the crowd.

There is no let-up after the funeral. If she had hoped for a modicum of leniency from them, a sliver of decency and respect at such a torrid time, then she was sadly deluded. They follow her around school, throwing insults, trailing in her wake, always there. Always close by. Mocking, scornful. A relentless tirade. All her father's death has done is give them more ammunition. More reasons to hate her. More reasons to drag her down.

There are times when she can, albeit briefly, watch them. If she gets lost in a crowd as the bell rings, or is seated at an angle in the canteen, she can observe their dynamics and try to work out what their next move will be. And on occasions, she can slip away unnoticed. But not often.

The ringleader shows no mercy, her jibes and insults coming thick and fast. A couple of the girls have enough civility to look shamefaced and pretend their attentions are elsewhere. They could hardly be described as bashful or diffident, but at least they glance away, try to distance themselves from certain situations. Situations that overstep the mark. Yesterday, she was slapped, called a whore, forced to listen as her father was mocked, her mother branded a drunken slut.

She'd like to think she's becoming inured to it, that none of it matters anymore. But of course, it does. It hurts. Every second in their presence is an hour; every day a year. Time drags.

And going home provides no escape. The heavy drinking had begun almost immediately. Prior to her father's death, her mother had been a semi-functioning alcoholic, and although her mother's input to everyday life had been minimal, at least she got out of bed each morning, got dressed and showed her face around the house. After the funeral she lapsed into simply being an alcoholic. Seeing her mother slumped awkwardly in the chair or splayed out on the floor only exacerbates the girl's depression and sense of isolation.

There is nowhere to run, no safe place. Her glimmer of hope, the lady next door, has kept her distance, unwilling, she surmises, to become associated with a family of drunks, a family of unwashed losers. She is truly alone. Aunt Petra visits infrequently, tired of cleaning up after her drunken idle sister, tired of finding empty bottles strewn around the house. Soon she will stop coming around altogether. The happiness the girl hoped to find after the death of her father has disappeared into the ether.

She watches the gang of girls whenever she can, looking for cracks, fissures in their airtight chamber. There is still that one girl, the same one that awful day down by the river. The quiet one. She's the weakest member of the gang, the one most likely to break away. Perhaps she has a conscience. Or perhaps not.

Maybe she doesn't like to get her hands dirty, preferring to watch from the sidelines.

The girl suppresses a sob, furious with herself for feeling this way. She doesn't think she will ever be able to forgive them for how they treat her. Especially, her, Tanya Sharpe, the ringleader.

One day, things will definitely improve. Karma will play its part and they will all get their comeuppance. She only hopes she's around to see it or perhaps even be the one who delivers it.

21

2019

Light falls in great waves over the dark asphalt, spreading across the lines of parked vehicles. It diffuses and dips over the red brick wall that surrounds the railway station, shadows spreading over the concrete floor. Commuters rush past, hurrying home after a busy week, their faces angular, lined; tense expressions gradually melting into relief as they slip into taxis or slide into their own vehicles and fire up the engine.

I circle around the car park for the third time in Wade's vehicle, hoping to spot a space. The lock on the passenger door of my car seemed secure enough but I didn't want to take any chances, not with the recent damage. The railway station is in one of the roughest areas in town and owners who park their vehicles here do so at their own risk. Car break-ins are a common occurrence.

A horn sounds behind me. In the rear-view mirror and I see a man gesticulating wildly, telling me to move and get out of the way. I raise my arm and wave, hoping he'll see it as a friendly gesture, then slowly nudge forward, praying somebody backs out in time for me to take their space.

For once, luck is on my side. A large SUV edges out of a

corner space leaving me plenty of room to reverse in and leave hooting angry man to bother somebody else.

It only takes me one attempt to park up. I kill the engine and check my phone to make sure the train is on time. No messages from Wade which fills me with relief. I assume everything is running as it should be.

Climbing out, I click the key, double check to make sure it's locked and am slinging my bag over my shoulder when I feel the tap on my arm. I spin around to see a woman staring at me. Two small snotty-nosed children hang around her legs, pawing at her and writhing about as they vie for her attention. Despite the chill in the air, she is wearing a skimpy vest top with her bra straps clearly visible beneath. Her arms are large and flabby and the wedge of flesh protruding from her midriff hangs loosely over the waistband of her jeans. She searches my face for some sort of recognition. She looks vaguely familiar but I cannot place her. Her skin is pale, almost translucent, with a sprinkling of broken veins across the cheeks, and her mouth is puckered into a thin line of disapproval as she watches me, waiting for a response. I don't recognise her. Not immediately, although something deep within me stirs, a hand being dragged through murky waters, about to reveal something I would rather stay hidden.

'Kyle!' she shrieks, her hand slapping at one of the children as the two youngsters race around one another and kick at her podgy legs. A waft of nicotine filters over to me tinged with stale beer. She rolls her eyes, her voice loud, her accent thick and distinctly northern. 'Fucking kids, eh? Who'd have 'em?'

I manage a weak smile, glancing beyond her as I do to the clock in the distance. Wade's train arrives in ten minutes. I was hoping to grab a coffee before he gets in.

'Don't recognise me, do ya, Stella?'

I freeze at the use of my name. She's right. Despite the initial feeling of possible familiarity, I still don't recognise her. I had wondered perhaps if she was a parent of one of my pupils but they wouldn't know, or at least use, my first name. I always maintain a professional distance when speaking with them.

Her gaze bores into me as I wrack my brains, trying to work out who she is and how she knows me. I don't have to wait long to find out.

'It's me, Tanya. Remember?' She is smiling, her eyes searching mine, looking at me as if we are old friends. It takes a couple of seconds for everything to fall into place. My stomach ties itself into a knot. I shiver. Tanya Sharpe. Dear God, this desperate looking creature is Tanya Sharpe. I do know her. But we are definitely not old friends.

I nod, trying to muster up a smile, my mouth forming itself into a grimace. My teeth are bared, my lips feeling twisted and cracked as I grin manically at this person in front of me. 'Right, yes. Of course. Tanya Sharpe.'

Saying her name out loud knocks me off-kilter. I can't quite believe she expected me to remember who she is. Tanya has changed beyond recognition. She has gained at least five stone, yet is wearing clothes built for a woman half her size. And here she is with two small children; I stare down at them and then back up at her pale puckered face.

'Yeah, both mine,' she says with a laugh as if reading my mind. 'Got another one at home as well. How many you got?'

I shake my head. 'None. I can barely look after myself.' I laugh to show her I'm being self-deprecating, not trying in any way to be overbearing or superior. She would spot it. Her body may have altered beyond recognition but her mind, I feel sure, will be stuck in the same groove, that same way of assuming that anybody not on her wavelength deserves to be scorned and held to account.

'What you up to now, then? You got a job and a house and

stuff?' She looks me up and down, at my polished shoes, my blue suit and designer handbag which I attempt to push out of sight.

'I'm a teacher,' I reply reluctantly. I immediately regret my words and think about why I'm still living so close to the village where I grew up. I should have made a clean break, got out of here while I had the chance. Yet here I am, still living and working in West Compton, the place that showed no kindness or compassion to me as a child. The place I should have left behind.

At least Tanya's kids are too young to be any of my pupils and by the time they reach that age, I may well have moved on to pastures new. I refuse to tell her the name of the school. She knows nothing about me. I could be teaching anywhere in the North East. I will be frugal with any information I give out. Tanya is definitely not somebody I want to become friendly with. My memories of her are unpleasant, tinged with something dark, yet here she is, standing here, her smile wide revealing tombstone teeth, her eyes glinting as she chats amiably like the old friends that we never were.

'A teacher, eh? You always were a clever one. Not like me. I was a right thick cow.' She waits for me to correct her, to tell her that she did just fine. Ordinarily, I would, if only to fill an awkward silence, but Tanya is no ordinary person. She doesn't deserve any commendations or words of praise. She certainly doesn't deserve to be pandered to by somebody who spent many years in her shadow, terrified and unable to break free from her clutches. I lost so much sleep over this woman, this loathsome creature before me. I am not about to defend her or boost her flagging ego. Tanya will hear no tributes from me. If her life is shit then that is her problem. She deserves everything she gets.

My formative years were tricky, my home life rough-edged and chaotic. School wasn't much better with Tanya around, her monstrous bullying ways dominating everybody. Going to university was the best thing that ever happened to me. It gave me a leg up in life, dragging me out of an environment where the Tanyas of the world are only too ready to sneer and bully and drag everybody down with them, to keep everybody at their level because deep down they are terribly insecure and so full of self-doubt that they cannot handle people who succeed in life.

'Anyway,' I say breezily, hoping my smile appears genuine even though my face is warped and tight, my skin stretching like the fabric of Tanya's summer top; rigid and strained under such enormous pressure, 'it's been lovely to see you. Must dash.' I make a point of looking again at the clock and then at my watch, to stress the fact that I am running late, that I need to leave.

'Where you off to?' she says as I turn and head off down the narrow path that leads to the platform.

I shake my head and give her a wave. 'Sorry. In a bit of a rush. Got to go.'

The pavement thuds slightly, the sound like a beating drum as she runs to catch up with me, her two small children squawking at her side as she drags them along.

'Krista, for fuck's sake. Fucking shut up will you!'

I wince at her voice, at the way she screams and swears at the youngsters. They look up at me and smile, undisturbed by her outburst, clearly accustomed to their mother's brusque, unrefined manner. I smile back and avert my eyes away from them, focusing my gaze on the platform ahead. It's like stepping back in time, with me unable to extricate myself from Tanya's evil clutches. I'm a grown woman yet here I am again, at her mercy, her at my side, making demands on me, still trying to call all the shots.

'We should swap numbers, arrange a get-together, you know, for old times' sake.'

I nod but make a point of picking up my pace and looking again at my watch.

'We had some good times back in the day, didn't we?'

I almost choke on my own saliva. Is that what she really thinks? This woman is clearly mad. Mad and deluded. Does she actually remember those days with a sense of fondness? I think about how sad and lonely her life was and think that it obviously still is; so sad that she's still clinging on to some invisible vestiges of a past that in truth, was utterly dreadful and unimaginably horrible. Tanya was a vile bully who made miserable the lives of dozens of kids at that school, including me.

We are almost at the platform, the noise and crowds threatening to separate us, when she pulls me back and spins me around to face her. 'Here. Give us a call. Be good to chat about our school days. I'm in The Anchor every Saturday night. And a couple of nights during the week if I can get a sitter for these little ankle biters. We could meet in there and sink a few.'

The words, *over my dead body*, explode in my head.

I smile and nod, the sinews in my neck so taut, I am sure they must be visible. Can she not see how uncomfortable I am in her presence? Is she really that dense? I take the scrap of paper, watching through narrowed eyes, my teeth clamped together tightly as she winks at me. She turns and drags the two little ones along with her, their legs barely touching the ground as she pulls them to her side with her pale flabby arms. I watch, both horrified and mesmerised as Tanya merges into the crowd, her messy blonde hair bobbing about until she finally vanishes out of sight. Only then, do I tear up the paper she handed me and shove the tiny pieces into the side pocket of my handbag. I will enjoy disposing of them once we get back home. I visualise myself taking a lighter to her words, watching as the paper turns into a pile of grey crumbling ash. It will be like disposing of

Tanya herself. I was never brave enough to stand up to her all those years ago and in truth, am still a little afraid of her even now. I do know, however, that I would rather gouge out my own eyes with a blunt instrument than spend an evening with her at a local pub, especially The Anchor, an insalubrious place that is regularly raided by the police looking for under-age drinkers and drugs.

It's as I stride towards platform six that I realise I'm trembling. I clasp my hands together in front of me, my fingers locked to stop the shaking. I'm furious at my own weakness; for allowing myself to still be intimidated by her after all this time. I'm a grown woman, for God's sake. I've worked hard to remove myself from the person I was. The last thing I need is for Tanya Sharpe to breeze back into my life and drag me right back to the girl that I used to be. I've moved on. She hasn't. Still the same loud, graceless person she always was. Still the same bullying domineering ways.

I shiver and block out those memories. It's all too painful, too raw to think about. The passing of time hasn't erased the hurt. I'm a different person now. A better, stronger person. I've made something of myself. Done things I'm proud of; done things I'm not so proud of. But I'm in a better place than I was when I knew Tanya.

A train pulls up alongside me. The metallic drag of metal against metal plucks me out of my thoughts. I'm only too glad to be released from the misery of the past. Seeing Tanya has only served to strengthen my resolve to work towards a better future, to leave those unwanted memories far behind me.

I spot Wade's dark hair amongst the crowd. I am flooded with relief. I hadn't realised just how much I had missed him until now. He is a solid reminder of who I am, my life raft in a sea of uncertainty.

Tears threaten to fall as I fling myself at him and bury my face in his chest.

'Hey, hey! I've only been gone a couple of days.' His voice is full of concern as he pulls me back and stares deep into my eyes.

I blink and smile up at him, trying to conceal the tremble that is travelling up my body. Whether it's the recent letter or the accident or seeing Tanya, I am both elated and exhausted, and terrified and relieved all at the same time.

There are things I need to tell Wade, things I should have revealed to him a long, long time ago. 'Come on,' I say as I grab his hand and squeeze it tight. 'Let's get you home.'

22

The evening is a blur. We spend it wrapped in one another's arms. Spread before us on the coffee table is a collection of half-eaten Indian food and an empty wine bottle with two garnet-stained glasses beside it.

'Shall I open another?' Wade stands up, looks at me, his face quizzical, his expression dark and enigmatic as he searches my features for something I cannot give. His gaze is relentless, probing deep into my soul. I want to reach up to him, become nestled in the safety and solidity of his embrace and lose myself forever.

'Well, we're off tomorrow, so why not?' I wave my crystal glass at him playfully.

'You're a very bad influence, you do know that, don't you?' He leans down and kisses me. I can taste the garlic and wine on his lips and feel an unexpected flush of excitement at him being so close by. I'm a teenager again with a crush, a young girl unable to contain her feelings, swept along by lust and exhilaration.

I close my eyes and breathe deeply, complete contentment washing over me, settling somewhere down in the pit of my belly. When I open them again, Wade is standing over me, watching me, his expression one of mild amusement. 'I should go away more often. I can't remember the last time I saw you this happy and relaxed.'

He winks at me and I have no idea whether it's the sound of his voice or the fact that he is so trusting or if it is simply a release of all the pent-up anger and fear and frustration that has been building up over the past few weeks, but I unexpectedly burst into tears.

Through misted vision, I see Wade's expression change from happy to horrified. He sits down next to me on the sofa and places his arm over my shoulder. It is solid, reassuring. 'Hey, hey! What's up? One minute you're all laid-back and content and now this?'

I am not sure whether to move closer to him or move away and pull myself together. Too late now. He's seen the cracks in my veneer, the flimsy façade that disguises how broken and damaged I really am. I can't keep this to myself any longer. I have to tell him. So I do.

Leaning into him so I don't have to see his reactions, I tell Wade about my childhood, about the abuse I endured and why I simply cannot forgive my mother. And then I tell him about the letters. I'd like to say the whole process was cathartic but as I sit here, consumed by misery and anxiety, I'm not so sure it was. I am exhausted by it all. I've aged twenty years in twenty minutes. I don't tell him everything. I can't. And I don't tell him about Glenn. There's no need. Why bring up something that is no longer relevant? Glenn has been eliminated and isn't on my radar anymore. He's part of a past I am trying hard to erase.

'Have you still got the letters?' Wade's voice is quiet. Careful. Even his movements are measured and slightly contrived so as to not upset me any further. This is why I was drawn to him; to counterbalance my traumatic childhood with his steadiness and reliability. I know that now. Wade is everything I am not.

I nod, my voice too sore and croaky to say anything else, then go and collect the letters together, shuffling them into a neat and tidy pile in a bid to detract from their contents.

When I come back with them held tightly in my hand, Wade has cleared the table. He takes them from me and we sit side by side on the sofa. He lays them out on the coffee table one by one in such a precise and methodical fashion that it unsettles me. The sight of them there, squared up in front of me, the white paper incongruous against the dark wood, makes me feel quite sick.

He reads them all, his eyes sweeping over each word and then turns to look at me. I know what's coming next and my stomach tightens with dread.

'Two things,' he says in a low gravelly voice. 'Firstly, why didn't you tell me about this before now? And secondly, have you informed the police?' His easy, careful manner is slowly turning to one of brusqueness and efficiency. He has slipped into work mode and is now doing what he does best – sorting out problems that involve people being difficult or unfair towards one another.

A rush of heat blooms on my flesh coating me with a thin layer of perspiration. I wipe at my upper lip, my fingers as heavy as stone, and then rub at my eyes like a small child caught stealing from the sweetie jar. My voice trembles as I speak, a thin rasp in the silence of the room. 'I'm sorry. I should have told you. I don't know why I didn't. I was worried and when I worry, I find it hard to open up and talk.'

Wade knows this to be true. We've been together for ten years and he is all too aware of my faults and idiosyncrasies. We met when I was doing my teaching degree at Northumbria University. Wade was doing his master's degree and the attraction was immediate. I had passed him quite a few times on campus and thought he was the most handsome man I'd ever seen. Never in a million years did I expect him to approach me and speak to me. I was acutely aware of how damaged I was, always convinced my emotional baggage was visible to anybody who came into contact with me. I kept myself to myself and shied away from social events. While other students partied hard and drank themselves into a stupor, I sat in my squalid little apartment and read, or ate or slept. Anything to stop me from mingling with people who weren't like me. I also had a job. I needed the money. Support from home was zero and so I worked as often as I could at a café in town, serving greasy food and cheap coffee to the people of Newcastle.

And then one day, Wade walked my way. We talked. He smiled and spoke in a gentle voice making me feel reassured about the world in general. I needed to know that it wasn't filled with bullies and bad people and Wade showed me just that. He was the security I craved, my haven after so much uncertainty and fear.

And now I've lied to him, kept things from him even though he has been unerringly kind and supportive.

'Okay. Doesn't matter now. What's done is done. It's how we handle it from this point on that's important.' His voice has softened somewhat but still has an air of gravitas to it. An iron fist in a velvet glove.

I swallow and nod. 'I don't want to tell the police.' I look up at Wade, an obvious plea in my eyes. 'Please.'

Wade sighs and looks away, then turns back to me. 'All right. But tell me one thing, please. Why not? I just don't get it. I honestly don't know why you wouldn't want them to help.'

I'm not sure I understand it myself. I have a fear that once the police get involved, they'll begin combing through my every move. They'll want to know who holds a grudge against me. They will ask me hundreds of questions about my past, keen to unearth any dirty secrets, dredging and digging and I don't think

I can face it. I shrug and shake my head. 'I can't face all the questions and knowing looks they'll give me. All I want is a peaceful life.'

This is not so far removed from the truth. For once I am not lying.

'Look, we'll strike a deal.' Wade sounds and looks exasperated by my inability to give reasons for being so uncooperative.

I hold my breath, wondering what he has in mind. Wondering if I am in any position to actually refuse.

'No police involvement as long as you don't receive any more of this utterly spiteful and pointless drivel.' He holds up one of the letters and shakes it in the air, his face dark and brooding. 'The minute you get another one, I'm calling them in.'

My chest and throat tighten. Dare I hide any future notes? Am I really that devious and secretive? I refuse to think about it. I don't want to go down that route so instead I nod and pray to a God I'm almost certain doesn't exist that there are no more. Because if there are, and Wade keeps his word, which I know for sure he will, and he informs the police, then I dread to think what will happen. Only I know the dark secrets of my past. Glenn has been all but eliminated, but as misdemeanours go, he was a minor blip. I've been lying to myself that Glenn was the only one with a grudge. Lying is easier than thinking about the unthinkable. Lying is a way of concealing my past, pretending it never happened. Pretending I didn't do that terrible thing, that awful thing that I've tried so hard to forget.

I nod and tell him that I agree. What choice do I have? Even as I'm sitting here, looking into his eyes, saying all the things he wants to hear, I'm still not sure I am up to this. Wade has led a simple life; he has nothing to hide, no shadowy past, no dark secrets. Just a steady, average existence. Mine has been a bumpy ride along a cliff edge. I'm constantly terrified of dropping over and plummeting to the bottom, my body falling apart as I hit the floor, splitting in two, releasing a host of demons into the ether. The past ten years with Wade have taught me how to act normally, how to conduct myself in social situations and not let my anger and fears bubble up to the surface, but underneath it all, I'm still that terrified little girl, the youngster who did a terrible thing to keep herself safe.

And now it would appear, it's all coming back to haunt me.

23

I'm desperately relieved when the weekend is over, when Monday morning arrives and there is no letter. Is this how I'm going to be from here on in – checking the post every single morning with my heart in my mouth? Watching and waiting for the morning when Wade finds it before I do? Because he will. Since Friday evening he has been up and out of his seat as soon as he spots the postman striding up and down the road. This is his new project; keeping me safe from an invisible maniac. And there is no way the mystery notes are going to suddenly cease. I'm not that lucky. One day soon, another will arrive. And then he'll be as good as his word and will call the police. That's when everything will come apart. That's when my nicely ordered life will disintegrate.

I am being treated like a delicate porcelain ornament. It will be a relief to get into work where teenagers curl their lips at me, where they make snide remarks when they think I am not looking. The memory of Jack Phelps seeps back into my mind; the thought of his words twisting at my intestines until I can no longer eat my breakfast. I furtively pick up the bowl and empty the contents into the bin before Wade notices how little I've eaten, then stand staring out of the window as I finish my coffee.

'Right, I'm off,' I say a little too breezily. I place the cup in the sink, aware that I am in danger of play-acting in my own home. Nothing feels natural; every movement, every single word is artificial and theatrical. We can't continue like this indefinitely, me carrying on like a cardboard cut-out. At some point we have to go back to living a normal life. Whatever normal is.

'I'll contact the insurance company today, see if they've heard anything from the tractor driver. I'll pass on his details and let them do their thing,' Wade says. He is busy reading the news on his tablet, his gaze directed at the screen and for once, not at me.

I lean over him and kiss the top of his head. He looks up then and pushes the tablet to one side. 'Bye, kiddo. Have a good day. I'll see you tonight,' he says softly.

I'm relieved Wade is sorting out the insurance. It's one less thing for me to worry about, and besides, he enjoys taking charge and tackling all the admin tasks that I find indescribably boring.

'See you later. I'll be in at the usual time. No meetings to attend, thank God,' I murmur as I roll my eyes and head out into the hallway.

I grab my keys and unlock the door, before taking a glance behind me. Wade is looking at me, his dark eyes narrowed in concentration, his lashes fluttering slightly as he watches me leave.

I shiver and step outside.

The car park is almost empty as I pull up into my usual space and lock up. I spot Jonathan, the head of the English

Department, striding through the main doors and run to catch up with him. His briefcase swings by his side, before he suddenly stops, stretches out his arm to place his security fob against the metal plate on the door frame and pushes open the door. I manage to get behind him in time to sneak through before it closes.

'Morning, boss,' I say sardonically.

He turns and smiles at me, his face already flushed with the exertion of walking from the car to the building. A dark arc of perspiration circles his armpits, a stark contrast against the soft creaminess of his shirt. 'Morning, Stella. Another early bird, eh?'

I nod. 'I like to get things organised before the rest of the world wakes up. I've always been the same.' I don't tell him that I have terrible problems sleeping, that I toss and turn for most of the night, worrying about anything and everything; the future, the present, the past. They're all there every night, forcing me awake, presenting new dilemmas and problems. And as fast as I solve one, another appears, ready to grind me underfoot.

We walk to the English department, Jonathan holding open the door as I step through to the main office. 'How's our friend Jack been since coming back from his exclusion? I tried to call in to see you the other day but Allison caught me and we spent over an hour discussing the new SEN budget. Or rather, the lack of it.'

I think about Jack's choice of phrase, calling me a bitch, the connection to the letters and do my best to dismiss it. It's a tenuous link and I'm clutching at straws here. Jack Phelps is many things – disaffected, challenging – but he's not angry or even bright enough to be behind such a dark and nasty affair. 'He's fine,' I say with a smile. 'Still hates me and still loathes Shakespeare and all aspects of English grammar with a passion but apart from that, we're all good.'

Jonathan's laugh fills the empty room. 'Well, so far today I haven't got any meetings penned in so you know where I am if you need me.' He gives me an inoffensive affable wink and we part to prepare for the day ahead.

In school, there are days when time stretches out before me, when every lesson is arduous, like wading through treacle or trying to clamber out of quicksand. And then there are days when everything slots together with ease; students are responsive, the noise levels stay within an acceptable level and I manage to remain cheerful and not end the day like a washed-out old rag. Today is one of those days. Each and every lesson runs like clockwork, the pupils are receptive; even staff who usually look as if they've lost a tenner and found a penny, seem happier and lighter.

The sun is that little bit brighter as I stare out of my classroom window, the sky that little bit clearer. I decide that I will go shopping after work. I still have enough energy and think that perhaps a wander around town on my own will do me good. I text Wade to tell him of my plans. He replies, saying that he has to stay late anyway and could I pick up some food on the way home.

I am heading out of the class and about to make my way down the corridor towards the exit when Marion from the school office rushes towards me with the headteacher Andrew Holland by her side. Andrew is looking down to the ground, his expression unreadable. Marion looks stricken.

They reach me and stop, Marion's chest rising and falling as she gasps for breath. She looks up to Andrew for a reaction, her fingers fluttering over her face like the wings of a small bird. I wait as he clears his throat and indicates for me to go back into the classroom, nodding towards the door. Andrew is a young, fresh-faced headteacher, many of the staff believing him to be lacking in experience. Personally, I think he's an okay guy but right now, he is starting to scare me. His sombre expression, his inability to convey what is happening here, all serve to unsettle me. A thousand possibilities for this unplanned liaison are racing through my brain; a serious complaint from the parent of one of my pupils, somebody close to me is gravely ill or worse still – dead; or I'm about to lose my job due to some serious misdemeanour or budget cuts.

My head is spinning by the time we sit down at one of the desks. Andrew twists at his tie, perspiration starting to cover his slightly equine features. He stares at me from beneath his dark knitted brow. 'Really sorry to have to catch you like this, Stella, but we didn't want you going out in the car park on your own and seeing it,' he says, further deepening the feelings of concern and unease that are currently burrowing into my brain.

I don't say anything. I've never been very good at guessing games and I'm too worried and too old to suddenly start sharpening my conjecture skills, so instead I wait with a pounding heart to find out what is going on.

'Somebody has vandalised your car. A member of staff saw it as they left the building and came back inside to report it to Marion who went out to take a closer look.'

I smile and shake my head, suddenly relieved. I am both amused and entertained by their reactions, thinking them to be excessive for the amount of damage on the door. 'Ah, I had an accident and while I–'

'Not the dented door or the scratches,' Andrew says breathlessly, throwing Marion a quick side glance. 'We can see that that was from something else, that it was caused by an accident. This is something quite different.'

'How different?' I murmur, my throat suddenly dry. A tic takes hold in my jaw. A pulse judders in my neck. I press my fingers into it and clear my throat to alleviate the uncomfortable sensation that is building there. Marion places her hand over mine and leans forward, then smiles at me in her best matronlike manner. 'It's probably best that you come outside and see it for yourself.'

I'm speechless. Andrew is standing to one side, his head dipped slightly as he surveys the damage. Marion is watching me with her hawk-like expression, assessing my every move to see if I'm going to shout or cry or slump to the floor and scream at the heavens above that it's unfair and why have I been targeted like this. She is expecting me to turn and ask, why my car? But I don't do any of those things. Because I've been expecting something like this. After all those notes, I knew something else, something bigger was about to take place. I just didn't know what. And now I do.

I circle the car, like a predator tracking its prey. I squint, narrowing my eyes, assessing the damage. My back aches, my vision becomes blurred. I suddenly feel dizzy and lacking in energy. All four tyres have been slashed and the paintwork on the driver's door has one large word gouged into it – *BITCH*.

A piece of paper is tucked under the windscreen wipers, barely visible beneath the black rubber strips. I'm reluctant to pull it out while Marion and Andrew are here. I have a fair idea of what it will say and don't want them to see it. The last thing I want is for my work colleagues to suddenly become acquainted with certain unpalatable aspects of my private life. Shame and disgust washes over me. Them being here and seeing the car is bad enough. I'm now trying to limit the damage to my reputation, to show them that this means nothing to me even though it means everything.

I have an overwhelming urge to pull out my phone, book a taxi and go home, to hide away and pretend that none of this is happening. I let out an unsteady breath and turn to Andrew, claws at the ready, a streak of anger rushing out of me. 'We need CCTV in this car park. And lights for the winter. This isn't the first time this has happened. Remember the time Bill Tate had his windscreen put through by a disgruntled parent?'

I'm deflecting the blame, pointing the finger at an innocent man, I do know that, but I have no idea how to react. For some unfathomable reason, I feel culpable, as if I've committed this atrocity myself and am compelled to protect my image. Whether it's having the word *BITCH* scrawled across my door for everyone to see or whether it's the uneasy sense of guilt that is slowly creeping over my flesh as we all stand here, staring and doing nothing, I'm not sure. What I do know is, I now have to call Wade and tell him what's happened and then see what his reaction is going to be. Unlike letters that are posted through my door or slipped into my pigeonhole at work, this is too public. I can't hide away from this and act as if it hasn't happened. No more pretending. No more covering up. Everybody knows now. It's all out in the open for the world and his wife to see.

BITCH

Andrew nods and murmurs to Marion to get some quotes for installation of cameras at certain positions in the car park.

'Should we inform the police?' Marion asks, her voice squeaky with concern.

I shake my head. That's the last thing I want to do right now. Andrew doesn't press the issue. We both know that police involvement puts the school in a precarious position. The media would get hold of the story and make all kinds of assumptions about pupils and teachers and poor behaviour, and would ultimately paint Westland Academy in a bad light, printing stories that have no bearing on the actual event. The gutter gossips would have a field day with an incident like this. Life inside those walls is difficult enough as it is, a fine balancing act.

Letting the press get hold of this incident would make it a hundred times worse.

'Come back inside, honey,' Marion coos as she tries to take my elbow and guide me back to her office.

'Honestly, I'm fine,' I say a little too sternly as I shake my arm free. 'I'm going to book a cab and then call my insurance company.'

Marion looks genuinely hurt and surprised by my abrupt manner. Another thing to feel guilty about. Another worry pushing me deep into the ground. I wink at her, smiling sheepishly. 'You never know, Marion, what with the crash and now the graffiti, I might actually get a new car out of this sorry little mess.'

A look of relief passes over her face. Her eyes crinkle up at the corners as she lets out a low laugh at my words.

Andrew is already heading back inside, keen to distance himself from this situation. Can't say I blame him. I would do the same if I could. I pull out my phone and call a local taxi firm, already trying to work out how I'm going to break this bit of news to Wade as I punch in the number and wait.

24

1999

She considers saying nothing, just standing instead, adjacent to the quiet one of the gang, and eyeing her up and down. But the temptation proves too great and, in the end, she says the first thing that comes into her head.

'Why?'

The quiet one doesn't respond; she lowers her head and kicks at a stone, knocking it around her feet until it tumbles out of reach, disappearing down a drain with a metallic rattle.

The girl asks again. 'Why? Why do you hang around with them and why are you all so mean?' She knows this encounter could go either way. She is aware that the quiet one could go running back to her little legion of demons, tell them what she has said, but something is driving her on, making her question their motives. She has to fight back. At some point she has to try to claw back some of her dignity and what better time to do it than right here and now? It may make no difference, but she feels compelled to speak up; she has, after all, nothing to lose.

There is no response but she can see the guilt in the quiet one's eyes. She can tell by the flush that is creeping up her neck that a conscience of sorts lurks somewhere deep down in her soul. She is different from the others. Not necessarily better. Just different. She is their possible weak link, the pinprick hole in their hermetically sealed tomb.

The two of them are alone in the yard. The rest of the gang have split up and the quiet one is on her own. No reinforcements, no suit of armour protecting her. That's rare. They never walk anywhere unaccompanied, always travelling in a pack. But today the quiet one is by herself. Tanya Sharpe is nowhere to be seen. Probably towering over some unsuspecting child much smaller than she is; or sitting outside the headteacher's office awaiting another reprimand that will wash over her like liquid mercury. Admonishments and sanctions have no effect on the Tanyas of this world. They are immune to punishments, wearing them with pride, like a badge of honour, using them to elevate their status. Without their tales of regular admonishments, they are nothing; just hollow husks with no substance or depth.

The quiet one looks up at the girl with the dark brooding eyes, her mouth set in a thin line of unhappiness. The girl doesn't say anything else. She doesn't have to. There is a silent recognition between them. They are both Tanya's victims; one being forced to mete out the insults and abuse, the other receiving them. Both of them dragged along in the slipstream of Tanya's spiteful wicked ways.

They are both so deep in thought that they don't see Tanya approach them from the corner of the sprawl of asphalt. She is upon them before they can do anything about it. She stands, watching them, hands on hips, lip curled in a vindictive cruel sneer. The girl's skin prickles. She swallows down the sense of dread that has suddenly settled on her, nipping at her guts and stripping her courage away bit by bit. She has to stop this. She has to stop showing her fear. Her obvious weaknesses only serve to fuel Tanya's hatred of her. Tanya Sharpe laps up her victims' terror like a wild animal sucking dry the carcass of its latest kill.

'What's going on 'ere then?' Tanya's voice slices through the quiet. Her lank ash blonde hair hangs limply over her shoulders and her pale skin is almost translucent under the harsh glare of the midday sun. Her eyes are black with mascara, her cheeks pink with roughly applied rouge. The girl looks at her, at her skinny legs slightly bowed in the middle, at her large hooped earrings, and wonders if this brute of a being ever reflects on her actions. Does she ever have any moments of quiet when thoughts of what she has done blooms in her mind, filling her with guilt and shame? Probably not. Why would she? She isn't adversely affected by any of it. Tanya leaves her victims feeling wounded while she departs, feeling victorious, surrounded by people who continually back her up and help to perpetuate the myth that she is a deity capable of anything. It's all within her power. She holds the heart of her victims in the palm of her hands, whether she chooses to crush them or leave them intact all depends on what day it is and which way the wind is blowing. There are no set rules that her victims can live by to keep themselves safe.

Nobody speaks. Tanya continues to observe the two girls. She looks at the quiet one then over to the girl. Tanya spits out the words to the quiet one. 'Pick up that stone and hit her with it.'

The girl goes cold. Her skin prickles with dread. A voice inside her head tells her to move away, to turn her back and keep on walking until the pair of them are a speck in the distance. Her body refuses to co-operate leaving her frozen, unable to move a muscle. She is rooted to the spot.

'I said pick up that fucking stone!'

The quiet one moves over to a small, heavy looking rock. Its sharp edges make the girl's stomach fold in on itself. The quiet one doesn't pick it up. Her head is lowered, her gaze glued to the ground. The girl can't see her expression. Just as well. She may not like what she sees there.

'Oh, for fuck's sake!' Tanya's voice is an exasperated roar. She kicks the stone even closer to the quiet one. It lands directly at her feet and sits there, an inanimate object, threatening. Menacing. 'Now pick it up.'

The girl's heart pounds in her chest like a bass drum, echoing in her head. The ground turns to liquid under her feet. She needs to walk away but can't seem to move. Her legs refuse to comply with the messages her brain is sending. She is a target waiting to be hit.

Her eyes widen in horror as the quiet one bends down and wraps her hand around the rock, her fingers clasped around its rough hard edges, caressing its surface with her long nails.

'Now hit her with it,' Tanya hisses, flecks of spittle flying out of her mouth as she stares at the small bone-white fingers wrapped around the rock. 'Hit her with it or I'll use it on your head instead.'

Before she can do anything, the girl feels a hard object being rammed into her skull. Stars blind her vision and vomit rushes up her throat, burning her gullet. She slumps down onto the concrete, her hands covering her head. Pain bounces behind her eyes, pulsing white-hot flames that lick and burn at her brain. She lets out a sob and gasps for breath, feeling another source of heat close by.

She looks up, sees Tanya's leering grimace just inches away from her own face, smells her sour breath and gags. 'Don't ever fucking speak to any of my mates again, yeah? Or the next time, you'll have more than a tiny bruise on your greasy little head.'

Pain continues to pulse through her. Everything feels laboured – breathing, moving, thinking. She is left on her own as they stride away. She remains on the floor. Only when Tanya and her stooge are safely out of view does the girl get up and inspect her hands, scanning them for blood or brain matter. There is nothing. Apart from the throbbing pain and ringing in her ears, there's no sign that anything has even taken place.

25

2019

I wait until Marion and Andrew are safely out of sight before pulling out the note from under the windscreen wipers, and shoving it into my pocket.

A few members of staff are now strolling across the car park, stopping and surreptitiously glancing my way. It doesn't take long for bad news to spread, to bring people flocking so they can gawp and thank God it isn't happening to them and that it isn't their car that has been defaced. I turn my back to them, pretending to be speaking into my phone, booking a taxi that is already on its way. I'm too exhausted to bother with any of them.

I walk, my legs weakened by shock and fear, and make my way to the end of the road where the cab will park up and wait. I'm immediately more comfortable being away from the school site. My brain is in overdrive as I rake through a thousand different ways in which I can break the news to Wade, none of them seemingly easy. Police involvement will be unavoidable, unless of course they, as a sadly depleted force lacking in manpower, choose to ignore our report, claiming their resources are stretched too thin to warrant any sort of inquiry. I desperately hope this is the case although experience tells me somebody will call and start asking questions that I don't want to answer, combing through my past, delving and digging until they unearth the truth.

My head aches as I perch on a low stone pillar and wait for the taxi to arrive. At least half a dozen vehicles pass by me, their occupants peering at me quizzically from behind their sun visors. By tomorrow morning, I'll be the talk of Westland Academy, my name on everybody's lips as they discuss my misfortune, wondering what I did to deserve it. I try to block that thought out, to pretend that I'll be able to pass people in the corridor without having to discuss this latest event. Tomorrow morning is our weekly early morning diary meeting. I bite at my lip and shudder. All staff are required to attend, to listen and take notes as Andrew goes through any important dates and events. It's unlikely he will mention my car, but all eyes will be on me, watching, scrutinising. Waiting for something to be said. The thought of it makes me go cold.

It doesn't take too long for my taxi to arrive. It screeches to a halt beside me and I open the door and slide in, relieved to be hidden from the staff who are driving past on their way out of the car park, relieved to be away from the inquisitive glances of all the passers-by.

'Jesus, Stella. What the hell is going on? Why you?' Wade and I are sitting at the kitchen table across from each other. His hands are splayed out across the knots in the pine, an action that makes my skin crawl and my stomach plummet. It's a position of authority, one that demands respect. His words aren't empty rhetoric. He is waiting for an answer to his question. An answer that I simply cannot give.

I shake my head, my eyes aching from the effort of staring at him, from insisting that I have no idea why this is happening to me. I no longer know what to think. Do I really have the answers to his questions? Or am I lying to myself? Are my secrets hidden so far down inside me, I don't know how to retrieve them? Words needed to verbalise my early life have failed me on so many occasions, I fear I have lost all ability to ever say them out loud.

'Well, we definitely need to call the police now, don't we?'

I avert my gaze and nod, my face burning with shame and worry. I've eliminated Glenn. But I haven't eliminated everybody, have I? Not really. I've been kidding myself all along and my refusal to tell Wade everything that happened to me has now blown up in my face.

Before I can say or do anything, he stands up and speaks into his phone, enunciating every syllable. His voice is clipped, efficient, lacking in any kind of emotion. My flesh puckers, goosebumps standing to attention on my arms when I realise that a visit is inevitable, that an officer or a number of police officers will visit our house. Wade is nodding and sounding more confident than ever as he speaks to the person on the other end of the phone.

He flashes me a confident smile, talks some more, says a final goodbye, then disconnects the call and turns to me. 'They said that somebody is going to come out to look at the car. They should be there within the next hour. We'll take the letters and meet them in the school car park.'

My stomach flips. It's now or never. Wade needs to hear it from me before the police do; the story I've never said out loud. The part of my life I hoped to forget about. I should have told him before now. I should have admitted it to myself before now. Because after eliminating Glenn, Barry is the only other person I can think of who would do this. I have no idea why after all these years, he would suddenly decide to come after me, but his name is all I have left. God forbid that there are any more enemies lurking in the shadows, wishing me harm.

I like to think I'm a fairly decent person who has made mistakes. Mistakes borne out of a past that was traumatic and dysfunctional. My brain hasn't always responded as it should when presented with difficult situations but I'm getting there. I'm a vastly different person to the one I was all those years ago when I was being continually abused by my stepfather. I've grown up, learnt from the past, learnt from my mistakes and worked fucking hard to get to where I am now. I just hope my nice steady life isn't about to be ripped away from me because of something I did when I was no more than a child.

'Sit down,' I say.

Wade spins around and stares at me. He isn't used to this; being subjected to my assertive manner, listening to me barking orders at him and it shows in his expression. His lips are pursed, a pulsing hollow appears at the side of his jaw.

'We need to talk. I've got something to tell you. Something I should have told you before now.' I'm trying to sound relaxed and at ease when all the while my insides are churning and grumbling in protest, a cold sensation shifting across my belly, telling me to stop talking, to shut up and keep my secrets to myself. Nothing good can come of this, I can just feel it.

Wade slides into the chair opposite me. He looks deflated, like all the air's been sucked out of him. I'm not sure what he's imagining this revelation is going to be. Maybe what I'm about to tell him won't be half as shocking as he expects. Or maybe it will. Wade's normal upbringing means his expected standards of morality are higher than mine. The bar on my early life is set pretty low.

'I haven't been completely truthful when it comes to my childhood. You know that I was abused, but I think I've led you to believe that it was just the occasional smack and neglect. It was more than that, Wade. So much more. What I haven't told you is that I was abused both physically and sexually.' I swallow the saliva that has already begun to gather in my mouth, swilling around like acid. I'm trembling. I can't seem to stop it. I don't want to look at Wade, to see his response. I cannot bring myself to do it. I feel too ashamed, blackened and charred by what happened to me. By what I did. 'My stepdad, Barry,' I say, the air around me thick and muggy, stopping me from breathing properly. 'After my dad left us and Barry moved in, I did something to him. Something bad. It was to make him stop. I had to do it.'

Wade doesn't move. We're frozen in time, two people suspended in the moment, too afraid to do anything, to say anything. Wade thinks Barry just left, went on to live the life of a drifter. That's what I let him believe. It was easier. Lying is becoming second nature to me now. So much simpler than telling the truth.

'What?' he says eventually. 'What did you do, Stella?'

I close my eyes and exhale loudly, a vertiginous sensation swirling over me. 'I stabbed him.' Tears blur my vision at the memory of that particular evening; Barry's murky shape looming over me as I lay in bed all those years ago, his fingers tugging at the bed covers, his voice silky smooth, telling me to be silent, that he was just being loving towards me and that I needed to hush and just lie back and enjoy the moment.

You'll enjoy it all the more if you relax and don't cry. Sshhh. We don't want anybody to hear now, do we?

Wade throws himself back in his chair, an unwelcome look of incredulity etched on his face. I hoped for understanding but instead I've got this. He looks horrified. Not compassionate or caring but disgusted and repulsed instead.

'What? You did what?' Wade's mouth is twisted into something I don't recognise and it scares the hell out of me.

Everything is separating, coming apart, unspooling before me and I'm not sure if I'll ever be able to get it back.

'He used to come into my room nearly every night. I was no more than a child, only twelve or thirteen years old for heavens' sake and I was utterly terrified, so I took a knife up to bed with me to protect myself. I only intended to use it to scare him away but there was a scuffle when I showed it to him. At first, he became flustered and angry. And then he laughed.' I'm sobbing now. All these years later and here I am having to justify my actions to somebody I had hoped would understand. Even as I say the words, the memory of that evening is so fresh, so raw, it still causes me pain; an open wound that continues to bleed.

'A scuffle?' Wade's voice has softened but only marginally. Not enough to reassure me that he fully understands how it felt. How it still feels. How could he? With his perfectly polished parents, immaculate house and shielded childhood, how could he ever possibly begin to comprehend how any of this felt? I used to lie in bed, dreading the creak of the floorboards outside my room, the shaft of light spilling over my bedsheets, the reek of Barry's body and the feel of his fingers as he crept into my room and slid onto the mattress beside me.

'I became scared and dropped the knife so I jumped out of bed and scrambled around on the floor for it. He stood over me laughing. And that's when I did it,' I say through a series of hiccups and faltering breaths.

'Did what?' Wade asks cautiously, his voice no more than a whisper.

'I grabbed the knife and jammed it into his thigh as far as it would go.' My voice is a thin ribbon of fear. All those memories. All that damage and hurt and now it's back, the memory of that period in my life, making me question my actions when all I was trying to do was keep myself from harm, to protect my innocence and more importantly, my sanity. I keep my eyes averted, looking away from Wade's probing judgemental gaze. 'I pushed the knife in and held on to it as tight as I could, making sure it didn't come out. I just wanted him to stop hurting me. I just wanted it all to stop.'

'So, what happened next?'

I rub at my face, my skin cool and dry like parchment. 'He left. The abuse ended. I got what I wanted, not exactly the way I had planned it, but he left that night, dripping with blood and we never saw him again.' I take a shaky breath. 'And when I tried to explain to my mum what had been going on, that he had been creeping into my bed on a night and doing the unspeakable, she denied it, even blaming me for him leaving. She said it was me, that my bad behaviour had driven him away. I suspect he left because he had realised that I'd grown teeth, got up enough courage to confront him. Barry liked small terrified girls, children who were too timid to stop him. I stopped being that timid girl once I drove that serrated knife into his leg.'

The tick of the clock behind me booms in my head. My own blood roars through my ears, a swirling rushing sensation that makes me want to rest my head on the table, shut my eyes and sleep for an eternity.

'Why would he come back after all these years?' Wade says, his voice croaky and distant. 'It's a horrible story and yes, I wish you had told me this before now, but him reappearing like this doesn't make any sense. It's been, what – twenty years or so? What has this Barry guy been doing in the meantime? Why would you think this is him, Stella?'

'Because I don't know who else it could be!' I half scream. 'I've tried all my life to be a good person but when you come from shit, the stench always follows you around. It seems like no matter how hard I work at doing the right thing, shaking off the shackles of my past, it's always there, ready to remind me of what a crap person I really am. Like the other day at the station before I picked you up.'

'What?' Wade says. 'What about the station?' I can tell he's losing patience with me now. I understand his frustration. I'm going around in circles, not making sense. Wade likes order, routine. Not a useless messy specimen like me.

'I bumped into somebody I went to school with. Somebody I should have stood up to all those years ago. I hoped I'd never have to see her again after we left school, but like many things from my past, she reappeared when I least expected her to. There she was, right in front of me. Tanya Sharpe, the biggest bully I've ever had the misfortune to come across. She even had the audacity to suggest we have a get-together. Just me and her. As if the past didn't happen. She stood there as bold as brass, pretending we were good friends, for fuck's sake!' I'm panting now, gasping for breath. 'And you know the worst thing? I still let her take the lead. I'm a grown woman, no longer that pathetic little child and I still didn't stand up to her!'

The tears are flowing freely now, running down my face and dripping off my chin in great messy pools onto the surface of the table. I can't stop them. I'm not even sure I want to. Talking about it is a release. I feel as if I have atoned for my past sins. I feel as if I deserve some pity for what I did, for what I went through. Surely Wade can find it in himself to forgive me? I hope so. I really do. Forgiving myself, however, is another matter entirely.

I rub at my face, smearing make-up over my cheeks, catching sight of myself in the mirror on the opposite wall; a black river of mascara snakes over my skin, coiling and twisting until it reaches my jawline where it ends in a dark greasy smear. My stomach is heavy, as if it's full of jagged stones that are slicing at the lining of my gut. I swallow down hot bile and wince, the sour taste filling my mouth, causing me to grimace.

Wade looks at his watch and then at me. His voice is distant. I don't recognise it and it scares me. 'The police will be at the school shortly,' he says. 'We'd better get moving or we'll miss them.'

It's as I stand up, my head woozy with panic, that I wonder if this is it; if this is the beginning of the end.

26

What a fantastic sensation. I couldn't quite believe how amazing it felt, slashing her tyres and gouging her car with my knife. Energy surged through me as I did it. I felt like a God, like somebody powerful. I could do anything now, anything at all. If I felt that great just damaging her car, imagine how I'm going to feel when I actually get to damage her? I can see it now, the terror in her face as I slice though her skin. The blood, the screaming, the way she will beg me to stop – it's so fucking brilliant I can hardly contain myself.

Not long now. The hardest part is being nice to her, having to hold conversations and nod and smile in all the right places. I'm obviously doing a fine job of it though as there's never been a flicker of anything in her eyes. No recognition, no suspicion. She has no idea. I love that she thinks she knows me when all the time, she doesn't have a clue. She thinks herself clever and educated and yet she can't see beyond the end of her nose. I'll tell her that when it happens. I'll tell her how thick and stupid and short-sighted she is, how I know all about what she did. I'm going to tell her everything and I'm going to enjoy the look on her face when she realises what this has been about – all the threatening messages and the words scrawled on her car. Everything I have done is for a reason.

Having to live with what she did has been so fucking traumatic, and now she's going to pay. She deserves everything that comes her way. Everything. And I'm going to make sure she gets it.

27

Vanda, the site supervisor, is waiting by my car as we arrive, looking over the damage. I can see her as she sucks at her teeth and shakes her head, her hand trailing over the scratched paintwork. I kept Andrew abreast of what Wade and I were doing and he contacted her to let her know that we were on our way, asking her to keep the main gates to the car park unlocked until the police arrive to inspect the damage. 'Thanks, Vanda. I really appreciate this. Sorry if I'm keeping you here later than normal.'

She shakes her head, smiling at me thoughtfully as she plunges her hands deep into her pockets. 'I don't finish till seven, love. Not a problem at all.' She eyes me cautiously, keeping her voice low as she speaks. 'Who the hell would do something like this?'

My blood speeds up, rushing through me, rattling through my body, hurtling through my head. I can't see Wade's expression but am acutely aware of his presence behind me, his attentive ears, his keen eye for detail, searching for hidden meanings in my words. I swallow hard and choose them carefully. 'No idea, Vanda. Hopefully the police can shed some light on it. They should be here in a few minutes.'

She nods, her expression sorrowful and sympathetic. If ever there were somebody who knows when to speak and when to stop talking, Vanda is that person.

Backing away, leaving Wade and me alone, she heads into the main entrance of the school. It's a sprawl of a building with a royal blue modern curved roof and a huge frontage, a large expanse of glass that glints eerily in the early evening sun. Behind it, Vanda's lone shadow moves about, possibly the only person left inside. I think about those long dim corridors, the empty classrooms and dark cupboards, and swallow, relieved to be out here in the dying sunlight.

'Jesus Christ,' Wade says, his voice a low growl behind me.

I squeeze my eyes closed, wishing I could disappear. I don't want to turn around and see his expression as he inspects my car, or hear what he is going to say next. I just want all of this to go away. I want to live in a world where none of this is real.

'What the hell is wrong with people who do stuff like this? The insurance company is going to have a field day with this and the damage from the crash. They might even write it off.'

I let him ramble on, knowing he doesn't really want an answer from me anyway. He is untethering his anger, setting it free. He continues muttering, his voice a low rasp, his breathing laboured as he bends forwards, squatting to get a closer look at the damage.

I don't join him. I don't need to. The sight of it is already burned into my brain, etched into my thoughts and chiselled deep into my memory. Somebody out there really hates me. Perhaps it's Barry. Perhaps not. And if it's not... well, we will have to cross that bridge when we come to it.

The sight of a police car manoeuvring into the car park makes me dizzy. I reach out, place my hand on the bonnet of my car to steady myself. At least Vanda has left us alone. She doesn't have to listen to the questions they are going to ask, to be privy to the grimy ins and outs of my dirty little life.

The heavy thud of the closing door, the sound of the two officers' footsteps, heighten my fear and compound my misery. I can't look at their faces and yet am unable to tear my gaze away from their shiny polished shoes, their thick trousers with razor creases so sharp they look as if they could cut stone. They exude authority. It radiates out of them, tying my stomach in knots, sending a swell of unease under my skin.

Wade straightens up, puts out his hand for them to shake. They reciprocate briskly, clear their throats and ignore my presence as if they are at an alpha-male conference. I'm glad of it. I want to slink away into the background like a wounded animal retreating into its lair.

Their voices are white noise behind me, a crackle of syllables, sounds bursting into the air with no meaning or relevance.

A hand jolts me out of my trance. I jump, startled as Wade gently turns me around to face the two police officers.

'PC Whiting here is asking if this could have been done by a pupil? Somebody with a grudge?'

Jack Phelps' face leaps into my mind. I swat it away. Impossible. He's not clever enough. Jack operates at a basic level with knee-jerk reactions to situations. He doesn't plot or scheme. He is too dense, too lacking in sophistication for this sort of subterfuge. I've thought about this before. To point the finger at him would only add to his problems. The odds of living a half-decent life are already stacked against him, with his drug-dealing father, absent mother and violent brother. Me blaming him would simply compound his issues. Allegations against boys like him stick like mud, even false ones.

I shake my head, trying to look perplexed by the whole

situation. My body tenses as I wait for Wade to bring up the subject of Barry, to tell the police about him and tarnish the air with the very mention of his name.

He doesn't say anything, instead pulling out the sheaf of paper from his pocket. The letters. I freeze, my breath suspended in my chest, pockets of air beating at my lungs, begging to be released. The ground is soft under my feet, bouncing and tilting as I fight to stay upright, gravity doing its damnedest to pull me down. I think about the letter that was tucked under the windscreen wiper. The one still sitting in my pocket with the words *Die bitch* scrawled on it.

The officers scan each one, their expressions dispassionate. They see worse than this every day. Druggies that mug old ladies, alcoholics slumped in the street, people beaten black and blue. Dead bodies hauled out of cars and burning buildings, burnt and crushed beyond recognition. I bet they've experienced it all. This is nothing to them. A handful of notes written by some mad, sad old lunatic who has too much time on their hands, and a damaged vehicle. This is small potatoes.

I wait as time moves slowly, every movement laborious and stilted, every breath an effort.

'Right,' I hear one of the officers say, his voice distant, disembodied. 'We'll take these with us, see if we can get any evidence from them.'

I feel faint. Now it's real.

'As for the car, we could dust it for fingerprints but to be honest, I doubt we would find any. Whoever did this won't have needed to touch the bodywork. Looks like it was done with a standard knife. No flakes so it probably wasn't a jagged edge. Have you informed your insurance company?'

Wade assures them that it's all in hand. I have no idea if he has contacted them or not. I'm beyond caring. I just want this to end.

'Right, well we'll take a look at these,' the officer says as he places the letters in a bag and seals it up, 'and we'll be in touch in due course.' He holds up the bag and stares at it before depositing it in his top pocket and tapping at it with the palm of his hand.

The police leave, my letters sitting snugly in PC Whiting's jacket. It's out of my control now. There's nothing else I can do.

Later, on the way home, Wade asks me repeatedly if I'm okay. I tell him that I'm fine, just shaken up. His gaze lingers on me, scrutinising my every move. A sense of foreboding dwells in me.

'I'll email those photos to the insurance company when we get in,' he says, tapping at the steering wheel. The dull rhythmic thud annoys me beyond reason. 'And I'll transfer some money from our savings account to pay for the tow truck. I didn't want you driving it in that state.'

I nod, unable to speak. I'm wondering what's next, what little gem I might discover when I get out of bed in the morning. Whoever is doing this has made a conscious decision to up their game.

Resting my head back on the soft leather, I cast my mind back to Barry, to his slovenly ways, his loutish behaviour and think that, like Jack Phelps, all of this is rather beyond his capabilities. So, then who? Who hates me so much that they would go to these lengths?

Barry's face still bothers me, looming in my mind. Where has he been all these years? The only person who could possibly answer that is my mother. And I can't ask her. I just cannot face going to see her. It's out of the question. Especially since now, with the benefit of time and hindsight, I don't think Barry is the one who is behind this.

It continues to niggle at me all the way home. Something isn't right about this whole sick scenario. Barry is or was, a coarse, thuggish individual. Letters are too refined for him, too subtle. A brick through a window is more his style.

And Wade is right – why now after all these years? I chew at my lip pensively. The thought that his injury is now causing him pain and I've left him with long-lasting damage that deteriorates with each passing year, punches its way into my brain. Surely that's not it? I visualise Barry now; a drunken wizened old man, seated in the corner of some rundown pub, a walking stick at his side, his long grey hair settling in greasy strands around his shoulders, his clothes reeking of tobacco and mildew. I picture his narrow, crinkled eyes, as hard as steel as they follow the movements of every young woman that passes his table, his fingers clasped together in his lap, itching to reach out and feel the softness of their skin, erroneous and incompatible against his rough nicotine-stained flesh. I almost retch at the thought of it, at the thought of his gaze slyly undressing every single female in the vicinity.

My head is pounding as we pull up on the drive. How many circles do I have to go around in before I work out who is behind this? I don't want to go down the self-pity route, the avenue that will have me burying my head in my hands and sobbing *why me* over and over. I just want it to be over.

Before I have a chance to change my mind, I turn to Wade, uttering the words I never ever thought I would hear myself say, enunciating every syllable, if only to prove to myself that it really is me who is saying it. 'I think we should visit my mother and ask her about Barry. See if she knows where he is now, what he's up to.'

The lull causes me to suck in my breath, the hiatus hanging in the air between us before he finally responds. 'Right. As long as you're okay with it? I think it's a wise idea but only if you want to go through with it?'

I don't. I definitely don't want to go through with it but my choices are being slimmed down daily, my options reducing at an exponential rate. It's something I have to do and the sooner I make the visit, the sooner I can come home and eliminate him from my mind. 'I'm going because I have to, not because I want to. I think we both know that, don't we?'

Rather than answer me, Wade grasps my hand, his warm, soft fingers curling around mine, much needed reassurance in a shaky and unstable world. We sit like that for a period of time that feels infinite.

I want to stay here, next to him, to shut out the rest of the world, pretend none of it is real – the letters, the vandalism. I want to act as if it has happened to somebody else. I can do that for a short while, if we stay like this. I can think about things other than the impending visit to my mother's house; pleasant things, delicate things like the way the sun rises and settles over the geraniums in our garden, or the way the moon casts its gentle glow over the rooftops on a clear night, silvering the sky and bathing the ground in soft shades of grey.

If I shut out all thoughts of the impending visit, then I can shut out all thoughts of *him* and that final evening when I drove the knife deep into his leg, all the while cursing myself for not being vicious enough or accurate enough. All the while wishing I had had the guts to lodge it deep in his heart instead.

28

Placing her hand over her swollen belly, she stares down at the protrusion there, trying to imagine the tiny body beneath her own skin, the softness of its limbs, the gentle curve of its spine as it lies, cradled inside her body, nestled deep in her uterus. Protected from the blows and horrors of the outside world.

A blur of blues and greens interspersed with red brick buildings pass by. Neon lights and insipid-looking people, their skin grey and dead, are a smudge in her peripheral vision as the bus hurtles through town, picking up speed before stopping again. The hydraulic hiss of the doors echoes down the aisle as they open and passengers pile off, replaced seconds later by more who bustle their way into seats, grumbling about the weather, and the crowds and the price of this and that. She smiles, turns away to stare out of the window. Nothing can dent her happiness today. Not this grimy bus, nor the mumblings of disgruntled people sitting around her, beside her. Nothing. Today is a good day. The best of days.

Not all days are like this. Some are better than others and some are unutterably awful. But right now, she can see beyond the dark mist, through the thick curtain of misery that regularly envelops her. Soon she will be laid on the couch in the midwife's room, a pair of warm hands draped over her abdomen as they check for a heartbeat, take rough measurements, ensure her baby is facing the right way ready for birth. It makes her feel secure, knowing somebody cares, knowing that somebody, practically a stranger, will take her under their wing, look after her and her child and keep them both safe. It's all she's ever wanted – to feel protected. To feel wanted and loved. She had no idea it could be so all-pervading, this sense of belonging. This sense of being cared for and nurtured.

The last few years have been difficult. More than a few years, if she is being truthful. She tugs at her sleeves, the scars on her wrists suddenly too painful to gaze upon. Her skin has healed. Her mind is still raw, the wounds too deep to ever heal properly. Perhaps they never will. But this baby... She gently pats her tummy, flushed with love, alive with the joy of it.

Staring out of the window, she thinks of the baby's father, feeling his absence keenly, like a sharp pain to her heart. She remembers his reaction to her news that she was pregnant, telling her he was too young to be a dad. 'Can barely look after meself, babe,' was his reply. 'I'm only eighteen. Too young to be tied down with a bairn.'

She still sees him around town occasionally, watches from afar as he dives out of view whenever he spots her, dragging his latest girlfriend with him. Young bimbos with painted lips and pushed up breasts, their balcony bras affording a clear view of their generous cleavages. Not that she cares. She isn't jealous. It's just that she doesn't want to be alone, didn't plan it this way. It just happened. Her mother is still on the slippery slope into oblivion, unaware of where she is or what day it is. There's no company or comfort to be had there. That's why she is applying for a flat for herself and the baby. There's a waiting list and she knows it'll be hard, just her and the little one. The flat will be poky and damp but no worse than the house she grew up in. Money will be tight, but again, she's lived through worse. Far worse. If there's one positive thing to be said about poverty and being subjected to violence and thuggery, it's that it prepares you for everything, making even the most hostile of situations appear palatable and manageable. No matter what gets thrown her way, she will survive it.

Her scars tingle and itch. Once again, she pulls down her sleeves, trying to cover up the thin silver lines that criss-cross the pale skin on her wrists. Reminders of a past she would sooner forget. The past that has damaged her, but hopefully not irreparably. She trails her fingers over her swollen abdomen once more, a shiny new future presenting itself to her. The world is a brighter place with this new life growing inside her.

The loud shush of the doors drags her away from her thoughts. She blinks, looks up and her breath catches in her throat as she sees *her*. Heat travels up her body, a flickering trail of flames that creep up her spine, curling themselves around her neck, settling in her face; a flare of deep warmth sitting just below the surface of her skin. She brings up a trembling hand, places her cool fingers against her burning flesh to alleviate the fiery sensation that is pulsing there.

She can't quite believe it's her, the quiet one, here on this bus. She doesn't know why she can't believe it. They both live in the same town, but she is acutely aware that they move in different circles, their social strata completely divergent.

Chewing at her nails, she lowers her gaze and looks away. It's been two years since they left school and yet her blood still runs cold at the sight of her. She'd like to say the bullying stopped once puberty erased their childish thoughts and their brains developed, but that didn't happen. They continued with their onslaught right up until the final day of school.

Her hand rests on her bump as she squeezes her eyes shut

and recalls that incident. The incident that could have been stopped but wasn't. The incident that *she*, the quiet one, could have prevented but chose not to. She snaps open her eyes and stares as the quiet one takes a seat opposite, then sits and thinks back to that day. That awful day, the indignity of it, how any remaining decorum she had managed to hang on to was stripped away and lay strewn at her feet.

It had been a particularly blistering day, the sun hot enough to crack concrete. Hordes of youngsters were hanging around the schoolyard, listless, weary, too warm to do anything except kick at stones. The girl had been flooded with relief. It was her last day at that hellhole of a place, her days of torture finally coming to an end. She could leave these people behind, start a new life, maybe even take the opportunity to reinvent herself.

The slight tug on her bag awakened a sense in her that she was all too familiar with. Without turning around, she knew who was behind her. She could envisage their leering faces, Tanya's grimace as she stood, legs apart, nodding at the others to do her bidding. Her stomach tightened; her muscles ached at the thought of what was to come, what dreadful scheme Tanya had in mind.

'Turn around, freak.'

She did as they asked. No point in railing against it. Any resistance simply fuelled Tanya's anger, augmenting the bullying a hundredfold. There was nothing to be gained from fighting back. That much she did know. She had learned from bitter experience to put up and shut up.

'What do we have here then?' A callous roar of laughter spread around the group as Tanya dipped her hand in the bag that was slung over the girl's shoulder, and produced a sanitary towel, waving it about in the air above her head.

The girl had felt her cheeks burn with shame and humiliation, dipping her gaze away from the sea of sniggering faces that surrounded her. The circle grew larger, people gathered, their mouths locked into a rictus grin. She wished for a great hole to form at her feet and swallow her alive. *Anything but this. Please, anything but this sort of humiliation.*

'We got ourselves a bleeder!' Tanya's voice was a loud growl, attracting the attention of everybody in close vicinity. More people flocked, their eyes twinkling and glinting with mischief and disdain.

Before she could stop her, Tanya's hand dug even deeper into the bag, bony fingers rummaging, dragging, pulling out the contents, opening up and disposing of more plastic wrappers, allowing the sanitary towels to spill all over the floor – pens, pencils, books, her intimate sanitary products spread at her feet, a tiny ocean of white cotton strips, incompatible and ugly-looking against the sprawling grey asphalt of the schoolyard.

'Fucking hell, freak! How much blood are you expecting to lose? There's enough here to catch a bucketload.'

The girl had looked around for a friendly face, imploring somebody, anybody, to step in and help. She had spotted the quiet one half hidden behind Tanya's tall, willowy frame, her face turned away, her gaze resting on a point in the distance, a look on her face that told the girl she was refusing to get involved. Refusing to take sides and help. It was their final day. She could have done something. In a matter of hours, they will all be going their separate ways, free of Tanya and her controlling ways. She could have stepped in, stood up to Tanya and her cohort of lunatic friends. She could have done something, stopped them, told them to leave her alone. Yet she didn't. She let it all happen. It was pointless expecting Tanya or any of the others to back down – they were all beyond redemption, but her, the quiet one, she had a look of somebody who had a conscience, somebody who actually gave a shit. And yet on that day, like all the other days, she did nothing. She let it all take place.

Before the girl could do anything, they had pinned her down and were tugging at her clothes, pulling at her trousers, tearing at the button, dragging the zip, trying to yank them down. Only the screams of an approaching teacher who was sprinting across the yard, stopped them. She had noticed that something was amiss, alerted by the huddle of onlookers who were whooping and cheering, their voices carried across the yard by the gentlest of summer breezes.

By the time Mrs Hancock had reached the baying mob, the girl's trousers were halfway down, her worn cream knickers visible to everyone, a small spot of menstrual blood smeared on her inner thigh.

'All of you! Move away right now! I want to see every one of you in my classroom in five minutes!'

'Fuck off, Hancock. This is our last day at this shithole of a school. What you gonna do – give us detention?'

Hoots of laughter boomed in the air. Mrs Hancock helped the girl up off the floor, covering up the young female's near nakedness with her own ample body. The girl rearranged her clothing, shuffling and jerking about, all the while tears spilling, her voice a dry scratch as she sobbed.

That was years ago and yet only yesterday, still crystal clear in her mind. Always hovering, ready to intrude at the slightest provocation. The bus takes a corner, jerking her back to the present, away from the darkness, away from the memories that try to tip her over that precipice, showing her the bottom and reminding how far she could fall, how far she actually fell time and time again. But not now. Not today. She has a whole new life inside of her, somebody to protect, somebody to care for. Somebody she will make sure never has to endure what she endured in her formative years. All that violence and fear and hurt. All that damage.

She looks up. The quiet one is still there, staring ahead. If there was a flicker of recognition at her presence, she is concealing it well.

Torn between fury and fear, the girl stands up, approaches her, a dull beat starting up under her ribcage, her blood fizzing with dread. She stops, places a protective palm over her bump, considering her options. Does she really want to put herself through this? What could possibly be gained from a public confrontation other than a sense of mild satisfaction that will also be coupled with complete humiliation at bringing it all up again?

Walking down the aisle of the bus, she decides to get off early, walk the remainder of the journey to the clinic. Easier than sitting here staring at the back of her head, being subjected to the deluge of flashbacks that cripple her with anxiety. Most she remembers with frightening clarity, some are slightly dimmer, but they are all, without exception, lodged there in her brain, so deep-seated that she fears they will never diminish.

It's as she is making her way past the seat that it happens. Call it a bizarre coincidence, a stroke of luck, but as the bus makes a sudden turn, she topples sideways almost losing her balance and that's when their eyes meet, catching sight of one another at exactly the same time, their faces frozen, their expressions saying everything that needs to be said while their mouths remain closed. It's a matter of seconds, but that is all that it takes. The recognition is there, the look of horror and another look of what? Regret? Shame?

Perhaps. Perhaps not. Not enough time to analyse in any great detail. But there is definitely something there.

Then it is gone, that moment. Vanished into the atmosphere with the swirling dust motes that circle between them.

She continues walking towards the door, her legs trembling, her body suddenly coated with sweat. Thinking about the impending visit to the midwife, she covertly dabs under her arms with a tissue, wipes her upper lip with shaking fingers and tucks the tissue back in her pocket.

The doors open with a hiss. People tumble out onto the pavement like scurrying ants. She turns once more, glancing up the aisle to where the quiet one is sitting. Their eyes lock; an intense moment of pain, a brief longing to change what cannot ever be changed.

Another hiss and a whoosh as the doors snap shut and the bus turns the corner, leaving behind a trail of acrid fumes and a dry gassy scent that causes her to cough and splutter. She wheezes and closes her eyes against the wave of gritty heat that is thrown up from the gutter.

A drop of rain falls, cooling her bare skin. She stares up at the greying sky, the elongated spray of clouds that are spread above her like pulled candy floss. More rain comes, increasing drop by drop, second by second until it is coming down in sheets, soaking her through. She is accepting of it, enjoying the cooling sensation, the cleansing feeling as each spatter hits her limbs, her body, her distended midriff.

She goes under the nearby awning of a bakery, the sort of place that sells artisan bread and wholesome luxury foods and waits, watching as people scurry past, umbrellas held close to their bodies, faces creased with annoyance as they weave their way past the crowds, navigating their way through the spokes of brollies, becoming tangled with one other, arms bumping, feet splayed to avoid puddles that have suddenly accumulated on the pavement.

Rain batters at the awning above her, the sound as it hits the coarse fabric like a series of gunshots. More people pass. She notices how angry everyone looks, how pissed off they are, how brash and sullen they seem to be. She wonders what life has thrown their way to make them all so miserable. She studies their faces, trying to work out who was the bully and which of them was the bullied. So many aggressors. So many victims. She likes to do this, to convince herself that she wasn't the only one, that plenty of people have been subjected to the same levels of animosity and persecution, because if she were to ever think that she had been singled out, that she was such a bad person that nobody else suffered like she did, then she is convinced that she would go completely mad.

She stands for a short while, then smiles as the sun makes another appearance, a hazy ochre sphere peering through a split in the clouds, its rays illuminating the cerulean sky. The rain eases, steam hisses up from pavements. She steps out and spreads the palm of her hands up to the sky. It's stopped. A sun shower. That's all it was. An unexpected addition to the day. Like seeing her on the bus, the quiet one. Totally unexpected.

Taking off her thin jacket, she wipes away the excess moisture from her skin and heads off down the High Street towards the clinic thanking God she has something to look forward to, a new life within her, something that gives her a reason to live.

29

I'm thinking that I need to take things a step further, drop a few clues. Get her remembering. Get her thinking. It's been fun so far but I need to up my game, make her really scared. I want to see that mad uncertain glint in her eye every time she rounds a corner, see her quiver and cry at the slightest fucking thing. If I can knock her off balance and make her unsure of herself then it'll make my final plan so much easier to execute.

Execute. A good choice of word. I like it. It has a ring to it. It sounds so definite. So final. So gruesome. And bloody. The more blood, the better.

Anyway, if the next part of my game doesn't make her piss her pants then I'm not sure what will. I've checked everything out. No cameras outside her house, no nearby CCTV and neighbours so prissy and old-fashioned they all close their curtains at the same time every night. Sometimes it's as if these people actually want something bad to happen. She was even piss-easy to locate, her address online for anybody to find. People with any sense, remove themselves from the online electoral roll and stay out of the phone book, especially teachers, but not her. Name, address and postcode all listed in black and white. Unbelievably easy. She only has herself to blame for what happens next.

Anyway, in my opinion, those who don't protect themselves and have wronged others, deserve everything they get and more.

And she will get it. I'll make sure of it, if it's the last thing I do.

30

2019

I'm a young girl again, that naive, terrified child who is frightened of everything and everyone, even the people in her own home. I remember it well, being too worried to speak, too traumatised to do anything at all except exist. I was a shadow of a person then, a ghost in my own home. And now here I am again. Back to crouching and hiding, waiting for the next blow, wondering where it will come from. I've come full circle. There's no escaping the past, is there? Not really. It shapes who we are, forms our personalities. I'll never leave it behind. Ever.

I squeeze Wade's hand and he reciprocates, his thumb caressing the creases on my palm, putting me at ease. I shut my eyes and try to focus. Even breathing is difficult, laborious and unnatural as I attempt to slow it down, to get it under control. I've got to go in there at some point, into my mother's house. I don't think of it as my childhood home. No happy memories there within its walls, only heartache and horror.

My throat is dry, my skin coated with an Arctic frost. I cannot continue sitting here in the car outside the house like a perfect stranger. Just knowing she is in there is enough to make me dizzy and weak-kneed, to heat up my blood to boiling point.

She doesn't frighten me, my useless lump of a mother. That's not why I'm sitting here readying myself before I go in. She sickens me. I'm ashamed of her on so many levels, I don't know where to start. I am ashamed of how she lives, how she has always lived. I am ashamed of how she enabled the horrors that took place in this house to continue, doing nothing to stop them, refusing to acknowledge what I went through, what I was forced to endure when I was just a child, unable to defend myself. Until I got hold of that knife, that is.

Even then, she blamed me, telling me I had ruined her life, forcing him to leave like that when all he was doing was trying to care for me. She had, and probably still has, no fucking idea of what I went through, how much damage he caused. How he has shaped my life and left dents in my mind and my soul that can never be repaired. I hate him, and I hate her for not hating him, for choosing him over me, for choosing to believe what she wanted to believe. She had more compassion for a useless drunken brute of a man than she did for her own child.

I stare up at the house, at the line of roof tiles, at the swathe of brickwork, one blending into the other like paint on a canvas. My limbs are heavy. I feel a hundred years old. I cough, rub at my face and turn to look at Wade who is waiting patiently, his expression gentle, unassuming. Patient. Poor Wade, having to put up with all of this nonsense. Having to put up with me.

The sky is a wash of pale russet, the clouds stretched and elongated like a snowy mountain range.

'Ready?' he says softly, his voice low and steady. Comforting.

'Ready,' I reply, a tremor evident in my voice as I unbuckle my seat belt, open the door and step outside onto the pavement.

She is sitting bolt upright in the chair by the window, perched on the edge of the cushion like a frightened sparrow. The bones of her face protrude, her lean body is angular, more so than usual. She is practically emaciated, her diet undoubtedly one of cigarettes and gin. Her eyes dart around the room as we enter. She looks at the television, at Wade, at the faded patterned rug on the floor. Anywhere but at me.

'Afternoon, Maureen.' Wade gives her a cursory nod, smiling as he sits down on the sofa, patting the cushion for me to join him.

I don't say anything. I can't. Everything I want to say is jammed in my throat, locked solid, a heavy gathering of words and syllables that should form a coherent sentence but refuse to do so, staying instead, in my own head, useless and inexpressible.

Without missing a beat, Wade speaks for me. He was the one who made the phone call informing her of our imminent visit. He is the one who speaks now when I am unable to.

'How are you?' he says to my mother. She doesn't reply, shrugging instead and turning to stare out of the window. Her downward sloping mouth and piercing gaze say more than words ever could, anyway. She is still fond of painting herself as a victim, the woman whose husband left then died prematurely leaving her with a young child. And then of course, after my waster of a father passed away, she met Barry. Barry her saviour. Barry the manipulator, Barry the child molester.

I don't remember too much about my own father, only what my mother told me – that he spent most of his time in the pub. He left us when I was young and then died a few years later without ever coming back to see us. I do, however, remember Barry vividly. How could I possibly forget?

She continues to sit, mute, her mean pinched old body arched in permanent fury. I want to scream at her to stop being so rude and stubborn, to stop being a martyr and so bloody unwilling to speak about the unspeakable. This is something none of us want to talk about but we've no choice. The least she can do is manage a couple of words, to do me the honour of opening her slack old mouth and, for once in her life, speak truthfully and honestly. Is that too much to ask?

'Right,' I manage at last, 'who wants a cup of tea?'

The kitchen is as small as I remember and twice as dirty. I'm half tempted to go rummaging for hidden gin bottles and stashes of vodka but haven't the energy for it. What would I do if I found them anyway? Stalk into the living room holding them aloft and confront her, or act as if nothing is awry and tiptoe back in, carrying cups of tea and a plate of biscuits like we are one big happy family? One day in the not too distant future the police will come knocking at our door, informing me of her death. The neighbours will have been alerted by the inordinate number of flies congregating at her window and the stink of rotting flesh leaking out from under the ill-fitting kitchen door that has let in water for as long as I can remember. They will find her mummified body and then at long last, all of this will be over. A thing of the past.

I search for clean cups and locate the teabags at the back of the cupboard. The milk smells and looks surprisingly fresh and she even has a packet of unopened biscuits that are still within the sell-by date. I try not to think about how she gets by on a day-to-day basis. I shut it all out. I have enough issues to contend with without burdening myself with my mother's ails and problems.

'Well, this is lovely. Nice biscuits, Maureen. Chocolate digestives are my favourite.' Wade is babbling now. Her refusal to communicate has flummoxed even him; the man who can handle any crisis, any situation no matter how awkward, how tiresome. He is struggling to get her to open up, to greet us properly or even acknowledge our presence in her home.

I decide to grasp the nettle, to jump straight in and demand that for once, she does the decent thing and talk about Barry. She owes me that much. And more. Oh, so much more, yet she doesn't know it and I doubt she even cares.

'We need to talk, Mum.' My voice is brisk and efficient. 'I need you to tell me about Barry and what he's up to now.' My heart is thumping in my chest, a rock trapped beneath my ribcage rolling and banging against my sternum, forcing me to swallow hard and fight the urge to drop to the floor and cry. I take a deep gasp, ragged, uneven. I can't seem to think straight. I am hot and cold at the same time. 'When did you last see him?'

Making sure I catch her eye, I keep her gaze, never wavering or blinking, doing my utmost to look stern and imposing. The air in the room thins, the light begins to fade as more clouds shift in from behind the hills. She squints, turns away slightly, her head bent at a slight angle, then turns back and speaks. 'Barry? What about him?'

'When did you last see him?' I hold my breath, unwilling to lose the moment. She smiles, her mouth plastered into a lopsided grin. I scrunch my hands up into fists, keeping them hidden behind my back, clasping and unclasping them, the skin on my knuckles taut with annoyance and frustration. 'Mum? When did you last see him?'

She sighs, an exaggerated exhalation, before answering, her voice a low whisper. 'About two years ago. He was in the pub with Dom and Julie.'

I suppress an eye roll. If I want more information, then I am going to have to go along with her little game, begging and cajoling until she eventually tells me what I want to know. I watch her while I wait, assessing her lined face, her brown eyes and sagging skin. The years haven't been kind to her but then, she hasn't been particularly kind to herself. Maureen Ingledew has the face she deserves.

My foot taps an involuntary beat on the floor as I wait for more. In my peripheral vision, I can sense Wade becoming edgy, wanting to take control of the situation, wanting to get us back on track.

'And?' I say.

Still the same taunting smile, the same mocking tone, the dark glint in her eyes that tells me she's enjoying this. She thinks she's punishing me for what happened all those years ago, for the night I took a knife to the man who abused me, driving it deep in his leg, sending him running from this house, never to return. It will take more than this to stop me firing questions at her. A damn sight more, and deep down, I think she knows it.

'And what? Like I said, I saw him in the pub about two years ago. Not sure what else you want me to say.'

'Where is he now?'

'Why do you want to know?' Her voice is sharp; there is an edge to it that tells me she is about to clam up again. She is in fight or flight mode. This is the only bit of power she has and she won't give it up with ease. I need to move fast, to get as much information out of her as I can before her stubbornness forces her into a silence and then once again, she will have won.

'You tell me where he is now and I'll tell you why I want to know. Deal?'

Her eyes narrow, tiny dark slits in her furrowed face. Her mouth puckers into a tight thin line as she watches me, mulling over my words, deciding whether or not to grant my wish. For my entire life, I have asked for nothing from this woman. Not a damn thing. And now here she is, dangling me on a piece of string like a fucking marionette while she, the warped puppet-master, decides my fate.

The protracted silence is an eternity. She is staring out of the window now, her fingers drumming on the edge of the chair, my request being processed in her alcohol-saturated brain.

When she does finally speak, her voice is a nail being dragged down a blackboard, a thin jagged streak of a sound that grinds my bones into dust. 'He's dead. Died last year. And yeah, before you ask, it was liver damage that did it. And no, I didn't go to the funeral. Didn't seem much point really.'

The words, *with him not being my partner anymore*, are conspicuous by their absence. They hang in the air, heavy as leaden clouds ready to rip apart and empty their bellies over us. Not that it would make any difference. Here in my mother's house, it's been pissing down for the past thirty years. Everything is a permanent wash of grey, misery etched into every room, every single brick. It's a house full of hatred built on a foundation of mistrust and abuse.

I bite at my lip. Barry is dead. It's hardly surprising really. I'm not sure how to feel. I'm neither relieved nor disappointed. If I'm being totally honest, deep down, I always knew it wasn't him sending the notes. I just needed to eliminate him for peace of mind.

I can sense Wade waiting for my response. I could get up and walk out of here right now, leave without telling her why I wanted to know. Not keeping my word wouldn't bother me, not one little bit, and not where she is concerned. I owe her nothing. But I'm better than that; better than her, this woman who is biologically related to me but is so far removed from everything I hold dear that we may as well be perfect strangers. So instead, I tell her about the letters and the car, scrutinising her face for any signs of emotion. She continues to sit, her expression neutral, her eyes unfathomable pools of darkness that conceal the real Maureen Ingledew. She is in there somewhere but I don't know her. I never have. I doubt she even knows herself.

When no reply is forthcoming, I stand, Wade following my

lead, and make my way towards the front door. The shuffle of her feet indicates she is behind us, her tiny body barely making a sound as she approaches us and stands in our shadows.

I open the door and am more than a little surprised to turn and find her so close to me, our bodies almost touching, her gaze softening, searching mine for some sort of understanding.

'Call again soon, Stella. Please.' Then she turns, but not before I catch the sight of unshed tears brimming in her eyes.

With a pain in my chest and a buzzing sensation in my head, I step outside, slipping my arm through Wade's to stay upright. We climb into the car in silence. I can't speak. I can't seem to summon up enough strength to do anything at all except stare ahead at the green hilly landscape that stretches across the edge of town, and silently cry.

31

It was easy. A piece of piss. Why do people not protect themselves against crime? I know if I was her and I'd had somebody threatening me, sending me weird letters and damaging my car, I'd have a camera on every corner of my house. Maybe even a huge snarling guard dog. But not her. Completely wide open. Made it easier for me though so I'm not really complaining.

Her house was as nice as I expected it to be. As if she would know what it's like to be dragged up and have a shit existence. Some people have it all. They fucking waltz through life with no idea what it's like for others who have to scrape and struggle and still end up with nothing.

It was silent when I got there, no lights, no sign that anybody would disturb me. It didn't take me long either. At one point I looked up to the bedroom windows and thought about her lying there. It made me sick to my stomach, the idea of her being so close by, laid there with her husband in their big bed under their expensive covers, possibly even pawing at each other like a pair of rutting animals.

I did what I had to do and left. Nobody heard me, nobody saw me. I was like a thief in the night. I just wish I could be there to see her face when she wakes up and realises what I've done.

I hope she likes my gift to her. I chose it specially. It's a prequel to the big one. That's next. And I can't fucking wait.

32

I should get up, have a shower, get ready for work, but after sleeping the sleep of the dead last night, my body is as heavy as lead. I can't remember the last time I slept so soundly. No lying awake into the wee small hours fretting, even though I have every reason to worry myself half sick. Silly really, especially given that the perpetrator is still out there, wishing me harm, destroying my property and stealing my sanity.

Wade is beside me, his face turned away as a soft snore rumbles out of his throat. Outside, car engines fire up, doors slam, people murmur. The road is waking up, coming to life around us while we lie here, comfortable in our soft warm bed.

Guilt bites at me. It's a weekday. I have to go to work. Wade has to go to work. If I don't move in the next five minutes, then I'm going to be really late and–

The thunderous knock from below almost sends me crashing to the floor. Rolling to the edge of the bed, I catapult myself upwards, my spine stiff with shock. Wade jumps up, spins around, eyes bulging at being so rudely ripped from the arms of sleep.

We stagger around the bedroom, pulling on clothes,

crashing into wardrobes, colliding with chests of drawers, blindly banging into each other.

The knock from below comes again, loud, insistent.

Wade is downstairs in a matter of seconds, still fastening his jeans, his feet twisting under him as he slips and slides to the bottom step with a leap. I stand, the top half of my body leaning over the banister, watching as he opens the door to Jeff, one of our neighbours who looks pale in the harsh glare of the early morning light. The sun sits low in the sky behind him, framing him in the doorway. He stands immobile, his silhouette eerie in the dimness of our hallway.

'Jeff,' Wade says, rubbing his face and stifling a yawn. 'Everything okay?'

'I was just about to ask you the very same thing, mate.' Jeff shuffles his feet, embarrassment evident in his stance. I stumble down the stairs, wanting and yet at the same time, not wanting to hear what it is he has got to say. A stone sits at the base of my belly. I move closer, studying his face, wondering what is going through his head. His eyes dart about and a ruby web covers his neck and face. 'There's something here, something... well, you, um, you might want to come outside and take a look for yourself.'

The stone in my belly begins to roll about. A thudding starts up in my temple. *What now? What the hell is waiting for us now? A dead animal, more vandalism on one of the cars? What? What the fuck is it?*

I push my way through the door and follow Wade into the front garden, my bare toes curling in revulsion at the feel of wet grass under my feet. The pulse in my temple increases a hundredfold. Saliva builds in my mouth and I have to hang on to Wade's arm for fear of my legs buckling under me.

We are on the lawn, unable to stop looking at the front of our house, at the words written there. The same word, spray-painted on the bay window, the brickwork, the garage door, over and over again in bright yellow paint.

Freak, freak, freak, freak, freak...

Jeff sneaks us an apologetic sideways glance, his voice now a whisper. 'Sorry guys. I saw it as I came out and noticed that your curtains were still drawn, and just thought...' His gaze flickers, drops to the ground with an embarrassed sweep. He shoves his hands into his pockets, leaves them there as he speaks again. 'If you need a hand cleaning it off, I've got some stuff in the garage. A couple of bottles of white spirits that would do it.'

Wade doesn't reply. I also remain silent, unable to breathe properly let alone speak. I can hear my own heartbeat, the whistle of the wind as it rushes over the Cleveland Hills, the movement of every blade of grass underfoot as we stand together, too traumatised to say or do anything.

'Anyway,' Jeff says at last, 'I've got to be off, got to get to work but I can give you a hand to remove it when I get in tonight? Debs is working from home today so if you want that bottle of spirits, just give her a knock.'

Snapping out of his stupor, Wade rests his arm on Jeff's shoulder, an act of mutual friendship towards somebody who has stepped in during our hour of need without an ounce of judgement. And he has not tried to glean any information to feed to local gossips. Jeff is just a decent guy, trying to help. 'Thanks, Jeff. We really appreciate that. I think we might leave it until the police get here.'

Jeff nods and backs out of our driveway, giving us a small wave.

I can feel the heat of Wade's anger as it throbs within him, a slow building furnace with white-hot fury at its core. This is my fault. I've put him through this; lied to him, made him worried and confused and now look what has happened. I have no idea how to put any of it right or why this is even happening.

A thought suddenly nips at me as I stare at the graffiti, at those words, a distant fleeting memory that darts through my mind, a speeding object, gone before I have a chance to pin it down and identify it.

'Don't try to clean any of this off. I'm going to ring the police.' Wade doesn't attempt to disguise the contempt in his timbre. I wonder who it's aimed at – the perpetrator, or me for bringing this his way?

He stalks off inside, leaving the door ajar. I stand for a couple of seconds before following him, feeling the eyes of the entire neighbourhood on me, tracing my movements, thankful it wasn't their house that was targeted, wondering what we have done to deserve it. They will be in their kitchens, preparing breakfast, gossiping about who we have upset, who would do such a thing to us. They will suspect some infidelity from one of us. I know I would.

The door closes behind me with a muffled click. The house is in silence as if it is in mourning for the tragedy unfolding in our lives. Wade appears in the kitchen doorway, his head cocked to one side, his phone cradled under his chin. The sight of him suddenly takes on an unsettling portentous form, his broad shoulders filling the narrow space, his height casting a long shadow across the floor, a bleached ghostlike figure with spindly arms and an elongated body. His skin is a ghastly shade of grey. I have done this to him. This is all my fault.

I listen as he speaks once again to the police, informing them of our latest episode. Shame washes over me. The elusive memory from earlier still niggles at me, dancing in and out of my consciousness, too difficult to reach, too intangible to pin down and dissect.

Wade disconnects the call and slips his phone into his pocket. 'They're sending somebody round but can't give a time.

Apparently there's been a pile up on the A19 so they're short of people.'

'I'll need to ring work, let them know I'll be late in.' Already I'm panicking, thinking up a thousand different excuses. Anything but the truth. Astrid will know immediately. I never call in sick. She will ring me the first opportunity she gets and then I'll have to lie to her as well.

Everything begins to pile up in my head. Lie upon lie upon lie. The Jenga stack is close to toppling.

I make the call to work, speak to Marion, tell her I've been up all night with a stomach bug and have to listen to her own tales of when she had a stomach bug and lost over half a stone in a day and how I should drink plenty of fluids otherwise I could end up being admitted to hospital just like her neighbour's friend's daughter who had to be hooked up to a drip and couldn't be discharged until she had had a solid bowel movement and had eaten two full plates of toast.

By the time I end the call my head is spinning and I am dizzy with exhaustion.

'I've messaged the office, told them I'm working from home this morning,' Wade says, standing over me as I sit on the sofa, bleary-eyed and still reeling after the abrupt start to our day. 'I want to be here when the police arrive. This is getting really serious now. I'm going to get a shower. I suggest you do the same and then we need to sit down and rake over everything, try to work out what the hell is going on here.'

He goes upstairs before I have a chance to reply. His patience is wearing thin now. Everything seems to be spiralling out of control, our life together splitting and coming apart. Somebody out there hates me; really, really hates me, and try as I might, I cannot work out who they are or why they harbour such a deep-rooted grudge against me. As fast as I eliminate people, more damage occurs. I have no idea who could be behind all of this. I begin to shiver and wrap my arms around my body for warmth, lowering my head and fighting back tears. I think I may actually be losing my mind.

I shut my eyes and think again of that elusive memory. I try to catch it, to clutch it tight and hold on to it, but still it refuses to reveal itself. Perhaps if I let it go, it will come back to me when I least expect it. The police are on their way. They're going to ask me if I have any enemies, anybody who wishes me harm. I need to remember, to provide an answer to their questions, to give them something tangible, not just partly eclipsed memories that dance around my brain.

The clank of pipes and creak of floorboards overhead as Wade showers and dresses reminds me that I need to get ready, to prepare myself for the next stage of this scenario, this existence of ever-growing madness that has supplanted my previous orderly life.

My stomach is clenched, knotted into a tight ball of apprehension as I sit, ramrod straight on the sofa, waiting for the knock on the door that will alert me to the police's arrival. Wade is in the dining room setting up his laptop. He is going to do some work while we wait. I think of our neighbours, the thoughts that will undoubtedly pass through their minds when they see the words painted on the front of our house. They will make their own secret assumptions, judging us, thinking Wade and I are a bad lot, involved in unsavoury pastimes. I don't blame them. It's a natural thing to do. And yet I still have no idea why somebody would do this to us. Or I should say to me, because Wade has been inadvertently dragged into this seedy turn of events because of something I have purportedly done or not done. The letters were delivered to me. It was my car that was vandalised. Poor Wade is guilty by association.

I listen as he sets up his laptop, hearing the plastic snap of his briefcase on the table, the rustle of papers being handled, the tap of his fingers on the keyboard. None of this has anything to do with him. It's all my fault, everything that has happened has been aimed at me and yet here he is, having to set up his office at home while we wait around for the police so we can log another complaint against an unknown perpetrator who is hellbent on revenge for something of which I have no memory. Were it not for the fact that this is a serious string of offences, I would laugh out loud, but this is real, and it is serious, becoming more so by the day.

The sitting around and waiting is torture. I end up jumping at every squeak, every passing car, every single sound that filters in from outside. Waiting for something to happen saps me of energy. I watch TV, try to read, and eventually decide to do nothing as I am unable to focus on anything productive, so I sit instead, staring outside, my eyes glazing over until a beep from my phone snaps me out of my trance.

As expected, Astrid has sent a message asking how I am and whether or not I need anything doing or getting. I reply that I'm fine and still in bed, napping and trying to recover. The last thing I need is for Astrid to call around after work and for her to see the state of the house. She would become heavily involved, whether I wanted her to or not, doling out advice, listing possible suspects, perhaps even telling Wade about Glenn.

Once again, the word, *freak*, lodges itself in my consciousness, tugging at me, demanding to be noticed whilst its associated memory still roams free, unchained and untethered somewhere deep in my brain. I lean forward, place my head in my hands and close my eyes. There is something there, something important. Something that will allow me to understand why I've been targeted, why this is happening to me.

Before I can consider any further options, a knock comes at the door, stilling my blood. I stand up, watching as Wade rushes through the hallway, fumbling for the handle of the front door and yanking it open, speaking in a husky authoritative tone that is tinged with what – sadness? A sense of weary acceptance?

With liquid legs, I stand up ready to greet the police, to spill the contents of my overstuffed head and tell them what little I know in a bid to find out who it is that has damaged my car and my house; who it is that knows where I work; who it is that thinks I'm a bitch and a freak and has promised to do God knows what to me.

By the time the two officers enter the living room, I can barely hold myself upright, the room a swirling kaleidoscope of colours, the floor dropping away under me. I cling on to the chair and clear my throat ready to speak.

33

2018

She assesses his reaction to her words. His eyes are glassy, unresponsive. It's to be expected, she supposes, after what she has just told him about trying to end her own life. She owes him this explanation. It's long overdue.

He has lived most of his life unaware of why she is the way she is. He deserved to hear it, no matter how distressing the details were. So she told him as much as she could, sparing no details, leaving nothing out.

He looks heavy, laden with worry, his expression riddled with angst as he mulls over what she has just told him.

It's a lot for him to think about, she knows this, but it had to be done. This has gone on for far too long now, their lives suspended, constantly interrupted by her inability to leave her past behind. For so many years she has carried that baggage around like a fell runner with a backpack filled with rocks. In the end she couldn't do it anymore, be dragged down by all that weight. Something had to give. And it did.

She lets out a deep rattling cough, her fingers clasped to her throat to alleviate the ache that has taken hold there. She barks, clearing the dryness that is lodged deep in her gullet. *Lucky* isn't a word she would ever use to describe her circumstances, but that is what the nurses and doctors told her she was when she woke up. She was still alive. Still here, saved by the gracious efforts of a thoughtful neighbour who heard her sobs and cries through the paper-thin walls of their flat and called an ambulance when they entered and found empty blister packets of her prescription drugs scattered over the living room floor.

The boy strokes her hand, his fingers trembling, his head shaking as he looks away from her to hide the sudden release of tears that he has been holding back for all of his life.

They sit in silence, side by side. No further words are needed. She has said enough, told him what she thinks he needs to hear, hoping it is sufficient to explain the years of heartache and depression and misery that have led them to this point in their lives.

Behind them, around them, the metallic clatter of hospital trolleys echoes and bounces through the hospital ward. The squeak of rubber-soled shoes against laminate flooring, the incessant muffled chatter of nurses and hospital staff, the swish of curtains separating nearby beds only serve to remind her of where she is, why she is here.

She rests her head back, closes her eyes against it all, against the tide of memories that are flooding into her mind, a tsunami of unpleasant thoughts, the ebb and flow of her disturbed, damaged mind washing up its debris for the looters to pick through. The mental health team will call later today to speak to her, to go through her options and decide whether or not she requires any further assistance. Is she going to allow them to probe inside her mind and help her through this event or will she curl up on her side, tell them to leave her alone and bury her problems deep inside herself? A sigh escapes from her slightly parted lips. This is it, the catalyst for transformation. Now is the time for her to open up, to accept their help and to modify her behaviour and thought patterns, to effect positive change in their lives so they can move forward, not be continually dragged to the yesterdays of her damaged, impoverished life.

The appearance of a nurse at her bedside tells her that visiting hours are over.

'What will happen now?' she asks the young woman who is busy taking notes and checking her fob watch.

Before the nurse can answer, another woman appears at the end of the bed. She stands next to the boy, says something unintelligible in his ear then smiles. He nods, leans forward, says his goodbyes and she watches, her eyes misted with tears, as they leave together, the tip-tap of their feet receding into the distance. Her boy, leaving her bedside, accompanied by a perfect stranger who will take him to stay with yet another family she has never met. He will live in an alien environment with people he doesn't know until she can get her life back on track and only then will she be allowed to have him back home where he belongs.

She tugs at the bed sheets, pulling them up to her neck, protecting herself from the jabs and punches that life continually throws her way. He is gone. She has no idea when he'll be back, if indeed he ever will be. The pain in her throat increases, her head thuds. She lies back, closes her eyes, ignoring the noises that surround her, the scrapes, the bangs, the rattles. The murmuring voices, the ringing telephones at the nurses' station outside her ward, the moans and guttural cries of other patients nearby.

A wet streak streams out from the corner of her eye, running down her face, soaking into the cotton pillowcase beneath her head. Perhaps it was the death of her mother that brought on this most recent bout of depression. Or perhaps it was seeing *her* again at the school, knowing she had got on with her life, forged ahead with a successful career and not given a thought to what she had done, to the damage she had caused by her ineffectual ways. Or maybe it was both of those things happening at the same time that caused the mighty collision of emotions, so strong, so powerful that it tipped her over the edge, pushed her down into that deep dark chasm. And she almost hit the bottom. Had it not been for the actions of her neighbour, she would have reached it, her body cold and lifeless, her child left without a mother. She may not be the best parent in the world but at least she is here, still breathing, still full of love and passion for her son, her only child.

Her body aches, her mind aches. She is so tired she could sleep for a thousand years and still wake up exhausted.

She lets the tears come, lying still, waiting until she is all cried out, then closes her eyes and slips into a welcome state of darkness.

34

2019

I feel drained. Completely and utterly exhausted. The police have gone over the matter of the letters and my damaged vehicle, and are now outside gazing up at the spray-painted words on the front of our house.

Freak, freak, freak!

Shut up, freak. It's only a bit of water...

A yelp forces itself out of my throat, unbidden. A swarm of angry wasps fill my head. Perspiration coats my top lip. I drag my hand across my face, wiping at the tiny pearls of sweat, brushing them away. I have no idea where that thought came from or what it relates to. I should know, but somehow that area of my brain feels impotent, a latent force that every now and again springs to life, releasing a blur of images, throwing out random words and phrases without any information to back up their presence. Somewhere, entrenched deep in my brain, is the answer. I just need to dig deep, ignore the peripheral unimportant stuff that distracts me, stopping me from getting to the nub of this thing.

Outside I can hear the gravelly timbre of male voices as the two officers and Wade survey the damage. From the window I can see their dark bulky forms, am able to observe their even darker expressions as they stare at the offending words, their long fingers pointing upwards, discussing who could have put those words there and why. I slink back behind the curtain out of view, too ashamed to be seen. I should have followed them, listened to what they had to say, but couldn't quite muster up the strength. So here I am, like a chastened child, feeling guilty and alone, as if I have brought on this latest occurrence simply by being here, by just existing.

I chew at a ragged nail, wondering what is next. Is somebody following me, taking notes on my daily routine? The all too familiar pounding of my heart starts up again at the thought of being stalked; the thought of driving to work with somebody in close pursuit, or lying in bed while somebody crouches in the garden, waiting, watching. I swallow down saliva, almost choking. I have to do more, face this situation head-on, not crumple under the strain. If I bend and break, they will have ultimate control over my life and I cannot let that happen. I cannot let this person win. All these things, these acts have been done on purpose to frighten me, to weaken me. I don't want to cower away, too frightened to live my life. I have to fight back, to show them that I'm made of stern stuff and not somebody who will buckle and snap. How can I fight back though? How am I expected to fight back against an unknown assailant? How can I beat an invisible threat that is constantly one step ahead of me?

Voices cut through my thoughts. Wade is leading the two police officers back inside. They stamp their boots on the doormat, shaking off the excess damp. It's still early, the sun not yet high enough to fully warm the earth and dry the moisture from the air.

'Right, well what we suggest next is getting some security cameras installed outside your house. Seems to me,' says the older of the two policemen, his dark hair peppered with flecks of silver, 'that whoever is doing this bears a real grudge and that means that they may come back and do something similar. You said you can't think of anybody that you've had issues with in the past?'

Everybody is staring at me now, their eyes locked with mine, waiting for my response. A pocket of trapped air flutters in my chest, my skin flares hot, everything blurs. The constant arrhythmic beating beneath my sternum is clouding my thoughts, stopping me from answering properly.

I sit down, clear my throat, shake my head vehemently. 'No, nothing comes to mind.'

'You're a teacher?' the younger officer says.

I nod and look up at him, wondering if he has a list of badly-behaved pupils' names in his head, local troublesome families who are regularly involved in criminal activities. He will know them all, the drug dealers, the violent offenders, the recurring low-level stuff that takes place in kids' homes day in and day out. Westland Academy is in a deprived area with a range of pupils, some from decent backgrounds, some from highly challenging circumstances. A real eclectic mix. It could be any of them and yet it couldn't. Apart from Jack Phelps whose name I've already opted to not mention, there are no obvious suspects, nobody who has had repeated sanctions meted out to them for poor behaviour. Nobody who hates me enough to do this. Or maybe there is. Right now, anything seems possible.

'If you can think of any pupil or pupils who might do this sort of thing as a way of getting back at you, or even as a prank, don't hesitate to let us know. Sometimes they do stuff and they don't realise how damaging their behaviour is. They see it as a joke, not even realising that they've broken the law.'

Again, I nod, doing my best to hold everything together, to stop myself from shaking and crying. After removing Jack Phelps from the list, I more or less closed my mind off to the idea that any of this could be traced back to my workplace, to a disgruntled pupil. The thought both terrifies and sickens me.

'I'll give it some thought,' I whisper, unable to project my voice far enough to convey any of the authority I manage to hold when I'm in class, in front of a group of fourteen-year-olds who would rather pluck out their own fingernails than do the work I have planned for them about the grammatical features in *Great Expectations*. All of a sudden, I'm the weak one, the person on the cusp of breaking down completely.

The officers nod and look to Wade for affirmation that we will both be more vigilant, buying security cameras and constantly looking over our shoulders in the hope of spotting the offender.

'Right, well we've given you the crime number so don't hesitate to contact us if you hear or see anything suspicious or out of the ordinary,' the older officer says.

I lower my head, now desperate for them to leave, for Wade to lead them out so I can clear my thoughts and delve into the rogue memories that are tucked in the back of my brain, the ones that I just know have the capacity to unlock this damn mystery.

The officers hang around, talking animatedly to Wade about the local football team and how crime amongst supporters is beginning to resurface, a throwback to the 1970s and 80s when the real supporters became too frightened to attend matches.

By the time they leave, my spine is stiff from sitting so rigidly, my posture locked at an unnatural angle. My stomach aches, my head throbs and my flesh burns even though I feel unnaturally cold and can't stop shivering. And still the memory refuses to present itself.

'I'm going to go out and get some stuff to remove the paint. Are you okay here on your own? You look really pale.' Wade is staring at me, his shoulders hunched, his eyes dark and inquisitive.

'I'm fine. Just a bit shaken up, I think.'

'Right, okay. Well, I won't be long. Maybe while I'm out you could start thinking about what the police officer said. Start thinking of names of kids at school who might be behind this.' Wade tips his head at me, as if his words will suddenly conjure up an image of the person behind this, as if I would keep such a thing secret and let these vile acts continue while I remain mute. Sometimes it's as if Wade doesn't really know me at all.

I listen as he walks about the house gathering up his wallet, his car keys, and only begin to relax as I hear him leave the house, hear the opening and slamming of his car door, then the crunch of gravel as he backs off the driveway and heads into town. Tension and worry have turned me into a nervous wreck, my senses attuned to every little noise around me. I'm not sure how much longer I can go on like this, always fearing the worst, suspicious of everyone. And I'm not sure what it is I've done to deserve it.

Wade will expect to come back to a list of suspects. He actually thinks it is that easy, as if an errant pupil will suddenly slip into my mind, a forgotten misdemeanour popping up, prompted by the words of a policeman who assumes I haven't already thought this through prior to his arrival. My brain actually feels bruised and sore after ridding it of Glenn and Barry as possible suspects. There is nobody else. Nobody.

I make a cup of coffee and sit and sip the steaming liquid, going over everything again and again until I am dizzy with it, an exhausted gibbering wreck. Amongst all the thoughts that are rolling around in my head, something is still lurking, something dark and squalid. Something that doesn't want to present itself because it's too distasteful to consider.

My eyes hurt, everywhere aches. I should really go back to

work. I also need to help Wade clean the walls, to assist him with scrubbing at the brickwork until my hands are raw and blistered, and every last trace of those words has been removed.

I look at my watch and try to work out who will be covering my lessons. I always leave a stack of cover work in a tray by my desk for whoever is dragged in, and so far, have never had to use it. I only hope the supply teacher finds it and follows my plans. We're nearing the end of the year. Exams are looming, targets need to be met. I can't afford for any of my pupils to lose focus. While my private life is unravelling, I like to think that work is something tangible, a place I can go to, to forget everything that is happening at home. I enjoy the routine, the solidity of each day. Even when the likes of Jack and his cronies are playing up, I still love delivering those lessons, hearing the whirring of the cogs in their brains, seeing the look of realisation and joy on their faces as they struggle with a concept only for it to suddenly slot into place. I hate the bureaucracy that accompanies every single thing we do, but at its very essence is the learning, the imparting of knowledge, and that is what I love.

Outside, cars pass by, slowing down to gawp at our house, at the words written there.

Freak, freak, freak.

Fucking hell, freak! How much blood are you expecting to lose?

I go hot and cold simultaneously. My scalp itches. Stars burst behind my eyelids. I concentrate on my breathing as the elusive memory slowly but surely edges its way into the forefront of my mind, sliding its way in, turning everything to shit. Such a repulsive memory. It's no surprise I repressed it, kept it hidden away in the darkest reaches of my mind.

I shut my eyes, try to blot it out. There's no connection. There can't be. It's too tenuous a link. That event was years ago. We were still at school, just kids. I think of Tanya and her relentless bullying of that poor girl – what was her name?

Remorse ripples through me. All that she had to endure, all the misery she must have felt and I can't even remember what she was called.

I retch and place a hand over my mouth. What sort of a monster am I?

It was the worst of the bullying on that particular day. Whether Tanya did it because she knew we were leaving school, or whether her bullying had reached a new low was anybody's guess, but regardless, had the teacher not come flying over the yard at breakneck speed to break it up, that poor girl would have ended up naked, her clothes ripped off her back by a baying mob. There was no way Tanya was ever going to stop.

I bite at my lip as I recall how she looked at me, that girl, her eyes pleading with me to bring it to an end. And I would have if I could, but what she didn't realise was how feeble I was. I was never one of Tanya's friends, one of her unruly cohorts. I had been press-ganged into it. Everything I did, I did with my arm forced halfway up my back. I was weak, vulnerable. I had no idea how to break away from her clutches, how to help that poor girl. So instead, I stood idly by, watching it all unfold, doing nothing to stop it. I had the strength to stab my abuser, a grown man, but did nothing to help a child who was being so badly bullied it could actually be categorised as assault.

Monica.

It comes to me in a flash. That was her name. I rummage for more memories. I don't know her now, wouldn't even know how to find her. I can't even remember her surname. This can't be her, out for warped revenge all these years later. And anyway, it would be Tanya she would target, not me. I was an innocent bystander. I wielded no power. That I'm actually considering her as a suspect is ludicrous. She is a grown woman; the idea that she would stalk me, threaten me with hate mail, daub my house with paint and vandalise my car, is preposterous. It's too ridiculous for words.

I drain my coffee and head into the kitchen already blotting out those thoughts. I did nothing to help her. No matter what she may or may not feel about those days, I whisper an apology to her, to Monica, for my idleness, my inability to intervene and be a force for good. I say sorry to her for everything she endured, for Tanya's cruelty, for being too messed-up and vulnerable to step in and help her. My useless father had left us, only to be replaced by Barry. It was a harrowing time in my life. My mind had shut down, I wasn't functioning as I should have been, but that's no excuse. I should have helped and I didn't. I was a useless human being and I am now so filled with horror and remorse, not just at what happened, but because I had forgotten that it even took place.

If Monica were to ever meet me, I wouldn't expect her forgiveness. I don't deserve it and I certainly won't forgive myself. I do remember seeing her once on a bus, only a few years after we had left school. I was too embarrassed to acknowledge her so instead, I blanked her, pretended to not see her or recognise her. I had the chance then, to make amends, to apologise. And I didn't. I let that opportunity slide. Once again, I cowered, hid, refused to own up to my failings.

By the time I finish my penance, tears and snot have mingled over my cheeks and chin, smearing and blending into one sticky congealed mess on my face. No more than I deserve for my feeble ways and lack of consideration for that poor girl.

Outside, I hear the roar of an engine, the opening of a car door and quickly rush to the sink, splashing my face with cold water until my eyes sting and my skin is numb.

'In here,' I shout as I dry myself, straighten my clothes and get ready to put on a show of happiness, the casual façade I've worn only too well over the years. It's taken me until now to realise it, that it's a veneer that covers the real me, a darker side of me that lurks underneath. The guilty bystander, the person who did nothing and allowed that girl to suffer. I've always suspected I had faulty genes, inherited from my parents, and now I know it to be true. I'm a bad person, a dark, evil person. A wicked girl and now a wicked adult. I have a lot of thinking to do and a long way to go before I can ever truly consider myself atoned for what I didn't do.

I think of Tanya, of bumping into her recently, how repugnant a person she really is, and silently apologise to Monica again before striding through to greet Wade in the hallway with a wide smile.

35

My estimation about having blisters and sore hands isn't so far removed from the truth. We have been scrubbing now for over an hour. It's a painstaking process and already we've been through two bottles of turps. The smell is overpowering, giving off an oily haze that fills the air around us and clings to my skin. I stop and step away from the front wall of the house, trying to escape the stench.

'I think I know a better way,' Wade says, wiping his hands on an old rag and moving back to take a look at how much we have managed to remove. 'I've got some old brake fluid in the garage. I can use it to get rid of the paint off the windows. Nasty stuff but it'll do the job.'

'I'll keep on scrubbing at the brickwork while you sort out the glass.' It's difficult to keep the weariness out of my tone. I was hoping to make it into work this afternoon but it looks like today is a lost cause. By the time we finish up here, it will be early evening and the skin on my fingertips will be a thing of the past.

He's right. Wade gets kitted up in protective clothing and uses the brake fluid to clean the glass. A couple of swift wipes and the words disappear leaving a small smudge of yellow paint behind that Wade soon removes with a clean cloth. By the time he has finished, it's as if the graffiti was never there at all.

'I don't want to use it on the bricks. It's powerful stuff and it might damage them so we'll have to keep going with the turps I'm afraid.' He bags up the cloths and disposes of them in the wheelie bin before going inside to wash his hands.

It takes another two hours for us to remove the last traces of yellow paint off the brickwork. My arms ache, my throat is dry and I'm almost certain the lining of my nasal passages has burnt away to nothing from the overpowering smell, but at least those words have been removed. My sense of relief is tinged with fear. What's next? An axe through the door? Waking up to find somebody at the end of the bed carrying an offensive weapon, ready to do God knows what to us? The sooner we get some cameras installed outside, the better. I have no idea of costs and quite frankly couldn't care less. We'll find the money. We have savings set aside for emergencies and this I class as an emergency.

Our evening is spent sitting quietly in front of the television with a takeaway.

'So, you definitely can't think of anybody?' Wade shovels the last of his food into his mouth. I have barely touched mine. The sauce is too salty and brackish, every mouthful like a punishment to my stomach.

'Wade, there is nobody I can think of who would do this. The kids I work with might be from challenging families but that doesn't mean they're budding psychopaths. They're just kids for God's sake. I can't for the life of me think of one single child who would gouge my car or spray-paint our house. They just don't have it in them.'

He doesn't reply, doesn't try to push it any further. We're both tired, pissed off, ready for bed even though it's not quite 8pm.

I stand, scoop up the remnants of our food and head into the kitchen. I feel Wade behind me, loitering, trying to decide what to say. He steps forward, wraps his arms around my waist as I lean over the sink and stare out of the window into the encroaching darkness of the late spring evening. The ridge of the hills is a silhouette in the distance. To the left I can just about make out the line of lime trees that frame the long lane that leads into the next village. Each one was planted in honour of soldiers from neighbouring villages who lost their lives in World War One. I continue to stare out at it, squinting until the last vestiges of daylight disappear, blanketing everything in complete darkness.

'Come on,' Wade says softly. 'Leave the dishes until the morning. I'll get up early and do them. Let's have an early night for once.'

He switches off the light, takes my hand and gently ushers me upstairs.

36

I wish I could have seen her face when she discovered my artwork. It would have been a fantastic moment to see her wide-eyed expression, maybe even see her cry when she stepped outside and looked up at the outside of her house.

I wonder if she called the police or just got out there with a scrubbing brush and cleaned it off? I hope her skin falls off with all the chemicals she would have had to use to remove it.

I also hope that every neighbour in the road stopped and gawped at her house, thinking there's no smoke without fire and that the person who lives there must have done something to deserve it. Because she has. She deserves that and more. And I'm about to make sure she gets it.

My life is completely fucked up because of her and what she did. I can't get to everybody who ruined my life but I can get to her. She is close by every single day. It's too good to be true. I itch to gouge out her eyes or wrap my fingers around her skinny throat every time I see her and now it's almost here. The time has come. I'm sick of waiting. I've given her plenty of warnings, given her a nice little build-up to my thrilling climax. I've planned it all so well. Got every little detail sorted in my head. Then she'll know what I've had to put up with because of her.

No time like the present as the saying goes. So tomorrow is when it'll all happen. I hope she's ready for me, for the knife I plan on sticking into her.

I can't fucking wait.

37

Wade is taking another day off work to sort out my car insurance and keep an eye on the house. He is also planning to fit some security cameras that will link to our phones. No holds barred. He has suddenly turned into a steroidal security guard, ready to fight off any would-be intruders with his bare hands. I should be grateful for his presence, yet all I feel is washed out and unable to concentrate on anything except putting one foot in front of another.

'I'll drop you off. I need the car to go out into town to get the cameras.'

I nod, too tired to disagree. I had wanted to take Wade's car, have a slow drive in to school, give myself time to clear my head before work, but as it is, Wade will talk animatedly all the way there, going over the whole damn thing again and again as he has done for most of the morning, dissecting every part of it until I want to scream.

I'm all out of words. I have nothing left to say. I have had to crack open a past I desperately wanted to keep buried. I have had to visit my mother and step foot in that house with all the dreadful memories that it holds. And I have had to visit a man I once slept with and accuse him of stalking me. I don't have the headspace for it.

This person may not have physically assaulted me but they have caused me immeasurable anguish, playing with my emotions, taunting me, threatening me, making me doubt my own thoughts, my own sanity, and I am done with it. All I want is to get back into school, get my routine back and carry on with life; the life I had before somebody turned it upside down, shaking it about like a snow globe, then watching as the flakes of my life flutter around me in freefall.

As expected, Wade talks incessantly all the way to school, going over possible suspects – neighbours, pupils, ex partners – they are all on his radar. He will spend all day fixing cameras, raking over old conversations with everybody we have ever met, looking for cracks in their words, something that will lead him to our mystery suspect.

I no longer care who it is. I should, but a dense mist has settled in my mind stopping me from seeing things clearly. The thought of Monica has stayed with me, but I cannot marry her with any of this, that fragile wisp of a girl that I haven't seen for years. It doesn't add up.

The traffic is heavy, every set of lights against us and we arrive far later than I am comfortable with. Already I'm irritated. I won't have enough time to prepare. Wade doesn't seem to notice. His mind is still focused on security and keeping an eye out for prowlers.

'Ring me when you're ready to be picked up.' He leans over to kiss me, his breath heavy with coffee and cologne, his eyes scrutinising me, watching my every reaction.

'It'll probably be at about 5 o'clock but I'll text you if I'm going to be any earlier.'

He nods, squeezes my hand. I swallow down the rock-like

lump that has risen in my throat, pull at the handle and let myself out.

Considering it is 8am and lessons start at 8.45, the building is still relatively empty. It's getting close to the end of half term. People are tired, jaded and wondering if their efforts have been enough to get these kids some decent exam results.

I sneak past reception, hoping Marion is busy elsewhere. I'm not in the mood for one of her conversations that somehow always come back to her family. It could be a serious talk about the state of the economy in Uganda and Marion would still end up steering it back to her husband's most recent ailments and her daughter's latest fallout with her best friend's neighbours. I also don't want to discuss my car. She will have thought of a thousand questions since it happened and will be ready to fire them at me.

Fortunately, she is on the phone, half turned away. She catches sight of me, gives me a dismissive wave and a thumbs up and then continues with her conversation. I'm sure to see her later. She will find a reason to visit my classroom with some paperwork. I just know it.

In an eerie sequence reminiscent of a horror movie, the energy saving bulbs turn on as I head down the corridor. I try to blot out any negative emotions as I reach my classroom. Today is about putting some distance between me and recent events. Today is going to be about immersing myself in teaching and learning. It is the only stable thing in my life at the minute, a constant and something I can hold on to.

'You're back!' Jonathan peeks his head around the door and steps inside as I dump my bag down on my desk and sink into the chair like an old woman, fatigued by life, exhausted by every bloody little thing.

'I'm back,' I murmur, doing my best to muster up a smile.

'You won't mind if I don't get too close, will you? I'm not too good with sickness bugs. I'm a crap patient. I swear a lot and lash out like a wounded animal.'

Jonathan always has the ability to make me laugh. I shake my head at him, wishing I could give the real reason for my absence. 'I'm not contagious now. You can come in if you like. I won't throw up all over you or anything like that.'

'Ah well that's good to hear because I'm not too hot with cleaning up vomit either, but I'm not taking any chances. As well as being a shit patient, I'm not a risk-taker so if you don't mind, I'll quickly bugger off. Good to have you back, Stella. And as always, just holler if you need anything.' He leaves with a smile and a wave, his large bulk squeezing back through the door.

I am immensely grateful he hasn't mentioned the matter of my car. Perhaps later, I'll speak to him about it, reassure him that it won't affect my work here even though my head feels about to explode from the pressure.

It doesn't take me long to get back into work mode, stacking textbooks into a pile, sifting through yesterday's output from the pupils, deciding it's a pile of rubbish and throwing it in the bin. Word searches and quizzes about *Hamlet* for God's sake. Who would even consider that a proper lesson? It's a holding activity, no more, no less.

I am carried away by time, the clock ticking idly, my thoughts immersed in preparing for the day ahead. Tutor group first thing, then my Year 10 class. An easy start to the morning. I can break myself in gently, take my time and unwind, not spend the day taut and uneasy like a coiled spring.

The buzz of my phone causes my heart to start up again, a low heavy thudding in my chest; that's all it takes now for my body to slip into a state of panic, my responses wound tight, ready for the next occurrence. I lean into my bag, retrieve it and stare at the screen. It's Wade.

Thank God for B&Q and early opening hours. Got the cameras. See you tonight x

A mixture of emotions race through me. I should be grateful for Wade's patience and thoughtfulness and protection plans, and yet sometimes his sweet nature and endless tolerance of god-awful situations drives me to distraction. I often wish he would shout and swear and gnash his teeth and then at least it would allow me to do the same without feeling like I was out of control. Instead, we pad about the house like a pair of monks who have taken a vow of silence, when what I really want to do is throw things about and unload my anger and frustration to free myself of the constant heavy sadness that wells up inside me.

I slip my phone back and try to focus on the day ahead. I have too much to do and not enough room in my head for thoughts of home and delivering lessons.

The sound of the buzzer overhead drags me back to life. 8.45am already. I prepare myself for the thunder of footsteps outside, for the sudden crush of youngsters as they pour in for registration and tutorial. In the distance I can hear them, the vibrancy of their youth, their chatter and bustle, getting closer and closer until finally the door snaps open and they arrive, rosy cheeked, smart yet dishevelled in their dark green blazers and white shirts. The boys wearing black trousers with razor creases, the girls strolling in with their checked skirts hitched high, displaying long, slim legs underneath. Bags thump on the ground, pencil cases are opened, an array of coloured gel pens scatter on the tables, rolling around noisily, spilling onto the floor. This I can handle, all this chaos and noise and mayhem. This is my world.

I take the register, listening to the guffaws as I mispronounce Aine's name yet again. She smiles and gives me a thumbs up as I correct myself and move on.

We spend our tutorial time looking at the dangers and the benefits of social media. I ask them how often they use their phones to access social media and am horrified when they tell me that, apart from during lessons, they use it almost all day long. There's little I can say that will stop them so we talk instead about the benefits of keeping in touch with people and how they should treat online conversations with same sort of respect they would employ in a face-to-face situation.

'Not everyone is nice to your face though, are they? So they're gonna be even worse online.'

'That's a valid point, Josh,' I say loudly, hoping to catch everyone's attention. 'So what would you suggest doing if somebody is rude to you online?' There is a sudden hush as I wait for his answer.

Josh shrugs listlessly. 'Dunno really. Give as good as you get or just ignore them, I suppose.'

'That's the thing, isn't it?' I say, watching them cautiously. 'Speaking generally, we don't go around shouting at people in the street but as soon as some people go online, they seem to develop another persona. It's as if they've reinvented themselves or are hiding behind their keyboard and can suddenly say anything they like.'

'You'd be gobsmacked what some pupils in this school get up to, miss!' Candice is laughing but I think there's definitely a grain of truth in her words.

'Well, I'm sure you're right there, Candice. When you're dealing with people, what you see isn't always what you get. That's why you need to be careful, to make sure you keep yourself safe online and don't get involved in arguments or chat to people that you've never met before. They might have a hidden agenda that could put you in a risky situation.'

I look around, at the sea of young faces and wonder how many of them go home every evening to dysfunctional families, mothers who drink, fathers who beat and abuse them. Or how many are the victims of benign neglect, going home to families who simply ignore them, letting their kids go their own sweet way with no guidance or love? Both are equally damaging and can often alter a child's life trajectory irreversibly.

The lesson leaves me marginally deflated at how little I have helped these pupils. They file out buoyant and bubbly while I sit feeling as if my soul has been scooped out, leaving a huge hole where my emotions should be. I castigate myself for not trying harder. For not being a better version of me. Sometimes being kind and thoughtful just isn't enough. I need to do more. I have a lot to make up for. Many wrongs to right.

I look up to see Damon in front of me.

'You're right, you know,' he says softly. 'About people having hidden agendas and that what you see isn't always what you get.' He dips his head, dejected.

'Everything okay, Damon?' A sensation I don't care for opens up inside me, a cold hefty weight growing and unfurling, pushing at my ribcage.

He shakes his head. His face is pale, his gaze still lowered to the floor. My stomach tightens. My first thought is that he is about to make a confidential disclosure, that our talk has stirred up something, given him enough courage to speak about an event that is deeply troubling to him.

Year 10 begin to march through the classroom. I stand up, usher them back outside, close the door then sit down and gesture for Damon to do the same. He shakes his head, his gaze still downcast.

I think about Damon's home life, trying to recall information passed over to me. I know he's been taken into emergency foster care on more than one occasion. I also know that Mum recently attempted suicide. I think of the first and only time she attended a consultation with me, picturing him with her, trying to remember the dynamics between them. The image of her in my mind is unclear, refusing to come into focus. Then slowly, the fog in my head clears, dispersing, allowing me to remember her face.

And that's when it all slots into place with sickening clarity.

I swallow hard, look up to him. He is staring at me, his eyes narrow and full of hatred. He grimaces.

And that's when I see the knife.

38

Sunlight filtering in through the blinds intensifies the metallic glint of the blade, heightening my terror. My chest constricts. Breathing feels impossible. I shriek, jump up, the chair toppling backwards, crashing onto the floor. Nobody will hear. Nobody will be alerted to my plight. The noise outside the classroom is too great, too many youngsters talking, shouting, whooping, being belligerent and boisterous. Soon though, if they don't quieten down, Jonathan will appear, roar at them to stop the racket and then he will see. He will look through the glass panel of the door and notice what is going on. He will see Damon holding the knife and he will call the police and intervene.

Damon.

Jesus Christ. Damon is the quietest boy I have ever taught. The quietest boy I have ever met. Shy, introverted, sensitive. And he is holding a knife to my face, so close that I can hardly breathe.

I step back but he is too fast for me. A young lad, half my age and twice as fit, he pushes the blade into my cheek and steps to one side, yanking my arm up my back so high I am sure it is about to twist out of its socket. A burning pain flames its way up my spine, twisting under my shoulder blade and flaring into my neck.

'Say nothing. Make no noise. Not a fucking peep.' His voice is low, intimidating, intense.

My insides melt, turning into liquid. I don't recognise this person. There is nothing of the Damon I know in him. I begin to let out a little groan and wince as the knife is pushed harder, closer into my face, jabbing at my cheek. There must be blood, there has to be. My hands are trembling, my knees knocking together uncontrollably. I shouldn't be frightened, I know this lad, and yet terror is rippling through me, bursting through my veins. Living through abuse doesn't prepare a person for a situation like this; all it does is make me aware of how bad it can get. Abuse doesn't make people tougher. It weakens them, stripping away their strength and dignity leaving them exposed and vulnerable to further damage.

I am being pushed forward, his hand an iron vice on my twisted arm, the sharp edge of the knife now dangerously close to my temple. Saliva fills my mouth; tears blur my vision. I am unable to breathe. My mind freezes, starts to shut down.

'Keep walking. Put one foot in front of another. Don't speak, don't cry out or I'll stick this blade straight into your eye.' His breath is hot on my neck, a rancid odour pulsing from his mouth, wafting close to my face. I want to throw up. I pant repeatedly to stem the tide of rising vomit that is threatening to stream out of me. I swallow it down, feeling its burn in my gullet as it settles back in my stomach.

I don't nod to show him that I am following his commands. I don't do anything except go where he is directing me to. We shuffle along, our feet sticking and twisting on the floor tiles as he propels me forwards.

'Stop.'

I do as he says, our bodies almost colliding, my heart like a battering ram in my chest. 'Here,' he growls as he briefly leaves go of my arm and shoves a piece of fabric in my hand. 'Put this on. Cover your eyes, and then put your hands behind your back. Don't say a word. Make one sound and I'll shove this blade straight in your neck.' He prods it into my skin, twisting it slightly to let me know that he means every word. I cannot believe that he does. Not Damon, not this sensitive, obviously damaged young man. As frightened as I am, I should be able to talk him round, make him see sense. But not just yet. Maybe later. For now, I need to follow his commands, be biddable, silent. Be the victim he wants me to be. I can do that. Being a victim comes easily to me. I've had lots of practice.

The knife at my throat is sharp, murderous. If I decide to talk with him, the time has to be right.

I reach up and wrap the piece of material around my eyes, tying it awkwardly with trembling hands. My fingers are numb, as if the blood supply has been cut off. I wonder if fear can do that to a person, slow down their blood supply, shut off their senses. I wonder if I'm going to die.

'Tighter. Don't try and fool me. I'm not an idiot. If I tell you to do something, you fucking well do it, okay?' He is hissing in my ear, flecks of saliva landing on the side of my face. I suppress the urge to wipe them away. I have to do exactly as he says. I can see now that this isn't a fresh bout of anger. This is something that has been building for a long time, slowly festering and blistering, turning him into a dangerous individual. I have no idea what he is truly capable of, this young lad that I have taught for the past few years and I am now under no illusions about him. This is real. This is actually happening. I feel certain that Damon will kill me if I don't do as he says. I thought I knew him. I don't. I don't know this young man at all. Not the one who is holding the knife to my throat. The Damon that I know is a gentle, thoughtful soul. A kind, thoughtful boy. This entity before me is his hidden anger unfurling, uncoiling and springing to life. And it's a terrifying thing to experience.

I pull the fabric tighter until my eyeballs burn with the pressure and the side of my head throbs. Still I feel the blade touching my neck. I imagine the thin fragile skin on my throat pulsing with fear under the sharpness of the jagged knife. I think of my bulging veins, my raging blood pressure, and wonder how much blood I would lose if he decided to push it in just a bit further, how long it would take for me to die as my veins emptied and my organs shut down, deprived of oxygen as blood spills out around me in a great red sticky mess.

I finish tying the fabric just as a knee is jammed into my spine and my body is pushed up against a wall. My face is pressed hard against the smooth surface making it hard for me to breathe. The cold metal of the blade is removed and my hands are roughly pulled together.

'Don't even think about trying to move. I've got the knife right here, ready to push into your back if you try anything. It will go straight into your liver and you'll die within seconds.'

By the time he finishes speaking, my hands have been tied so tightly I feel sure my circulation has been cut off. My fingers are hot and swollen and my hands are throbbing. He removes his knee and spins me around. The blade is back against my skin, jabbing, pushing hard, reminding me that death is close by.

'We're going for a little walk. Don't speak, don't think about shouting for help. If I hear you even breathing too loudly, I will slash your throat. Understand?'

I nod, hot tears leaking out of the corner of my eyes. Crying won't help me but I can't seem to stop. I pray it doesn't exacerbate his anger, make him so furious that he stabs me right here in my own classroom, the place where I have always felt safe and hoped my pupils did too. I have no idea how it has come to this. I should have known, should have put all the pieces together yet I didn't. I was too wrapped up in the notion that the mystery letter writer was linked to my recent history, my secret infidelity, that I omitted to think about my other past, the past where I did the most damage by doing absolutely nothing at all.

He pushes me forward, my feet and legs unsteady as I stumble blindly across the floor. His hand grips my upper arm while the other holds the knife under my chin, pressing against my throat. I daren't swallow for fear of catching the blade. My breathing is laboured. I am sweating and shivering at the same time. I'm not sure I can do this. My dexterity and co-ordination are failing me. I have no idea where I'm going, where he is taking me. Perhaps to my final resting place, but then why not just kill me here? Why take me outside past the line of other students to somewhere else? I wish I could see inside his head, work out what he has planned for me.

I don't have time to think about it as the door is suddenly opened and I am bustled outside to a cacophony of screams and cries, a noise that both soothes and terrifies me in equal measure. There are other people around who can help me, and yet at the same time they are powerless. The grip on my arm is tightened; hot, strong fingers making sure I don't escape. My head pounds, my chest wheezes. I want to scream but can't.

My feet scramble for purchase. I have no idea where I am being taken. I imagine the crowds parting, bodies toppling sideways to allow us through, youngsters terrified, unable to comprehend what they are witnessing. Things like this don't happen around here, not in the village of West Compton in North Yorkshire, not in our school. Not to me.

It's too surreal. I think of incidents in other schools across the nation and worldwide; teachers and pupils shot and stabbed. Children hiding under desks, screaming for their lives, parents and carers gathered outside the school gates desperate for information, wondering if the child they packed off to school that morning will return alive that same evening. And now it is happening, right here. And I am part of it. I am right in its centre.

Damon drags me along. We stumble and walk, our bodies occasionally banging into each other, our feet slipping and squeaking on the cheap laminate flooring. All around me I can hear shouting and shrieking, male voices booming, female voices screaming, a discordance of sounds that are jarring and unnerving, echoing in my head, knocking me off balance. I struggle to stay upright, the fingers clasped around my arm the only thing from stopping me from sliding down onto the floor.

The hand tightens. A voice hisses in my ear. 'Just fucking walk, okay? Remember, this is a sharp knife. Sharp enough to slice right through your windpipe. Keep moving. Just keep moving.'

Any hopes I had of talking him round quickly dissolve. We're beyond that now. I have always had a bond with Damon, a connection that helped us to form a good solid teacher–student relationship, but this isn't the same Damon. The gentle, erudite lad I once knew has departed and been replaced by this stranger, this person beside me who will have no qualms about killing me.

Was the other Damon an act and is this the real Damon? Was this dark soul always lurking deep beneath the surface of the jovial sensitive boy I thought I knew? Or have his anger and hatred of me grown to such a pitch that he will go to any lengths to get even for what he feels is a great injustice?

I want to ask him why he is doing this, what he hopes to gain from this dangerous endeavour but it's too risky. Adrenaline is pumping through his system, obliterating his reasoning. He will slit my throat if I try to speak.

The noise around us continues; cries and shouts, hollering

and sobbing from terrified schoolchildren as they watch me being pushed and yanked towards a destination unknown. I wonder if anybody else knows about this; or is this Damon's solitary plan? I quell the idea that more people are waiting for us, that the place he takes me to is full of others who also wish me harm. *Dear God, no. Please no.*

There's no time to think about it as a metallic clank comes from somewhere close by followed by a blast of cold air that hits my face. I am jostled through a doorway and after a few steps, feel a softness under my feet. We are on the grass; perhaps the school field, perhaps the patch of lawn next to the car park. In truth, I have no idea where I am. We have walked down corridors, through many doors. Westland Academy has lots of pathways and grass verges. I could be anywhere. I want to escape, to break free of his grasp and run for my life but know that he would catch me and then I will be done for. All I can hope for is that the police are on their way, perhaps even watching us now, tracking our movements. Working out a way to save me.

A silence now surrounds us. It's as if the usual sounds have stilled in readiness for our appearance – birdsong, the chatter and whoops of youngsters nearby – they are all conspicuous by their absence. We are in a void, a vacuum where all logic and normality has been blown away into the atmosphere. All that remains is Damon and his fury. And me, his victim, the reason for his burning white-hot anger. I am the cause of this. The blame lies squarely at my feet.

We stop walking. There is a sudden loud creak – metal grating against metal – and I am pushed forwards, hands roughly forcing me towards a strange place that smells of rubber and dust and old socks. The air around me warms and I stumble forward on to hard ground, my footsteps echoing loudly, my breathing taking on a different pitch altogether.

I am propelled headlong into a dark, smelly room, falling onto my hands and knees with a clatter.

'Stay down there and don't move.'

The creak comes again, like a metal door closing. There is a loud bang and then nothing. And then I know. I know now exactly where we are.

39

The large metal shed where the school stores its sports equipment is on the far side of the field and hemmed in on all sides by shrubbery and trees to hide its existence and deter burglars. One small window allows staff to peer in to locate items, but the whole of the inside is dirty and dusty and the last time I looked, so much grime had settled on the glass, it was almost impossible to get a good view of the interior. That's where we are. I recognise the smell, the musty, rubbery odour of discarded footballs and old equipment that is nestled at the back. I knew the sound underfoot as we stepped inside; it's a tinny echoing noise, dulled slightly by the items stacked high from floor to ceiling.

I listen as Damon uses the padlock that is meant to be on the outside. The heavy metallic clink of it against the door makes me queasy. He has locked us in, sealing my fate. I don't know how he has done it, whether he has used some sort of makeshift lock through which he has slotted the padlock, but I can hear the grating scrape of metal and feel sure I am going to die in here.

Has anybody watched us, I wonder? Do they know where we

are or has he warned them off, waving the knife about manically until we were out of sight? And how did he get the key? I think about how often he helps out around school, using his charm and easy personable manner, allowing staff to think he is trustworthy. He will have spoken to a member of the PE Department, told them he needed some equipment, a football to kick around at breaktime perhaps, and they will have believed him, handing the key over without question.

I try to steady my breathing, to control it and not let him see my fear but it's so fucking difficult. He is teetering on the brink; unpredictable, volatile, furious. Anything can happen. All the usual rules and regulations have been crushed underfoot. The new rules are that there aren't any. I have no idea what to do next, what will happen next.

I feel my legs being touched, hear a screeching, snapping sound and on instinct, I let out a howl of protest. My deepest fear is that this boy is going to do something to me that is worse than being stabbed, something sickening that I cannot bring myself to think about. Something sexual. I would rather he slit my throat. Anything but *that*. He is just a boy; fourteen years of age. I'm a grown woman, twice his age. The thought of *it* repulses me.

'Shut up!' His voice is shrill, like ice raining down on me. I am knocked sideways by a heavy blow. Pain rips through my head, beating and pulsing under my skin, settling deep in my jawbone. I inadvertently let out a whimper of pain and there is another heavy blow before blackness descends and I slip into oblivion.

My feet are being bound together as I come to. A crushing pain slices through my skull forcing me to remain still. I am half lying on the floor, my back propped up against something metal. The surface is hard and uncomfortable, not conducive to human flesh resting on it. It takes me a short while to remember where I am, to recall what happened. A creeping sense of disbelief grows in my mind, ballooning and distorting as the memory comes back to me. This cannot be real. It's a dream; it has to be. It's a dystopian alternative reality where the impossible is possible, where the unthinkable has happened.

I swallow down my feelings of dread. Got to start thinking straight, be rational, logical. I cannot allow fear to muddy my thinking. Therein lies the road to ruin. Or certain death. Damon will smell my terror, use it to maximise his hold over me.

This boy is familiar to me. There has to be a way to get inside his head. He's distressed, angry. He's not a natural-born killer. I have got to try and reason with him, make him understand that I forgive him and won't hold this against him. He can walk free out of here with no comeback or retributions. I have no desire to press charges or take any further action. He is furious, resentful, upset with me. And I get that, I really do. He has every reason to feel that way, but doing this isn't the answer.

'Damon,' I whisper, my voice hoarse, 'please, Damon, let's–'

'Shut up! Shut up or I swear to God, I will slit your throat and smile while I do it.'

I lower my head, knowing my pleas aren't working. I may not be able to see but I am able to detect futility when I hear it. Right now, my impassioned imploration is falling on deaf ears. I need to appeal to his sensitive side, the part of him that displays empathy and compassion. It's in there somewhere. I know that for certain. This isn't him, not the real him. The real Damon has gone into hiding but I can get him back. I just need a little time to coax him back out.

Outside, noises begin to pick up. I can hear voices in the distance, anxious desperate voices. I wonder if the police have been called, whether or not they have surrounded the place, are outside right now, bent on one knee, rifles aimed directly at the window and the door. I swallow. My eyes fill up, my stomach shrivels, a mass of tight knots and coils squirming beneath my skin.

I catch my breath, wait a few seconds then try a different tack. 'You have every right to hate me. I don't blame you for doing this.'

No shouting, no threats. A prolonged silence interspersed with the occasional grunt and a series of rasping breaths. I continue, analysing every word before it leaves my mouth. 'I wish I could go back in time, change everything. I would have helped her. I want you to know that.'

He is upon me in an instant, so close to my face I can almost taste his sour breath as it wafts through the stuffy stale air. 'But you can't go back, can you? What's done is done. The damage is lasting and no amount of talking can change that!'

I'm breathing hard now, gasping for air in the growing heat. It's stifling in here and the smell is overpowering. Putrid body odour blended with old perished materials that are slowly rotting away. I suppress my gag reflex, swallowing down more vomit. 'No,' I say, doing my best to sound humble, contrite, 'I can't change things but I want to show you how sorry I am. I want to tell you what happened.'

He doesn't reply. I can't work out whether he is listening to me or planning how to kill me. One swift move and my throat could be sliced wide open, blood pumping out in gallons, my life ebbing away before he knows the full story, before I can tell him that my life and his mum's life weren't that dissimilar, that we both had useless fathers and drunken mothers, that we both suffered horrific abuse at the hands of adults who should have looked after us and cared for us. That I was so damaged, I couldn't even save myself let alone anybody around me.

'I was another person back then,' I whisper softly. 'It was a different version of me, a darker me, a damaged, fractured me. You have to believe that. I'm not excusing what I did because I can see now that what I did or didn't do, was completely wrong but I had it tough too. It was a wicked version of me for sure, doing nothing to help your mum, not stepping in to stop the bullying but there was a reason for that.'

'So what? I don't give a fuck about your life. You still did it, didn't you? You still bullied my mum, trying to actually fucking drown her! And you're not the only one with hidden depths, you know. The person you thought you knew isn't really me. It was for show. This is the real me. I also have a damaged, fractured version of me tucked away. I'm not the nice sugary sweet boy you thought you knew. That was an act. I have a darker side of me lurking, itching to be set free, and now you've seen it, there's no going back.'

His voice is rising in pitch. I need to calm him down, not rile him. I nod my head repeatedly to show him that I'm on his side.

'The thing is, I hated myself more than I ever hated your mum. Still do. What I did was terrible. Terrible and horribly wrong and I am so, so sorry.'

A voice rings around my head, strong and clear.

How long are you going to let your damaged upbringing define who you are? Who you have become? What you have become?

'I should have done something, stopped it all and I didn't. I deserve your anger and hatred. I know that, but please let's talk about this before it goes too far, before something happens that can't be reversed.'

I don't tell him that I too was a victim, subjected to abuse at home and Tanya's wrath if I dared to defy her. Trying to garner sympathy for myself won't work. It will just anger him all the more.

'I'd like to hear about your mum. I know that she is a good, kind person,' I say softly. I have no idea what sort of reaction my words will provoke whether it will engage or enrage him. I shuffle about, hoping his response is a positive one, a means of breaking out of this deadlock. If I could cross my fingers I would, but my hands are tied too tightly and stuck in position, my fingers swollen and useless, so instead I do something I haven't done since I was a child; I pray.

40

The empty silence seems to go on forever, an endless stretch of nothingness that increases my fears and anxieties with every passing second. With my eyes covered, I have no idea what he is doing, how he looks, whether his face is creased with anger or whether he is deep in thought. My heart crawls up my neck as I feel his body heat close to mine, hear the rustle of his clothes as he slips down next to me, his body almost touching mine. I can hear the low rasping of his chest, the rattle in his throat as he inhales and exhales, the effort of it echoing around us.

I begin to count in my head to pass the time, to take my mind off the sharp blade that is possibly still near my neck. I think about Wade and what he will be doing now. Does he know about me? Has the school or the police contacted him? My thoughts flit briefly to my mother. Will anybody get in touch with her about this situation? Do I even want them to? Then I think about what will be taking place outside this container. I can hear voices out there, too jumbled and distant to understand. Perhaps it's the–

'This is my fifth foster parent. Mum tried to overdose a few months ago. She's still in hospital – St John's. Do you know it?' His voice is a strangled cry as his words cut into my thoughts.

I nod and fight back the tears. St John's is a local mental health unit. Everybody knows of it. Many fear it. Rumour has it that once you're in there, you can never leave which is, of course, complete nonsense, just a local myth. St John's has been there for as long as I can remember and so many stories have circulated about it that plenty of people in town claim they would rather die than be admitted there. It has all the appeal of a Victorian asylum.

'She told me about you after seeing you at the parent consultation evening last year. She said you didn't recognise her. Said you could have helped her all those years ago but didn't. She called you the quiet one, said you never spoke. Never did anything actually. Just watched it all happen.' His voice breaks, his pitch becoming higher, more aggressive. He is unravelling, becoming completely unhinged.

I have to intervene, needing to choose my words carefully, to do my best to sound calm, peaceable. My heart is thrashing around my chest, my throat is tight and dry as I speak. 'Damon, I am so, so sorry. I cannot say that enough. I don't expect you to ever forgive me. I can't ever forgive myself, but I hope that in time, your mum will heal and you can go home to live with her again.'

My head is spinning. I'm about to pass out. The heat in this place is rising, the atmosphere thick with Damon's unabated hatred and need for revenge. Just in case he thinks I've forgotten about it, he traces the blade over my twisted bare forearm that is tied behind my back, running it downwards from the crook of my arm to my tightly bound wrist.

'This is the way to cut,' he says in a childlike sing-song voice that scares me more than his anger. 'Did you know that? Mum didn't. She slashed her wrists the usual way.' He moves the blade and rests it on the inside of my wrist. 'Like this. Left to right. If she'd cut lengthways, top to bottom, she probably wouldn't be here today. She would have bled out in no time at all. Do you know how long it takes for somebody to die when they cut themselves that way?'

Shaking my head feels impossible. I am trembling so much I can barely control my own breathing.

'If you do it that way,' he says so softly and calmly it terrifies me, 'you will die within a minute or two. Your heart gives out. It gets deprived of blood and just shuts down. The doctors can't stitch veins and arteries back together when you slice downwards. There would be no more Miss Ingledew. No more Stella. You don't mind if I call you Stella, do you? It seems like we're getting to know each other really well now. We may as well dispense with the formalities, don't you think?'

I'm nodding now. My reflexes have kicked in. I can't remember thinking that I should nod in agreement but I am. Something has taken over, some deep internal visceral emotion is directing me, forcing my brain to process his words and making me respond accordingly.

'That was a few years ago when she did that. The most recent attempt was pills. She was found by our neighbours and had her stomach pumped so she's still here. She lived to tell the tale as the saying goes. That's when she told me about you. And about her dad of course. He was a complete bastard as well. Just like you.'

I fight back a sob. Memories of Tanya and her gang taunting Monica about her father's illness and subsequent death fills my mind. How could I have forgotten about such awful cruel stuff? How could I? I am a savage, as bad as my mother, Barry, all those people I have spent years fearing and detesting. I am one of them.

'He once beat her so badly, she had to take a week off school until the cuts and bruises healed. She never knew which was worse, being at home with him or being in school with you. She thought that him dying might make things better but it didn't. But then, I suppose you know that, don't you? The bullying got worse; his death made her a target and her own mum, my gran, turned to drink. She died recently. Cirrhosis. To be expected, I guess. By the time she died, she was on a bottle of whiskey a day. It's a wonder she lasted as long as she did really.'

I listen to him speaking, not daring to say anything, not wanting to break the spell. I can't work out whether this is therapy for him or whether it is a build-up to something much worse. Something final.

Every breath is laboured, every pocket of air in my lungs heavily controlled as I draw oxygen in and exhale as slowly and carefully as I can.

'So I suppose her problems aren't all down to you. All you did was make them worse. You should have helped her.' His voice cracks ever so slightly, a subtle nuance in his tone as his speech picks up rhythm, getting louder with every syllable. 'We should all help people, for fuck's sake! Not make their lives worse. Why didn't you help her? WHY?' His last word comes out as a roar.

I wince, trying to make myself as small as possible, to distance myself from his anger. He is crying hard now. I can hear him as sobs wrack his body and I am powerless to help, my limbs bound, my eyes covered with a blindfold. Yet again, I am letting this kid down. What a useless person I am, a pathetic nobody who leads a double life and disappoints everyone around her time and time again. I know exactly how desperate he feels, how that emotional turmoil can rip a person apart. My heart aches for him, not only because of what he is going through, but because I missed the signs. I should have seen it in him. I should have noticed his quiet ways, spotted his pained expression in class, and I didn't. I mistook quiet for contented, and I did that at my peril. I've spent so long thinking about myself, concentrating on my own purported suffering that I have lapsed in other areas, been remiss in my duties, and this is the result.

'Damon, I cannot apologise enough. I am so, so sorry. I was a bad person back then, a dysfunctional person. It wasn't really me. It was a broken version of me, a secret me that I've hidden away for all these years and I know that is no excuse, but if you'll let me, I can make this up to you. I can meet with your mum, apologise and maybe even–'

'NO! I said NO!' The strength of his voice shocks me, makes me want to hide away, to curl into a tight ball and pretend none of this is happening.

I listen to his cries, to the thrashing of my own heart, the rush of my blood as it hurls itself through my veins. They all crash in my ears, an inharmonious jumble of sounds, roaring, surging through me, around me. Noise everywhere. Too much. Too much...

My own sobs merge with his, our cries conflicting and out of sync. It's a nightmarish sound. And there's something else coming from farther away, another noise that I can't quite fathom. I stop, try to catch my breath. I hear it again; a male voice coming from outside, echoing, authoritative, robotic. And then I realise what it is. My head rings, my chest gurgles as I listen to the sound of a megaphone outside, the voice imploring Damon to open the door, to drop the knife and let me go. He doesn't seem to hear it, to even be aware of its presence close by. He continues to cry; great big wet sobs that fill the stuffy air around us. I want him to quieten down, to hear what I'm hearing, to be susceptible to their words. I just want all of this to come to an end.

41

The voice outside has softened; it is now imploring, cajoling, using tried and tested methods to persuade Damon to let me go. If I could see, I am sure I would be able to get through to him. Making eye contact is so important. I would also be able to see his mood changes, to pre-empt his moves and match my words and movements to his oscillating emotions.

They have ditched the megaphone, possibly thinking it is too aggressive, too hostile. They are outside now, talking in softer tones, using one voice in particular that is mellow and genial with an authoritative inflection to it. I have no idea how many of them are out there. I try to not think about it. The thought of hordes of people, police and possibly even the press, sickens me. I just want to go home, to get out of here and escape to my little sanctuary; the place that Damon sought out and defiled with those awful words.

All I need to do is to loosen the binds that are keeping me prisoner here. Then I can hopefully talk to him properly, get him to put the knife down. Underneath it all, Damon is a sensible lad, a kind person. He is hurting; a frightened and desperate young man, I know that now, but aren't we all hurting and frightened? We have more in common than he will ever know. Every one of us has demons that lie dormant, latent dark secrets that hold us hostage in our minds, springing loose when we least expect them to.

Moving slightly, I lodge myself up against a pile of rubber mats, then with hot, semi-dextrous fingers, do my best to undo the fabric that is tied around my wrists. There is too much material tightly knotted for me to try and rub and fray it, so I frantically grasp about for a loose end and tug at it repeatedly, hoping to slacken the fabric enough for me to wriggle out.

My heart pounds and sweat trickles down my back as my fingers fumble about, my hands twisting frantically whilst I try to remain still. Outside the voice continues to plead and coax.

'Damon, my name is Alex. We know you're upset. All we ask is that you let Miss Ingledew go. We can talk about what it is that's bothering you, Damon. We just want to make sure that nobody gets hurt.'

I have no idea what sort of expression is on Damon's face as he hears those words but something tells me he is impervious to them. A bright lad like Damon will see straight through their rigorous methods and procedures. He is probably sitting here smiling as they speak, knowing they are wasting their time. I want them to continue talking, not only to distract Damon from my attempts to free myself but also because it's comforting to know somebody else is close by. Somebody with the means, the proper training and the determination to get me out of here.

I continue pulling and tugging at the fabric that is binding me, even though I don't know whether or not it will do any good. For all I know, I could be making the damn thing even tighter. This colossal effort may be a waste of time. My nails break and bend and my fingers ache as I pick away at every piece of loose material I can locate. It seems to take an age; pulling and scratching, tugging and grasping at anything I can get hold of, then when I least expect it, something miraculous happens. Just when I think that it is a useless endeavour and I should conserve my energy, I feel an unravelling, like an outer layer of skin falling away. The tension on my wrists lessens and although they don't spring free, I am able to slowly pick my way out of the many folds that are holding me together.

A thudding takes hold in my chest but this time it is excitement that is pulsing away beneath my breastbone and not fear. My breathing is rapid, hot and erratic. I have to calm down, to keep my new-found exhilaration under control or Damon will sense that something is amiss. I have a chance to do something. I cannot let my enthusiasm and impulsivity ruin this opportunity. This is my chance to escape and stay alive.

I have no idea what my next move is going to be. I need to take some time to think, time that I may not have, to form a robust strategy that will aid and not hinder my chances of staying alive, so I continue to sit, my hands wedged together behind my back. Wiggling my fingers, I will them to move properly, for the numbness to dissipate and sensation to flood back into my hands.

'Hi, Damon, I'm here with Alex to help you. My name is Cora. We want to make sure you're safe in there. Can you give us some indication that you're both okay? Perhaps a small knock just so we know everyone is fine?'

The metal shed rocks slightly and for one awful moment I think that the police are going to storm their way in. I think about that knife, wondering where it is right now, how close it is to my body, to my skin and vital organs. Then I realise that Damon is on the move. Is he standing up? Or is he pacing, a predatory look on his face as he prepares to plunge the blade deep into my stomach? Saliva fills my mouth. I swallow it down, run my tongue around my teeth. My mouth is gritty, tasting of sand and mud. My temple vibrates, my throat closes up. The heat is stifling. I feel certain that this time, I am going to pass out.

'Stop talking! Just stop it!' His voice sounds muffled, distant and disembodied. Perhaps he has sat back down, has his head buried in his lap, his voice muted by the fabric of his clothes. Or perhaps he has turned away from me. Maybe this is my chance.

I have no idea where the knife is. No idea where Damon is. I can no longer feel his body heat, hear his ragged breathing. Has he moved away to communicate with the people outside? Or is he standing facing me, the cold metal with its serrated blade pointed straight at me? I don't think he is. His voice is too thin, too inaudible. Too reedy. Maybe the time is right and I should just take my chance, here and now. Maybe this is the moment. Now or never.

Terror renders me incapable of any swift movements. My hands still ache and throb, my legs are weak, my back is stiff from sitting on a hard surface. I'm in no fit state to launch an attack on a young man half my age. And of course, I have no idea where that fucking knife is.

Waiting only increases Damon's chances of finding out that I've managed to untie my hands. What if he tells me to move? To stand up and walk? What if he spins me around and sees what I've done? Time is against me. I have to do something sooner rather than later.

I wait for my pulse to slow down, for the pounding in my head to stop, then let out one final ragged breath, inhale deeply and make my move.

42

As slowly and quietly as I can, I slip my hands from behind my back, every infinitesimal movement seeming to take an age. Bending my head ever so slightly, I remove the blindfold and look up to see the shadow of Damon at the door of the container, his back to me. His shoulders are shaking, his entire body vibrating as he stands silently, staring at a blank stretch of metal. I have no idea where the knife is and I am unable to stand up. My feet are bound with duct tape too tightly for me to make any sharp movements.

I blink to clear my vision, waiting for my eyes to adjust to the dim light. Damon's silhouette remains in front of me, silent, still shaking. My next move is unclear. I can't run away or launch an attack. But I can see.

My body is lead, weighed down by terror and dread as I wait for something to happen. Would Damon really kill me? That's what I need to focus on if I am to survive this incident and escape unscathed. Would this sensitive, clever youngster really stick that knife deep into my heart and watch me die? Or is it down to me to talk him round? To let him know that I'm not his enemy and that I want to help him?

My time for thinking runs out as he faces me, his features twisted with rage and confusion. He is still holding the knife.

'Just a light tap on the metal is all we're asking for, Damon. I promise, nobody is going to hurt you. We're here to help. We just want to keep you safe.'

He lets out an unrecognisable grunt and begins walking towards me, the jagged blade thrust out in front of him. My head swims, my throat closes up. The metal glints despite the shadows, despite the darkness. I have no idea what to do.

'Damon, we've been in touch with your mum. She wants to talk to you. She's been allowed out of hospital and is on her way here with your social worker.'

He stops moving, standing silently, an intimidating figure looming over me. He is just a few feet from where I am sitting. The oxygen around me rarefies. Adrenaline shoots through me, whistling around my body.

He turns again, grunts something incomprehensible, a jumbled stream of syllables, then lets out a deep rasping roar. I see a chance, the only one I might get, and lunge forwards, grabbing at his ankles, snaking myself over his body, screaming in his ear to drop the knife. It clatters to one side, the sound of the metal clanking and rattling somewhere behind me.

I reach out, my eyes wide, trying to see through the shadows, beyond the darkness, my fingers splayed as I attempt to locate that weapon. Damon is strong. I can't hold him for long. He is writhing under me, bucking and bending his torso, hollering at me to get the fuck off him. I try to press down on his abdomen, to weaken him and push my full weight onto his spine, pressing down onto his back as hard as I can.

Other sounds filter in from outside; people shouting, the sharp scrape of metal.

A cacophony of noise. Grunting, screeching and banging.

Damon's hands collide with mine as we sweep the area for

the knife. My fingers briefly touch upon something hard and cold before losing it again. With a sudden surge of energy, he throws me off his back and is up on his feet, his body arched as he scours the floor. I don't waste any time. With my feet still bound, I lunge at him again, trying to knock him off balance, hitting his ankles and shins with my fists, pummelling against his legs. Anything to stop him getting to that knife before I do.

He topples over and hits the floor with a thud. I let out an ear-piercing scream in the hope that the police hear me and increase their efforts, breaking in with weapons at the ready. My lungs burn. Every part of me aches, my muscles fit to burst.

Once more, I spread my wet palms out over the metal floor, frantically sweeping around for that knife. I have to find it. I don't want to die. I'm not ready. My knees are jammed into Damon's back but he shakes me off. I fall backwards, my hands landing upon something hard, something cold and sharp. I let out a gasp of relief. He turns to me, his face full of hatred.

The noise outside grows, an explosion of sounds – screams, shouts, pleading. And the powerful growl of machinery as they use a cutting device to break through the padlocked door.

'Give me the knife.' He is soberingly quiet, his voice a hiss in stark contrast to the jarring wall of noise outside.

I clutch it tightly, my fingers slippery against the cool, smooth metal handle.

He takes a step towards me. A loud bang erupts as the padlock falls to the floor and a rip appears, allowing a sliver of daylight in.

Like a feral cat, he pounces, his arms outstretched, his mouth twisted in an ugly unrecognisable grimace, a manic snarl that tells me he will do anything now. He has nothing to lose. He knows it. I know it. It's all coming to an end.

I move back, my body pinned against a pile of old sports equipment that is stacked in the corner. The smell of dust is overpowering as a heap of apparatus topples, spilling over me – tennis balls, racquets, baseball bats.

The knife falls out of my hand. It skids across the floor and disappears out of sight, hidden beneath the debris. We both scramble about, me disorientated, my feet still bound together, him larger, stronger, more agile, our bodies bashing into each other in the fight to retrieve that weapon.

Suddenly Damon stops, lets out a brash, caustic laugh, stands back up with the knife in his hand.

'Police! Don't move!'

I turn, expecting to see a swarm of bodies but still the door is intact. They must be close to getting in. Why are they taking so damn long? Where the fuck are they?

I thrust myself at him just like before but he steps back, holding the knife aloft and I land awkwardly on the hard floor, slumped in a heap. He is close by now, close enough to bring the knife down and jam it into my back. I struggle to escape, to wriggle away from him. With a sudden burst of vigour, I slither forwards, grab his leg and pull as hard as I can, knowing that he could stab me at any time. I thank whichever God is looking down on me as I catch Damon unawares and he stumbles and slides, the knife falling from his grip and bouncing across the floor. It spins around, the blade pointing towards us ominously, like some dreadful prophetic indicator of what lies ahead.

'Bitch!'

Gone is the sweet boy I once knew. He has been replaced by this person; this imposter who wants me dead. I initially doubted Damon's capacity to hurt me. I now have no doubts that he would slice me open in a heartbeat. He has gone beyond the point of no return.

Pulling myself up to my knees, I feel around for the knife, hoping it has bounced out of reach, hoping the police break in before we locate it.

No time to think. Damon spots something, dives forward, grapples on the floor and brings up the blade, his fingers gripping it tightly, knuckles taut and stretched, his eyes glinting as he begins to laugh, his voice guttural, hysterical.

Fear paralyses me. I need to snap out of it. I need to move. As if I am disconnected from reality, I sweep my arm behind me; it rests upon something solid, something substantial. I grasp it, feeling the heft of it as I bring up an old wooden baseball bat and swing it high in the air at exactly the same time that the metal blade rushes towards me.

'Freeze! Police! Nobody move!'

A loud crack, a swish of metal. Feet stampeding through the container, a welcome streak of light cutting through the darkness.

And pain. A terrible gut-aching pain. We both slump, Damon and I, our bodies collapsing in on each other. Slipping and sliding in a gathering puddle of blood. Warm, sticky blood everywhere. So much of it. A tide of thick crimson liquid pooling and spreading beneath our bodies.

The pain is crippling, a deep cramping; an inescapable searing ache. It's in my muscles, my bones, every part of me. I close my eyes, say a prayer remembered from my childhood, then count, too exhausted, too terrified to do anything else. Time is suspended. I think of Wade, my mother, Astrid. I think of Monica, Damon, every pupil I have ever taught. Suddenly, the pain begins to ease. Like the tide being sucked back out to sea, it leaves me and I am overwhelmed with a sudden dizzying sensation of weightlessness. Every muscle, every sinew in my body is as light as air. I am made of paper. I can float. I can fly; soaring above the ground like a bird. I can do anything at all. I close my eyes, fatigue swamping me, overwhelming me.

But not for long. Gradually, a coldness takes over, permeating every inch of my body, wrapping me in its arms, pulling me away. And lethargy. Lethargy, the likes of which I have never before experienced, enters my pores, sinks deep into my bones. I try to ignore it, to stay awake and fight it but it's hopeless. My eyes are heavy, like lead. I gasp for breath.

Close by, I hear Damon groan, a low boyish sound that tears at my emotions and I wonder if it is he who is dying or if it is me. Perhaps we are both losing the fight, our lives ebbing away from us. I blink and let out a long, ragged breath, close my leaden eyes.

Then nothing.

43

The human body is both frail and tough at the same time. It is a complex gathering of vital and not so vital organs all tightly packed into a small space in our abdomen with other important blood vessels and veins spread farther out into our extremities. How I am still alive is a mystery to the doctors who have spoken to me at length about my injuries. How I am still alive is a mystery to me.

Memories took a long time to resurface when I first came to. My head felt as if it had been trapped in a vice and on waking, I was introduced to a whole new level of agony. Waking at all seemed like a miracle. Despite the initial euphoria of realising I was still here, it felt as if a branding iron had been implanted into the lining of my stomach. Still does. The pressure of breathing causes me intense pain. There isn't enough morphine in the world to deaden the burning ache in my belly.

But I can live with that. Being able to feel pain has never felt so good. I am high on life, high on having survived a knife attack and losing over four pints of blood. By the time the medics got to me, I was on the point of slipping into a coma, my body going into hypovolemic shock due to massive blood loss. I suffered lacerations to my kidneys due more to the fall than anything else, and the knife punctured my right lung, missing my liver by a hair's breadth. Just one centimetre in another direction and I wouldn't be here. I'm trying not to think about it.

Doctors have said that my body will take some time to heal; months rather than weeks, but I am fine with that. Time is something I have plenty of. They haven't spoken to me yet about what is going on in my head. That is another matter entirely.

A police officer has been standing guard outside my door, and I imagine the press will still be camped on our doorstep at home. Wade has told them to piss off on more than one occasion and has taken great delight in it from what I can gather. He has never held any truck with the gutter press, journalists who avoid the real issues whilst feeding a distorted version of the truth to the public, offloading their sick and mean narrative to suit their own agenda. I imagine he will have smiled while he said it, perhaps even given them the finger. Wade may be a quiet and sensitive guy but he's not an idiot and doesn't suffer fools gladly. Confuse compassionate and caring with soft and stupid at your peril.

I have had some terrible nightmares but have been reliably informed they are probably caused by the morphine rather than the incident itself. Tall green monsters, grinning clowns, vampires and talking porcelain dolls have all invaded my head at some point while I've been in here. I administer my morphine pump frugally and am trying to do without it entirely but when the pain crashes over me like a tsunami, I find myself relenting and pressing that button rather than weaning myself off it. It is a necessary evil, killing my pain and messing with my head and I'll be glad when I no longer need it. It is still infinitely preferable to the other option. I could be lying in a coffin rather than this bed and will never forget that. I am eternally grateful for being here, for the efforts of the medical team who saved my life with their skilled hands and minds. If I live to be a thousand years old, I will never, ever be able to repay them.

'Somebody's looking perky today.' Dawn is at the end of my bed smiling, her head cocked slightly to one side. She is one of the nurses here and we seem to have bonded. I look forward to seeing her smile, to hearing her warm, reassuring voice.

'I'm getting there,' I laugh as I try to shuffle myself into a more comfortable position, an intense eye-watering pain ripping through my abdomen as I move.

'I always think that putting on make-up means we're on the up and up. A couple more days and you'll be able to brush your hair and put on a bit of lipstick, then you'll feel the difference.' She winks at me and gives me a radiant smile. 'You've got a couple of visitors by the looks of it.'

Behind her, I can see the outline of two people – one slim, the other a larger figure who suddenly lets out a booming laugh that ricochets around the room. Astrid and Jonathan bustle their way through the doorway, giggling and pushing each other like a pair of badly-behaved teenagers. I smile and shake my head at them. The sight of these two people makes me want to cry tears of joy.

Astrid points at Jonathan and widens her eyes dramatically. 'He started it! We've been halfway around the hospital looking for you. He said ward twenty-two was over the other side and I said it wasn't. Serves him right if he has a coronary right here next to your bed. Silly old duffer.'

Dawn is laughing now, her eyes glistening under the glare of the overhead lights.

'I thought I was supposed to be off work and recuperating, not having to sort out kids' squabbles,' I whisper, trying to suppress a wave of laughter that I know will hurt like hell. My stitches have yet to heal and making any unplanned movements, taking any deep breaths or trying to cough feels like a red-hot poker is being repeatedly rammed into my abdomen.

'We've brought you chocolates and flowers,' Jonathan says as he wheezes, struggling to catch his breath after the exertion of getting here. His skin is mottled and pink. Tiny pearls of perspiration sit on his forehead. 'Astrid wanted to bring you a bottle of rhubarb gin but I told her it was too expensive for the likes of you.'

He leans over me and plants a hot kiss on my forehead. 'If you wanted some time off work, Stella, you only had to ask, you know. This is a bit extreme.' His face changes, his eyes suddenly dark and sombre. 'Sorry. You know me. Sick sense of humour. This is how I deal with stuff. My mouth gets into gear before my brain in situations like this.'

'It's fine, honestly.' My voice is hoarse. 'Just don't say anything that will make me laugh,' I say, wincing as I place my hand gingerly over the bedsheets that are covering my midriff.

'She's right,' Dawn barks. 'If those stitches rupture, we'll never get rid of her and believe me, we need her out of here so we can have that bed.' She smiles and gives me another wink then slips out of the room, tucking a pen into her top pocket and humming to herself as she leaves. She gives the policeman outside my door a brief nod before going on her way.

I lean back, close my eyes for a second. When I open them, Astrid is staring at me, her expression grave. 'Damon?' she whispers incredulously. 'I mean, Jesus Christ, Stella, fucking Damon?' She is shaking her head now and looks like she might cry at any second.

'I know, I know,' is all I can manage to say, my voice weak and croaky.

'I've seen stuff like this on TV and it's always the loners,' Astrid says, her voice close to breaking. 'It's the quiet ones, the kid who sits alone eating his lunch, the one who never smiles and refuses to engage. Not the likes of Damon for crying out loud. I mean, why? Just why?'

I turn away momentarily to stem the flow of tears that threaten to escape, to give myself a few seconds to think clearly and get my next few sentences shaped into a coherent formation as I try to explain what happened, what went on that day and why a boy like Damon tried to kill me.

'It's a long story,' I manage to whisper without bursting into tears. 'Has he been named in the media?'

Astrid shakes her head. 'No, there's been a ban on naming him but it's all over social media. Every kid in school saw him. You can't keep them all quiet, can you?'

'I guess not.' A lump is stuck in my throat. I swallow it down, biting back hot tears as I relive the experience. 'I've been told by the police who are dealing with it to not say anything to anybody. I've only spoken to them briefly. They're coming back later today to take a formal statement.'

The thought of explaining why he chose me makes me want to weep for an eternity. How can I begin to explain such a connection? Once again, shame and guilt trap me, cornering me as I take a deep unsteady breath and plunge into a past that I had forgotten about, a past that appeared out of the blue, and ripped my world apart.

'I went to school with Damon's mum.' I stop, readying myself for the next part of the story. The difficult part.

Astrid shrugs, looks to Jonathan who is sitting, shoulders slumped, listening intently whilst trying to catch his breath. 'Right. So?'

'So, I was part of a gang who bullied her.'

'Oh, for fuck's sake, that's ridiculous! He tried to murder you because of something that happened years ago? That's just bullshit, Stella.'

I widen my eyes, subliminally signalling to Astrid to lower

her voice. I should have known this would rile her. Astrid is tough and unforgiving, expecting others to think as she does. As lovely as she is, as thoughtful as she is, Astrid doesn't always understand sensitivity or how difficult it is to rise up and break away from a damaged start in life, to throw off those shackles and survive life's difficulties. She is both gorgeous and friendly, and brusque and efficient at the same time.

'She was also abused by her father, so she had it twofold,' I say through gritted teeth, doing my best to manage my pain and get my story out there without crying.

Astrid starts to speak but I hold up my hand to stop her. She shakes her head in annoyance and leans back in her chair, a flush taking hold in her neck.

'When I say bullied, I don't just mean name calling or the occasional push or slap. She was cruelly targeted by a gang who even tried to drown her.'

In my peripheral vision, I can see Astrid stiffen, her eyes narrowing as she listens closely and assesses me. I feel sick at the thought of her and Jonathan hearing that I was part of those terrible bouts of bullying, part of that terrible gang, but it's about time I owned up to what I did, be the better person and not shy away from it. If only I'd found this courage all those years ago.

I almost tell them that I didn't take part, that it was my inability to stop it that has resulted in the whole catastrophe taking place. But I don't. Because deep down, I feel as if I deserve this. Monica and I had more in common than we realised, more mutual problems shared between us than things that kept us apart and separated us. If only we had known that back then. If only I had found the nerve to speak up and not be one of Tanya's subordinates. Monica and I were both from abusive families with alcoholic mothers who neglected us. I could have been a friend to her and instead, I allowed her to be beaten and degraded. I did nothing to stop it. And as a result, she ended up trying to take her own life. Her son spent most of his formative years in and out of care, his own mother too ill to look after him. He has every right to hate me. For years, I have hated my mother for being ineffective and useless and yet here I am, no better than she was. Perhaps I'm genetically predisposed to be an ineffectual human being, shallow and shiftless with no thought for anybody but myself. Like mother, like daughter.

I do my utmost to fill Jonathan and Astrid in on the grisly, seedy details without coming apart and weeping buckets, each word I utter like a physical blow to my body.

By the time I have finished speaking, they are both a sickly shade of grey, their bodies rigid with shock.

Astrid does her best to alleviate the obvious tension that has settled in the room. 'You were just a kid yourself, Stell, and as you said, a fairly damaged kid at that. You don't have to carry this shit around with you for the rest of your life, you know. You're allowed to forgive yourself and move on.' She takes my hand and laughs. 'Christ, you know what I'm like. If I had to be held accountable and punished for every stupid thoughtless prank I've ever done in my life, I'd have to spend the next forty years locked away in solitary confinement!'

Her words make me dissolve into tears. I try to pull myself together, feeling stupid and childish for crying in front of Jonathan, my boss. He gives me a tissue and handles the situation with his usual humorous bent. 'Dry your eyes, Stella. Crying is for women and babies and we all know you're neither.'

I laugh and shake my head at him. My shoulders shake violently as a bout of hysteria takes hold, laughter and tears mingling and merging. I wipe at my face with the tissue. By the time they both leave, I am completely exhausted, my eyes heavy and sore, my abdomen hot and tender. I had forgotten what a rush of raw emotion can do, how it can leave you both fatigued and delirious at the same time. I've been treading on eggshells for so long, I think I've lost touch with how to simply be me.

I make a promise to myself before I drift off into a welcome slumber: to be kinder to myself. And to stop being the keeper of dark secrets. It's too stressful, too damn exhausting. The time has come for change.

44

I'm nervous, jumpy and anxious to the point that my stomach is growling at me, my flesh puckering on my neck and forearms. Stupid really. I have no real need to feel this way. Everything is going to be fine. I don't know how I know that. I just do.

Wade grasps my hand as we sit outside the building. 'You sure you don't want me to come in with you?'

I shake my head. 'Thanks, but I'll be fine. This is something I've got to do on my own. It's about time I faced up to my responsibilities.'

He leans forward and hugs me, eyes full of concern and sadness on my behalf. 'Stop with this constant self-deprecation. You can't keep on punishing yourself for something that happened many years ago. If we're going to blame anybody for this whole thing, it should be Tanya bloody Sharpe. She owns this situation. This is all her fault.'

I suppress the animosity that immediately enters my mind at the mention of that woman and all the problems and hurt she has caused. I am willing to bet she has barely given Monica a second thought since leaving school. Tanya will have lived her life, oblivious to the trail of damage she left behind. She may have even read about this incident in the local paper and made no connection to her involvement in an event that almost cost me my life.

I reach up and kiss Wade, eternally grateful that he stayed with me throughout all of this. In the end, I admitted to my infidelity. I figured if I was going to come that close to death and survive, then we should start again with a clean slate. I won't pretend that everything was okay when I owned up and that Wade glibly accepted my confession with good grace because that's not how it was. It's not how life is. We shouted, we cried, we talked until the early hours; we spoke of separation and cried some more until eventually we decided that neither of us wanted to end the relationship. We may not be perfect but we both know that we are better together than we are apart. Wade is the other half of me. I couldn't live without him.

He also persuaded me to try again with my mum. It hasn't been easy. We have a chequered past, my mother and I, a lot of painful history to get over and many sins to forgive but we're giving it a go and you can't ask for more than that, can you? I visit her twice a week and whilst the conversation is often strained, it's improving. Every so often, I find empty vodka and gin bottles stashed away behind cushions and now that tensions have eased between us, I have found that I have the courage to confront her about her drinking. Sometimes, I cook her a meal and sit, watching patiently as she eats it, thankful she's getting some nutrients into her emaciated body. It's not an ideal situation and not quite the stereotypical mother–daughter relationship that most people have but it's better than complete silence and being permanently estranged. She certainly seems more contented, less oppositional and distant. I only wish we had found this happy balance before now. I find it terribly sad that it has taken this tragedy for us to both see sense. Coming close to death makes you realise how precious life really is.

I took some time off work to heal and gave my choice of career some deep thought. Despite everything that has happened, I concluded that if I didn't return to teaching and give it my best shot, anything else would feel less. This episode has taught me many things – the main one being that we all have something to give. I may not be the best teacher in the world or the most knowledgeable but I do have experience enough to help the children who need it the most; the hurting children, the damaged children. The quiet ones who look as if they are managing nicely. They are often not. It's a cover, a way of concealing all the hurt and the pain, of covering the scars that they carry on the inside. The deepest wounds are rarely visible.

I had a call last week from a major national newspaper offering me a large sum of money for my story. I didn't shout or yell, I didn't lecture them about morals or ethics. I simply put the phone down. Doing the right thing and being the better person is my aim in life now. I owe it to the world to be the best that I can possibly be. I owe it to myself.

My palms are damp as I wrestle with the door and wrench it open. Nerves are destroying my fine motor skills, taking ownership of my co-ordination. I take a couple of deep breaths and give Wade one last smile before I climb out of the car and close the door behind me.

Damon has been in here since the trial just over a month ago. I hope he's receiving the help he so obviously needs. I didn't expect him to agree to this visit. It was arranged by his social worker and the courts. They call it restorative justice although I'm still not entirely certain which of us is the offender and which of us is the victim. The lines of such cases are often blurred and difficult to define. There are no clear winners, that much I do know.

He received stitches to his head where I hit him with the baseball bat, and suffered concussion afterwards. I sometimes lie awake at night thinking about what would have happened had I not managed to grab that bat. Would he have continued stabbing me? Or would he have stopped, regretted his actions and helped me? I like to think it's the latter but unless he tells me in person, then I guess we'll never know.

Monica has refused my offers of contact and I'm not going to push it. Hopefully she will accept when the time is right. Damon is her only child and he is currently incarcerated in a young offenders institution. I don't blame her for blanking me. I would probably do the same. The memories she has of me are dark and unpleasant. Why would she want to sit opposite a woman who stripped her of her dignity and drove her to the brink of death?

The sun emits a trickle of heat, disguising the sharp breeze that threatens a cold winter. I look up, glad of the balmy autumnal warmth, trying to ignore the swathe of dark clouds that give the place an ominous, sinister feeling. The sprawling red brick building is immense and seems to go on forever. It looks dramatic and imposing. Vaguely threatening.

Sarah is waiting for me beyond the gate, standing next to a man in a dark uniform. Sarah is Damon's latest social worker. He has had many. Her red hair catches in the sunlight, shades of amber that contrasts against her pale blue coat. She raises her hand and gives me a slight wave, a small line of apprehension etched into her brow about what we are about to do.

It will be fine. I hope it will be fine.

My breath mists, a small cloud that curls and disappears as I walk up the narrow path, my mind focused on the young man inside and what I am going to say to him to try to make amends. I don't think there are words available to do just that, to say what I want to say, to apologise and help us move forward, so instead I will go inside, wait for Damon to arrive and see what happens next. He deserves that much.

And so much more.

My hands are trembling. I take a deep, shaky breath, press the call button and wait.

THE END

ACKNOWLEDGMENTS

This is a tricky one to write and as always, there are so many people to thank.

I'm going to start with a little explanation. This book was written long before Covid-19 appeared in our lives but was edited during the lockdown. It was quite a surreal experience and for many, a devastating time. For me, I found that for once, I had enough time to take on board the comments made by Clare Law, my editor, which helped to get this book into shape. I would like to thank Clare for her help and her words of encouragement.

My thanks as always to Betsy and Fred for allowing me the chance to get my story into print. You guys are unerringly kind and supportive, always ready to help and reply to my many questions no matter what time of the day or day of the week it is.

A big thank you to everybody who helped to promote this book and another thank you to all the staff at Bloodhound Books for everything that you do. You are stars that shine bright.

To my family and friends who are subjected to my solitude and absence whenever I embark on writing another book, I thank you. I may not say it, but I'm always with you in spirit.

Thank you to my ARC readers for providing those all-important reviews. You guys are ace!

And finally, a million heartfelt thanks to you the reader, for taking the time to purchase and read my book. I am humbled that you chose mine over the thousands of others that are out there. If you enjoyed *The Girl I Used To Be* and feel so inclined, a review would be most welcome.

I enjoy hearing from readers and can be found on social media at:

https://www.facebook.com/thewriterjude/

https://twitter.com/thewriterjude

CPSIA information can be obtained
at www.ICGtesting.com
Printed in the USA
JSHW081139170223
37906JS00001B/115